Sweet Surrender

WENDY MAY ANDREWS

CR&O

Sparrow Ink
www.sparrowdeck.com

ISBN - 978-1-989634-04-2

www.wendymayandrews.com

Can a lost love be rekindled?

When Lady Julianna ended her engagement to Lord Ackerley, Viscount Beaumont, during her first Season, she left London vowing never to return.

Seven years later she returns as chaperone to her niece and unfortunately Lord Ackerley is also in Town for the Season. Rumor has it the viscount is in search of a wife. Julianna is uncomfortably aware of the handsome nobleman at nearly every Society event she attends. Moving around the small circle of the ton stirs up feelings she has kept hidden. Embarrassed and ashamed that she made a mistake in ending their previous relationship, she tries to avoid further contact. Ackerley, stunned by her second rejection, pursues her to discover the truth.

Is it ever too late for a second chance at love?

Dedication

I love the Second Chances trope. We all make mistakes, sometimes they result in the end to a relationship. But the end isn't always permanent. This book is for those who believe in second chances. May you find your happily ever after.

Acknowledgements

Thanks to GermanCreative for my beautiful cover.

Very special thanks to my husband – the best partner life has to offer.

Chapter One

"Julianna?"

Julianna felt herself grow faint for a moment at the sound of her name spoken in that deep baritone. Despite the incredulity colouring his tone, she would recognize that voice anywhere. Of course, it was easier to handle due to the fact that she had been both expecting and dreading just such an encounter.

"Good afternoon, my lord." Proud that her voice did not betray any of her weaknesses, she prayed that her face did not give away her reaction to his rugged, handsome features, and the air of strength about him that she had always found so attractive. Time had been kind to Viscount Beaufort. He was more handsome than ever, blasted man. Gone was any trace of youthful fleshiness. His high cheekbones were highlighted by the traces of laugh lines around his eyes — eyes that were not laughing now. Their grey depths were blocks of ice.

During their previous association, one of the things that had attracted her to him was his size. She had enjoyed feeling dainty and feminine next to his athletic build. Now it felt as though he towered over her, and she felt it put her at a disadvantage. Julianna tried to ignore the sensation.

1

"Rumour had it that you vowed never to return to London and yet here you are."

Julianna wanted to cringe at the coolness in his voice but managed to contain her reaction. Offering a polite, cool smile of her own, she wished fervently that she had remained inside the fripperies shop with her niece and their maid instead of escaping to the busy street for a break from the tedium of shopping. She had thought the cool air of the spring afternoon would be a relief. It would have been if she had remained alone.

"Yes, I had made that vow in my youthful haste, but the need has arisen to be here, so here I am."

"Are you here for the Season?" he asked, or rather demanded, his tone turning fierce and his arctic gaze sharpening to scrutinise her.

His almost insolent examination made her wish she were wearing some of her newly acquired finery instead of a less than fashionable, though still serviceable, frock. She was glad that her maid had at least taken pains with her hair before she left the house for the day. She had to remind herself quickly of his question in order to answer him hoping she would not appear a simpleton at the delay.

"I am," she answered simply but then felt compelled to elaborate. "My niece is here for her debut, and I am to be her chaperone."

It would seem the viscount could not keep the incredulity from returning to his face. "You are going to chaperone your niece?" he asked with unmistakable emphasis on the "you" as though he considered her completely inappropriate for such a role.

Julianna squelched her residual feelings of anger and attraction toward him, maintaining her dignity with an effort of will. "That is correct, my lord. So no doubt I shall see you about. I wish you a good afternoon. I must return to my niece."

With those coolly uttered words, Julianna turned her back on her former fiancé and returned to the shop. As the door closed behind her with a small tinkle of the bell, she braced herself against the wall in order to rally her senses and bring the frantic beat of her heart under control.

Rolling her eyes heavenward she asked herself rhetorically, *Why does a man I vowed to hate forever have to be the only one who causes this reaction? It is nonsensical! And I will not have it.*

Pasting a smile upon her face, she entered fully into the shop and collected her niece and their purchases.

~~~

As she stood in the foyer awaiting the return of the footman, she felt the events of the previous day chasing around in her head. She ground her teeth in frustration and pushed the memory to the back of her mind as she braced herself for a confrontation of another kind. The footman beckoned for her to accompany him.

"I am quite certain I told you never to darken my doors again." Agatha, the Dowager Duchess of Westerley, spoke in a hard, cold voice as she stared down her perfectly straight nose at the young woman before her.

Lady Julianna felt the blood drain from her face, and a wave of nausea washed over her. In her mind's eye, she went back seven years to that awful moment when her grandmother had originally uttered those words. Julianna's hand instinctively reached toward her throat and the locket concealed by her modest neckline, seeking comfort from the familiar charm. Memories of the darkest period in her life flowed over her. Too much drama squeezed into such a short time, and she had been far too young to handle it all.

On that distressing evening seven years prior, Julianna had burst into this very same sitting room with tears streaming down her cheeks. The duchess, unused to emotional outbursts in her presence, had been shocked and initially expressed concern.

"Julianna, what has happened? Why are you not at the Roxboroughs' ball? Are you all right? Have you fallen ill?"

"No, I am not all right, Grandmother. I am no longer engaged to marry Viscount Beaufort," Julianna declared with the dramatic flair of a seventeen-year-old.

Confused, the haughty old woman, stood straight and proud, gazing at her granddaughter. "What are you talking about? Of course you are engaged to Beaufort."

There was a momentary pause while the older woman's face paled and she came to the brink of anger. "He has not behaved the cad with you has he?"

"No, he has always been the perfect gentleman with me," Julianna said with weary emphasis. Gazing at her grandmother with warring emotions clearly displayed on her face, Julianna almost backed down in the face of the Duchess' withering disapproval. She hated to disappoint anyone, but with a valiant force of will, she straightened her backbone even more.

Julianna cleared her throat almost delicately. She had stemmed the flow of her tears and now angled her chin proudly and managed to speak in a stronger tone. "I do not wish to discuss this. I have already informed the viscount, and now I am telling you. I have realized he is a philanderer, and we shall not suit. Now, may I please go to my room?"

A loud knocking resonated throughout the stately mansion. The duchess looked on in bewilderment as Julianna ran to the door of the sitting room and yelled to the butler in an uncharacteristic display of emotion and lack of grace.

"George, do not allow Lord Ackerley in. I absolutely refuse to see him." Her usual dulcet tones echoed shrilly off the high ceiling. "He is never to enter this house again."

The duchess found her voice again. "What is the meaning of this, Julianna?"

"I have ended my engagement to Lord Ackerley and I do not wish to ever see him for the rest of my days!"

"What happened to cause such a rupture?" the Dowager asked, still unclear on this sudden change.

4

"I do not wish to discuss it." Julianna struggled to maintain her uncharacteristic defiance. *"We just shall not suit."*

"I do not understand you. You must tell me what has taken place. You have seemed perfectly happy with the arrangements these past two weeks. What could have possibly happened at the Roxborough ball to cause you to suddenly change your mind?"

"I do not wish to discuss the matter." Julianna insisted once more before pausing. She lowered her vehemence toward the duchess and found a respectful tone. *"Please, Grandmother, do not try to talk me into it or ask me to discuss it. It is just too painful."*

"This is incomprehensible and unacceptable, young lady." The duchess paused momentarily. *"You cannot expect me to accept your broken engagement with no explanation."*

Julianna remained rigid and mute, but tears of distress streamed down her cheeks. The duchess pressed on, hoping to bring reason to the normally biddable and sensible youngster.

"My lawyers and I have been working hard on all the details with the viscount as to marriage portions. The paperwork is nearly complete. I will not be made a laughingstock. Where is your loyalty, girl?"

Julianna blanched at the thought of disappointing her grandmother.

"Grandmother, please," she persisted in pleading tones. *"You know family is the most important thing to me. You must realize I would not do this frivolously. Please do not press me. I stand by my decision."* There was a note of finality in her voice, and her firm little chin rose again to a proud angle.

"I will not listen to this defiance," declared the duchess despite her hesitation to hurt her beloved granddaughter.

Julianna loved the duchess but refused to be cowed. *"My parents always said I would be allowed to choose my own husband. I do not choose Lord Ackerley!"*

The Dowager Duchess of Westerley gave up trying to reason with her granddaughter and gave her final word on the subject. *"Your hen-witted parents may have said you would be allowed to choose your husband, but they are no longer here. No one under my roof is going to bring shame on the Templeton name or on the House of Westerley."* Her haughtiness rose in a *final attempt to make her normally biddable granddaughter submit to her will. "If you refuse to marry the viscount and refuse to explain yourself, then you are no longer welcome in this house."*

Julianna raised her luminous, tear-filled face and looked her grandmother straight in the eye. Agatha appeared profoundly surprised. "If that is your wish, I will leave at first light. I never wish to set foot in London again after this horrendous night."

"But you have nowhere to go, you foolish girl," the duchess almost pleaded, still expecting her granddaughter to crumble.

Julianna pulled a crumpled page from her pocket with a slight flourish. "As a matter of fact, I do have somewhere to go. Hartford, writes that Lucretia is terribly ill, struggling to bear him another child. It was such a delightful surprise to find out she was increasing, but now her illness has the household in an uproar. While he would never ask me to leave the Season in order to help, I am sure he will be happy to have me home to help the governess keep the children entertained and out of his wife's sickroom." Her defiance returned. "He will not turn me away!"

Julianna paused while struggling to regain a modicum of composure. "Since it is already such an advanced hour, I trust you will not put me out until morning. Good night, Grandmother." The overwrought young woman fled from her grandmother's presence, pounded up the stairs, and slammed the door to her room.

Now, seven years later, with the memory of their last encounter almost echoing in the room, Julianna tried valiantly not to quake as she stood her ground. She held her chin at a proud angle, unaware of her resemblance to the haughty old dame despite her heated cheeks. She waited calmly until the footman discreetly closed the door before she gracefully dipped into an elegant curtsy. "Hello, Grandmother, it is a pleasure to see you, too."

The duchess' flinty eyes warmed ever so slightly at her granddaughter's cheeky reply, but she would not allow herself to relent, continuing to glare at the rebellious young woman.

Julianna sighed with resignation as she arose from her respectful stance and acknowledged the older lady's original statement. "Yes, Grandmother, you did say I was never to return, but I thought it best to tell you in person that I shall be in London for a time. Odelia is here for her Season, so I must be as well."

"And why could Hartford not inform me of this development himself? Should I not be included in my great-granddaughter's debut into Society?"

A flurry of emotions flitted through her consciousness that she hoped didn't show on her face as she strove for a tactful, yet true, answer. Hart had said that only over his own dead body would his grandmother have any say in his daughter's debut. It would not do to tell the Duchess such a thing. The truth was that Julianna didn't want her grandmother to publicly shun Odelia just because she was angry with Julianna. She loved her grandmother dearly despite their history but would not put it past the cantankerous old lady to do such a thing. Loyalty to both the duchess and Odelia had prompted Julianna to beard the old lady in her den.

Julianna hit upon just the right angle of explanation. "The earl has come up to Town with us, but he is a bit put out by all the uproar required for Odelia's come out and I must admit he has escaped to his club. I did not think you would be most pleased to hear about our arrival from someone else, nor would a note have been sufficient."

Finally the old duchess smiled with a hint of warmth and she looked with some admiration at the young woman before her. "You just did not wish to face me in public for fear I would make a scene and ruin your niece's chances."

Julianna allowed a grin to break over her face. "No, your grace, I can honestly say I would never consider you capable of making a scene. The cut direct, perhaps, but not a scene."

Finally Agatha appeared mollified, at least for the time being, and let a chuckle escape from her thin lips. "I did tell you never to come here, but I suppose you did the right thing. You are correct, it would have been completely inappropriate to hear of your arrival from someone other than family, although you could have written me a letter in advance," she concluded reprovingly.

"True, but I learned from the best to never give away the advantage," Julianna reminded her gently, relieved to have weathered the storm and feeling somewhat more familiar with her relative. The younger woman knew not to relax completely, though, and was glad for her vigilance when her grandmother continued the interrogation.

"Are you not concerned that your tarnished reputation will harm your niece's chances?" asked the duchess not unkindly. "No doubt it would have been best for me to undertake to sponsor the young lady."

The duchess had unknowingly touched on one of Julianna's biggest concerns, but she managed to maintain her composure. "Well, Grandmother, you did not make such an offer to Odelia, and she has now reached the age to make her debut. And no, I do not worry about my tarnished reputation," was Julianna's flat response before she elaborated.

"I must admit that it did cross my mind when Hart first proposed that I should be the one to chaperone Odelia for her Season. But while you were willing to banish me, I was quite sure you would not have allowed scandal to attach itself to anyone under your name, so I am fairly certain I need not worry about my reputation. And while at the time my hasty departure from Town at the height of the Season might have been considered a touch irregular, the strength of my position as your granddaughter and the sister of the Earl of Somerton should smooth over any awkwardness with even the highest sticklers." Julianna concluded this last statement with a small, crooked smile at her grandmother.

She then continued on a more pensive note. "There is also the fact that while Odelia is quite pretty and will no doubt take, she will not be a diamond, so there should not be any viciously jealous mamas looking to discredit her by dredging up my past."

The duchess nodded, seeming to agree with the soundness of her granddaughter's reasoning. She was then struck with a disquieting thought. "If I agree to acknowledge you, you will not *now* be expecting me to sponsor her, will you?" she demanded abruptly with a degree of alarm despite her previous statement that it would be better if she brought out the young lady herself.

"No, Grandmother," Julianna laughed lightly. "That thought did not even cross my mind. Between Hart and I, we should be able to manage launching her rather successfully on our own merit. I have kept in touch with a couple of my old friends through the years, and they are willing to lend a hand since their children are much too young to be about in Society. One dear friend, in particular, is quite close with one of the patronesses and has promised us vouchers for Almack's which is quite a coup, or so I have been told." Julianna allowed a slight sigh to escape as she thought of the upcoming busy activities of the next several weeks.

A stern look came over Agatha's face as she again looked coldly at her granddaughter. "You aren't really looking forward to this, are you? It would all be much easier for you if you had married him back then."

Unwilling to discuss the subject and refusing to acknowledge even a degree of truth to her grandmother's words, Julianna forced a slight, polite smile to her lips as she rose gracefully to her feet. "Perhaps, but then I would not know my dear Odelia as well as I do." She stepped forward and quickly dropped a gentle kiss onto her grandmother's cheek. Then she offered a cheeky grin as she flippantly said, "Thanks for not throwing me out when you realized who your caller was."

Agatha laughed. "I guess it is about time I forgave you for being so stupid," she decided baldly. After a pause, just before Julianna exited the room, she called out to her. "You should bring your niece around to meet me. I have not seen her since you left London."

"Thank you, Grandmother, perhaps I will," Julianna replied, politely but without making a commitment. She then made her escape and nearly fled from the house.

With a heartfelt sigh of relief, she collected her abigail who had been waiting patiently for her, and they set out on a brisk walk toward the elegant townhouse of the Earl of Somerton.

Knowing all the details of her mistress' life as long time servants always did, after a couple moments of silence, the maid asked with curiosity. "'Ow did that go? Was 'er grace amenable?"

Julianna smiled kindly at the maid. "Better than I had expected, actually, Maizy. Thank you. The duchess did not have me thrown out on my ear at any rate, so that is a step in the right direction."

The loyal maid bristled at this. "'Ow could anyone ever even think of throwin' you out, milady?" she demanded, anger colouring her voice.

Julianna laughed. "Thank you, Maizy, but truly I was mostly funning. I admit, I was a bit concerned about my reception with the duchess, but of course she would never throw me out of her house."

Still worked up, Maizy declared fiercely, "Well she's gone and done it afore, so I cain't say as I'd trust `er not to go doin' it again."

Again Julianna laughed, although this time it was a bit forced. "That is only partially true, Maizy, but she is still my grandmother, as well as the duchess, and as such we must respect her position."

Instantly contrite, Maizy apologized profusely, "I never meant no disrespect to 'er grace, milady. I just cain't accept of her disrespectin' *you*."

"I know, Maizy, do not trouble yourself on this matter. It has been taken care of, and all is well. The duchess saw fit to forgive my past transgressions and is willing to be kind to our dear Odelia, which is all I could have hoped for."

Cheering up at this, the faithful but simple maid was distracted from the troublesome thoughts and began to bubble over with excitement about all the preparations the household was undertaking for Lady Odelia's debut ball despite it still being several days away.

Julianna smiled warmly at the young woman's enthusiasm but only paid half a mind to her chatter. As they walked along, Julianna was deep in thought considering all that was left to accomplish before the Season got fully underway. She was relieved they had arrived early for the Season to give Odelia some time to become accustomed to Town ways and get a bit of polish before the full Season got under way. It would give Julianna time to become reacquainted with her old friends and shore up her defenses before she next encountered *him* – the source of her disgrace –Viscount Beaufort.

As they neared her brother's townhouse, Julianna gave her head a shake to get herself out of the doldrums. Since they had just arrived in London two days prior, they had much to do in order to ready everything. The house was, of course, in constant readiness for guests, so she did not have much to worry about there. The earl had a well-trained staff, and they were fully prepared for whatever the Season would bring. But Julianna knew well that although Odelia's and her own wardrobes were fully adequate for life in the country, they left much to be desired for the various occasions they would be involved in over the next several weeks. They had many appointments over the next many days with the dressmaker, the cobbler, a hat maker, a hairdresser, and even a dancing instructor. Julianna wanted everything to be perfect for her beloved niece and was leaving nothing to chance for the younger girl.

Stop your wool-gathering, my girl, she told herself sternly. *You decided on this course after thinking it all through. Stewing over it now will not change anything. Just get on with it!* With those bracing thoughts, she strode purposefully up the front steps and entered the door being held open by an ever-attentive footman. With a gracious smile for the servant, she asked for her niece's whereabouts, and then headed in the direction indicated.

Chapter Two

"Aunty Jewel, you're back!" exclaimed Lady Odelia enthusiastically as she bounded up from the chair she had been lounging in. "How did it go with your grandmother?"

Julianna's smile warmed when she heard the endearment and it widened even further over her niece's interestingly worded question.

"You know she's your relative, too, don't you?" Julianna laughed. "It went quite well, thank you. The duchess has invited us to call on her together. I did not commit us to anything since your father has been quite clear that he does not wish to have much association with our grandmother. But it would actually be best for you to meet her since chances are good you will at some point run into her while making the social rounds. She is no doubt not as active as she once was, but I am quite sure that she does still participate in certain activities of the Season."

Odelia wrinkled her nose. "I have not seen her since before I was ten. She did not even come to Somerton for Mama's funeral."

Julianna's frown of sympathy was chased away by her usual optimism. "I am sure she had her reasons. Never mind about that now. Let us think about how much excitement you are to have over the next weeks."

There was a brief pause while both young ladies thought with widely varying enthusiasm about those forthcoming activities. Julianna then continued, "What have you been up to thus far today, my dear? Are you ready to head out to the dressmaker's shop?"

Odelia twirled around with all the energetic enthusiasm of a young seventeen-year-old set to enjoy her first Season. "I have been ready all day!"

With an indulgent smile, Lady Julianna preceded her niece from the room, calling for the carriage to be brought around. They set off for the dressmaker's shop and spent the rest of the afternoon choosing multiple dresses and gowns that they would require in the coming weeks. It was such a decadent activity spending the afternoon with fashion plates and fabrics, but it was the very foundation upon which the entire social scene was based.

"Is this not just the most thrilling thing we have ever done, Aunt Julianna?" Odelia asked with a delighted grin.

Julianna's returning smile could not quite match Odelia's for brilliance. "Oh, yes, my dear, it is quite lovely."

Odelia let out a gurgle of laughter. "How could you have grown up an earl's daughter and not love dressing up in lovely new clothes?"

"I was too busy in the stables wishing I could be a boy like my big brother to bother much with dresses and such. I was the bane of my poor mother's existence. She despaired of ever getting me to be pretty and make an eligible match."

"Well, you managed the pretty part, now let's get you properly dressed so you can escort me around and get *me* matched up," Odelia trilled, not realizing how insensitive her comment was towards her aunt's unmatched state. She wandered away to finger more of the fabrics as the modiste discussed various patterns with her.

Julianna became lost in thought. *How can she enjoy this boring activity quite this much?* Catching sight of her own reflection in a nearby mirror she cast a critical eye over her ensemble. *I guess this gown is a trifle out of date. I know I cannot go about Town looking like a dowd.*

As she fingered the fabrics, much as Odelia was doing, her mind flitted back to her unsettling conversation with the Dowager Duchess. She needed no reminders of her former fiancé; thinking about him was the main reason she had almost refused coming to London. Knowing he had never married made it all the more complicated. Even though seven years had passed, thoughts of him were never completely far from her mind. And for that reason, she determined almost fiercely, she must not look like a dowd the next time she ran into him as she went about Town during this Season. *But why can this whole process not be much faster? It would be so much better if I could just leave it in Odelia's capable hands.*

Looking at her darling niece chattering happily with the seamstresses, Julianna allowed a small sigh to escape her lips. *If only Lucretia were here. She would love to see her daughter dressed in all the finest styles. It is certainly a blessing Odelia inherited her mother's eye for fashion.* Julianne gave her head a shake, realizing she needed to stop her woolgathering and make an effort to participate.

With a decisive shake of her head, Julianna strode forward and engaged the modiste's attention. "*Non, madame*, this is not the look we would like to pursue. Please keep in mind this is *mademoiselle's* first Season."

"Ah, but of course. We were just experimenting," the modiste excused while whisking away the offending garment and presenting another, much more suitable one, shrewdly acknowledging Julianna's restored attention to the matters at hand.

"That dress would have looked absolutely marvelous on you, Aunt Jules," Odelia explained.

"It was not quite the style I am looking for either, Dee. Bear in mind that I need to look sufficiently severe to scare away any inappropriate suitors," Julianna explained with a twinkle in her eye causing Odelia to laugh with delight.

"That may be difficult for you to manage."

"Difficult perhaps, but not impossible, am I not right *madame*?" Julianna glanced ironically at the dressmaker as they shared a look of understanding.

After a few more selections were made, Julianna arranged for everything to be delivered at the earliest convenience to the earl's townhouse and the bills sent to his secretary.

"I know you are all grown up now, and this may seem like a silly question, but would you fancy an ice from Gunther's? I quite forgot how much work shopping can be, and I could use some refreshment."

Clapping her hands like a little girl, Odelia gave a little skip as she accepted the invitation. "I doubt I will ever be too grown up to enjoy Gunther's, Aunt Julianna."

"Well then, let us be off." The two ladies made their way up the street in fine accord.

Moments later, happily ensconced in one of the confectioner's plush chairs, Julianna leaned back with a contented sigh of relief.

With a girlish laugh, Odelia looked at her aunt in sympathy. "You do not really love to shop do you, Aunty Jewel?"

With a slightly guilty look and a rueful smile, Julianna shook her head. "Was I that obvious? I hope I did not ruin the experience for you."

"No, no, I had a lovely time. Do not trouble yourself on that head. I doubt anything could rob me of my enjoyment of shopping. It was a bit obvious it was not your favorite activity. But we really did order some marvelous items. That maroon gown will look ravishing on you, Aunty."

"Dee, you must remember, I am the chaperone. I quite decidedly do not want to look ravishing. To be honest, I am not quite sure how I allowed you to talk me into that particular purchase," mused Julianna.

"You could not resist how exquisite you looked in it," replied her niece with no sign of repentance, looking at her aunt with an impish smile and twitching eyebrows.

The two ladies grinned at each other but were interrupted before the conversation could continue.

"Lady Julianna Montgomery? Is that you?" demanded a fashionably dressed woman of about Julianna's age. "I have not seen you in years!" she continued to exclaim in a pleasant but overly loud voice. "What a delightful surprise! You have not changed one bit in the time since I last saw you! And who is this pretty young lady with you?"

Both Julianna and Odelia were blushing at the attention being brought to them by their overly exuberant visitor, but there was naught they could do to stem the tide of her exclamations. At last, with the final question she paused for a breath. And it finally dawned on Julianna who the other woman was.

"Lady Catherine, how nice to see you," she said in equally pleasant but much lower tones. She stood to offer a quick hug to her old school friend while a member of Gunther's staff stepped forward to offer the new lady a chair once it became obvious that the women knew each other. "Please join us if you have a moment. Odelia, this is Lady Catherine, an old friend of mine. And this delightful young lady is my niece, Hart's daughter, Odelia."

With a lilting laugh Catherine broke in, "No, no, Julianna, please, not old!"

Julianna chuckled too. "You are right; I should say a friend of long standing. We spent a delightful two years together at finishing school."

Odelia's expressive young face showed how surprised she was by this information. "You were sent away to school?" she demanded incredulously. "Why then was I not allowed to go?"

Julianna was chagrined. She had forgotten that old complaint and was embarrassed to have it come up in front of her former friend. But then she was surprised by Catherine's response.

"Odelia, I am delighted to make your acquaintance. 'Tis true that your aunt and I spent some lovely times together. She was lucky enough to have had quite a wonderful experience while at school, mostly because she was blessed with extraordinarily loving parents. But I do not believe your mother had such an experience, from the tales I remember hearing from my older sisters, and I do not think your father overly enjoyed his time away at Eton either. You shall have to ask him about it sometime." She then very adroitly changed the subject. "Now tell me, are you here for your first Season? What have you done so far, and how are you enjoying it?"

Odelia, somewhat mollified by the lady's brief explanation, allowed herself to be distracted by her questions and launched into a rapturous catalogue of all the delights she had enjoyed thus far and what they had planned for the next several days. As she listed their various activities, Catherine turned to Julianna with a twinkling eye and teased.

"It's hard to believe you have kept your looks! I do believe it would turn me grey."

Julianna laughed good-naturedly. "It's not as bad as it sounds. Do not concern yourself with me. Your time will come if you have any daughters."

A shadow crossed Catherine's face. "We have not yet been so blessed."

Julianna clutched her friend's hand in sympathy wishing wholeheartedly she had not said something so thoughtless, but then the other lady quickly recovered.

Shaking off her melancholy, Catherine again showed a happy countenance. "But being as free and unfettered as I am, you must allow me to plan some sort of entertainment in your honor. I am just so delighted to see you after all these years, Julianna!

You must pay me a visit and catch me up on all your news. We shall have a comfortable coze! And please allow me to throw some sort of an event for your Odelia. It would be so delightful, perhaps an informal morning dance just before the full Season commences so she can meet a few young people and practice the steps."

Julianna hesitated. She felt sad that she had not maintained better contact with her old friend and was surprised how delighted the other woman seemed to be over seeing her. They had not spoken since Julianna fled from her own abbreviated Season. On the other hand, her old friend clearly had sorrows of her own and was seemingly eager to host a gathering. It would no doubt be a wonderful opportunity for Odelia. Seeing her hesitation, Lady Catherine tactfully interjected.

"Well, think about it at least. I must run. I am expected at Mrs. Mortimer's at-home this afternoon. Please do come by soon, Julianna." As an aside, she added an important piece of information. "Of course, you know I married Viscount Chorney, do you not? We are at number 3 Curzon Street." Then in a flurry she continued, "Lady Odelia, it was a true pleasure to make your acquaintance. I look forward to seeing more of you throughout the Season."

With that, the energetic viscountess got up swiftly from their table and swept from the room. Julianna and Odelia blinked at the suddenness of it then turning to each other, they burst into laughter.

"Was she always like that?" asked Odelia with a touch of awe.

"Actually, worse," laughed Julianna. "It is obvious that maturity has tempered it a bit, but when we were young girls she was forever swirling into activity and often getting us into trouble with her starts. But she was always such a kind girl, and it seems obvious that that has not changed. It was generous of her to offer to have you as guest of honor to some sort of an event, and I feel rather churlish for hesitating to accept."

Odelia laughed. "Aunt Jules, you are never churlish. No doubt you had your reasons for not jumping on the offer," the younger girl defended with loyalty before continuing in more wheedling tones. "But if upon reflection you decide it is a good idea, I must say I am in full agreement." She grinned impishly at her aunt.

Julianna laughed, too. "Of course, you would, you insatiable chit. You just want to show off the skills you shall be learning from Francois, the dancing instructor who is coming by tomorrow morning."

"Well, of course!" Odelia rolled her eyes drolly. "What is the sense of going to the effort of learning if one does not get to show it off?"

With more laughter the two ladies got up and left the shop ready to complete their errands for the day.

Chapter Three

That night, over a snifter of brandy in front of a warm fire in her brother's library, Julianna confided in Hartford, the Earl of Somerton.

"Hart, I must admit to you, it feels quite strange being back in London after all these years."

The earl smiled kindly at his younger sister. "Are you being worn ragged chasing after my hoyden of a daughter? Are you enjoying it at all, or is it a dreadful chore for you? I never really considered your feelings, I'm sorry to say, sister. I rather assumed you would be delighted to come."

Julianna knew her brother quite took her for granted, but she loved him with all her heart nonetheless and would have been willing to do just about anything he asked of her. But she was happy to be able to say with all sincerity, "No, Hart, it is not too much of a chore." After a momentary pause, she inserted, "Except maybe the shopping." She allowed a low chuckle before returning to her usual seriousness.

"You know I would not miss Dee's Season for anything despite my reluctance to return to London. I love her more than I could ever properly express to you. After all, you allowed me so much say in the raising of her and Fletch when I came home after my own ill-fated Season. Although I would not say she is hoydenish, I do fear we shall have our hands quite full once the Season gets fully underway."

21

With a slight shudder, Hartford heartily said, "I shall be glad to leave all that to you as usual."

With resolution, his sister set her chin stubbornly and looked him in the eye. "Not this time, my lord," she began formally, making the earl eye her askance. "I was happy to have you out of my hair when the children were younger, but you are going to have to take an interest now. This is very serious and much more the father's place than mine. Your daughter is here to look over prospective husbands, and it is your job to guide her and protect her." Julianna stated these points forcefully before continuing in kinder tones.

"Odelia is such a sweet girl and quite pretty. With the generous dowry you have set up for her, I am afraid she may be the target of certain gentlemen with less than honorable pasts or intentions. I shall do my best to guide her, but you will need to show your presence on occasion to lend the air of protection she will need as an earl's daughter."

Hartford's face held an arrested expression as though this was a revelation for him. Since Julianna had returned to their ancestral home seven years ago, just before his wife's death in childbirth, he had been quite happy and comfortable leaving the running of his household in her capable hands. He had given little thought to the burden of responsibility he had left on her young shoulders. He resolved to give it more thought, but in the meantime he needed to acknowledge the reasonableness of her request.

"I will, of course, be visible at times, but please do not tell me you are expecting me to be tied to my daughter's apron strings throughout the entire Season, are you?" he demanded incredulously.

"Of course not, Hart, I only expect you to be a bit more visible than you usually are, especially whenever we are entertaining here at our house. As you hopefully know, we are planning an official ball for Odelia to mark her come out. You will have to lead her out for her first dance. That is to be held in ten days. As well, you should escort us to the theater and at least a few balls and such over the next several weeks. I shall let you know which invitations we have accepted, and you can let me know which you can join us for."

In kind tones Julianna continued, "I know you are very busy in the House of Lords and with running the estates, but this is important, too, Hart. I do not expect your constant attendance on us. I can handle most things, but I do think it is best for you to be visibly about during the Season, keeping an eye on which gentlemen are showing an interest in your only daughter."

"You are right, Jules. Thank you for bringing this to my attention. I know I rarely acknowledge how much in your debt I am for taking over my house for me when Lucretia died, but I really do not know how we would have survived without you. I know I have not been around the children nearly enough, but since my wife died I have found running the country to be the only thing that I truly enjoy."

Julianna clasped her brother's hand warmly. "No, Hart, I would not have survived coming home in disgrace if you had not given me full reign. You must not thank me, I am most grateful that you let me take over your house and children." Then she grinned at her brother. "We are really most fortunate that the children turned out so well considering they only had us to bring them up. They really are quite lovely young adults now, aren't they," she said with a great deal of loving pride evident in her voice.

"You sound just like a doting mama," laughed the earl.

"Maybe so," acknowledged Julianna, not really wanting to think about the fact that they really were not her children. She carefully brought a subtle change to the subject. "When do you think we can expect Fletcher to be joining us here in London?"

"Oh, did I forget to tell you?"

"Probably," replied Julianna dryly.

"I just had a letter from Fletch's tutor. John wrote they expect to be here within a se'ennight."

"What excellent timing!" declared Julianna. "They should be here for our ball. Hiring John was another stroke of luck for us, wasn't it? I so look forward to hearing all about their travels in person! They have not been the very best correspondents this past year, I must say."

Hart teased his sister, "Are you going to expect Fletcher to lend his appearance to Dee's Season, as well?"

"Well, of course! I think a big brother might be more protection than even a father," Julianna teased back not expecting the reaction she got from her brother.

The earl became instantly serious. "I was no protection at all when you came for your Season, so I do not see where you get that idea."

"Oh, Hartford, that is old news. Do not trouble yourself over my misbegotten Season. It is done and over with. You were tied up with young children and a sickly, pregnant wife, besides still figuring out the estates Papa left for you." Julianna then changed the subject again. "Now pour me a wee bit more of that lovely brandy and I shall be off to my bed. We have a dancing master coming in the morning so I had best get a good rest. I shall need all my energy keeping up with the young ones," she laughed.

After downing her glass, she bade her brother a fond good night and went off to seek her bed unaware of the brooding state in which she was leaving the earl. With Julianna's departure, Hartford spent some minutes thinking over all that his young sister had sacrificed in coming to look after him and his children.

There was a large gap in their ages since their mother had lost several pregnancies after his birth. Their parents had never intended to have another child after the losses, so when Julianna had come along they had been overjoyed. But it had meant that the two of them had lead quite separate lives. By the time their parents died in the carriage accident, Hart had been married with two children, but Julianna was still a teenager. He probably shouldn't have allowed their grandmother to bring her to Town for her Season when they were barely out of mourning for their parents but he had been too distracted by his wife's surprise pregnancy. Then his grief had made him selfish and he hadn't cared what Julianna might be giving up when she returned home.

"What do you think, Charlie?" he asked the faithfully attentive spaniel at his feet. "Should I have made my sister come back to London to find a husband after her engagement shattered her heart? Was I a completely selfish cad for keeping her at home with me and the children when she should have been establishing her own household?"

Charlie's ears cocked in response but he didn't have much to say beyond a feeble tail wag.

"You are correct, Charlie. I should have done more for her. No doubt our grandmother would have ensured that no scandal had attached itself to her so she could have returned and would have been welcomed back amongst the *beau monde*."

Charlie placed his paw on his master's knee, whining.

Reaching down to scratch the dog's ears Hart agreed. "Maybe you're right, Charlie. The duchess really should have made a push to rescue her darling granddaughter. She should have come and gotten her or at least talked some sense into her. But then where would the children and I have been? Maybe Julianna is right. It is all part of the past, and we just need to do our best for Odelia now."

Hart sat in thought for a few more minutes. "Julianna should really have a home of her own, filled with her own children. I have no idea how this can be changed though, at this late juncture. And really this is all the Duchess' fault, so she should cudgel her brain on the matter. Perhaps I will make a call on her to discuss it."

Not usually one for such self-reflection, after a few moments Hart resolved to think of it later, enjoyed a last swallow of his brandy, then took himself off to his own bed.

Chapter Four

The next day began later than usual for the country-bred lady but with Julianna up and about despite her rather restless night.

Maizy breezed into the room carrying her mistress' toast and chocolate. "Good morning, milady!" she declared with great cheer as she threw back the curtains to let in the sunshine. "I'm sorry to say so, but you don't look nearly rested enough this morning. Did you want me to close the curtains and let you sleep a wee bit longer?"

"As lovely as that thought sounds, Maizy, I have far too much to do today. I had too much on my mind when I went to bed last night, and it kept me tossing and turning for some time. But I think I have come up with some solutions, so it was not all in vain."

"You were worryin' about your niece again, weren't you?" demanded the ever-loyal servant. "You surely ain't the only one that should be workin' on this."

"Hush, Maizy. Odelia's mother is not here, and it really does not fall into the realm of what a father can handle. Hart has left all the decisions to me as to what Odelia should or should not be permitted to do as he is much too busy in the House of Lords to deal with most of it."

Somewhat mollified, Maizy demonstrated her curiosity. "What exactly has you so concerned? I thought you had all the details worked out before we even left the estate." She kept her watchful gaze divided between her mistress and the wardrobe from which she was selecting Julianna's gown for the morning.

With a heartfelt sigh, Julianna concurred as she took her seat in front of the vanity to allow Maizy to style her hair. "Most everything *is* worked out. But a few issues have arisen. One big question is whether or not Odelia should be allowed to learn the waltz."

The maid regarded her in the mirror with rounded eyes. "That is a tough one, isn't it, milady? You don't want her to seem fast, but you don't want her to be left out either."

"That is my exact dilemma!"

"So what did you decide in all that tossin' and turnin'?"

"I came up with a compromise. We have already arranged for a dancing instructor to come by today to help us perfect our steps. I shall ask him to teach us the waltz, but I will withhold judgment on whether or not she may actually dance it in public until I see it for myself and approval has been given by the patronesses of Almack's."

"That sounds like a right good idea, milady. And I can't imagine that took you so long to figure out. Was there something else worryin' your head?"

Julianna let another sigh escape but followed it up with a warm smile at her favorite maid. "You know me too well, Maizy! Odelia and I were in Gunther's yesterday and we ran into an old school friend of mine. When she learned I was to chaperone Odelia's debut, she offered to hold an entertainment of some sort in her honor. It is a terribly generous offer, but I cannot decide on the propriety of it."

"So did you come to any conclusions at all?"

"I must admit I only made a partial decision on the subject. I have decided to wait and see. Lady Chorney has invited me to come for tea. I shall hear what suggestions she may have and come to a conclusion from there. Really, what harm could it do? And it was very kind and generous of her to even suggest it."

"That sounds quite reasonable, milady," answered the maid deferentially but with a delightful twinkle in her eye, knowing how much her mistress was agonizing over every decision. "I just hope *you* can have a wee bit of fun while we're here in Town. It's not just milady Dee who should be enjoying herself."

"None of that now, Maizy. I must run. The dancing master should be here any moment. My hair looks quite lovely. You always do such a good job of it."

"You are most skilled at avoidin' certain things, milady. But I'm certain you'll come about all right and tight. Have fun with the dancing master." With a cheeky grin, the faithful maid left the room.

After a last glance to ensure she was appropriately dressed and everything was in place, Julianna left the room just as a maid approached to announce the arrival of the dancing instructor.

"Thank you, Jane. Please make sure Lady Odelia is also informed of our visitor."

It was a trifle unorthodox to have their lessons so early but they had been fortunate to be able to arrange them at all since they had not thought of it until they had arrived in Town. Despite the early hour, Julianna and Odelia were both ready to face the rigours the dancing master would put them through as he helped them practice all the steps they would need for the many balls and soirees they would attend over the next weeks. Both girls, of course, were quite familiar with the steps for the country-dance, the cotillion and the quadrille, but the waltz had yet to be introduced to the assembly rooms near their home estate, so Lady Julianna thought it best that they learn it. Despite the knowledge they already had, the skilled dancer had several suggestions as well as a few new steps to offer them.

Monsieur Francois Lemieux was a handsome, athletic young man forced by his family's straightened circumstances to go into trade. He usually found these lessons exceedingly boring, but was soon happily surprised to find he had finally been hired by someone with skill. He was delighted by Julianna and Odelia's proficiency and grace with the dances they were already familiar with and impressed with how quickly they were able to master the steps of the waltz.

He had brought a copy of *The Gentleman and Lady's Companion Containing the Newest Cotillions and Country Dances*. Julianna and Odelia had giggled over the subtitle of the book – *to which is added, instances of ill manners to be carefully avoided by youth of both sexes.*

"Does that mean the older folks do not have to avoid the instances of ill manners?" Odelia had asked drolly as she leafed through the illustrated manual. That was just the beginning of the hilarity.

Since there were two girls and only one man, the girls had decided they would take turns dancing with the instructor or on their own pretending to have a partner, which eventually caused them all to dissolve into fits of giggles and gales of laughter. The stiffly serious young dancing master also finally succumbed to mirth at Odelia's antics as she pantomimed accepting an invitation to dance with various imaginary lords or other gentlemen.

She dipped into a deeply formal curtsy. "Oh, my lord, I would be ever so honored to dance with you next," Odelia simpered coyly while batting her eyelashes madly as Julianna and Monsieur Lemieux howled with laughter.

It was into this chaotic scene of hilarity that a slightly dusty, but handsomely dressed young nobleman walked. After surveying the trio momentarily, with a slightly amused smile upon his lips, he cleared his throat loudly causing the other occupants of the room to turn in surprise. Odelia stared in delight, but it was Julianna who reacted most swiftly, dashing across the room with a whoop of joy.

"Fletcher Montgomery! What are you doing here? Have you just arrived? Of course you have, just look at you." With that disjointed series of exclamations she proceeded to fling herself into his open arms to receive the warm, bear-like hug of her favorite, if only, nephew.

Much less unconditional in her love, the young lord's sister declared, "Fletch, you are just in time to help us finish brushing up our dance steps. If Aunt Jules is done fawning over you, we can complete our lesson and let poor Monsieur Lemieux be off to his next appointment."

Fletcher swept his sister an elegant bow. "I am ever so gratified to see you missed me, sister dear," was his sarcastic reply before he pulled her into a warm hug, too.

With the greetings out of the way, he remembered his manners. "Sorry, Aunt Jules, I probably should not have come to greet you in all my travel dirt. Do you want me to go clean up, or should I do as this silly chit demands and help you polish up your dancing?"

With a cheerful laugh Julianna answered, "Well, considering hugging us has probably gotten us fully covered in your dust, we might as well continue. Besides since you have just returned from the continent, perhaps you shall be nearly as skilled in dancing the waltz as our friend Monsieur Lemieux."

"Glad to oblige. I'll do my humble best," he replied as his aunt introduced him to the dancing instructor.

"Monsieur Lemieux, please allow me to introduce you to my nephew. This is Fletcher, Baron Hanford. If you do not object, he could join us for the lesson so that we are equally paired."

"It is a great pleasure to make your acquaintance, my lord Baron. I have absolutely no objection to you joining with us. If you have nearly as much skill as your aunt and your sister, you will be a welcome addition." With that gracious speech, the lesson resumed.

The four, young people spent almost another hour in vigorous dancing, enjoying their energetic perambulations about the room. Despite their giddiness, with the help of both gentlemen the girls did manage to master the steps of the new dance as well as perfect their knowledge of the more familiar dances. Finally the dancing instructor declared they were ready to face the scrutiny of the *ton*.

After Monsieur Lemieux politely took his leave of the young baron and bowed gracefully over Julianna and Odelia's hands, the three young relatives adjourned to the morning room to be served some refreshments and get caught up on Fletcher's news of his travels.

"All right, Fletcher, I have been perishing of curiosity! Where did you learn the waltz? I only remember you having two left feet, and you were actually almost graceful in the ballroom just now," Odelia gave her big brother a backward compliment.

The young lord actually blushed at his sister's words. "Almost graceful, you say? Thanks ever so much, little sister. I must say I am shocked looking at you as well. Last time I saw you, you were still in the schoolroom. Now here you are with your hair up and your dress long, almost like a real lady," he teased.

Odelia's swift reaction was a swat towards his well-styled hair, which he not so gracefully dodged. Before things could escalate out of hand Julianna stepped between her two young relatives.

"Enough, you two! Dee, do you not want to hear all his stories? Please do not chase him from the room before he has had a chance to explain himself. And Fletcher, I was so surprised to see you entering the ballroom. Just last night your father told me he had received word to expect you within the next week, so I did not think to watch for you for at least a couple more days."

With the subject safely changed, she reached up to give her nephew another warm hug. "It is so nice to see you Fletch. I had no idea I would miss you quite that badly," she declared with a watery chuckle struggling to hold back tears knowing the almost twenty-year-old would shudder at the sight of his aunt crying.

"Well, I'm here now," the young baron stated pragmatically. "So let us sit down to some of Cook's scrumptious cookies, and I shall tell you a little bit about our recent travels."

So the three took their seats, and the ladies listened raptly as Fletcher related some of his adventures and exploits from his travels throughout the continent with his former tutor, John. After one of his more vivid stories was winding down his ever-attentive aunt chimed in.

"Where *is* John, by the way? He has stayed on here with you, hasn't he? Or did he instead decide to head back to Somerton to see his family? His poor mother must be anxious to see him since you two were gone for so long."

Fletcher's face showed a tinge of alarm as he momentarily worried that his aunt would ring a peel over him for his long absence, so he broke in defensively. "Well, we always kept Father apprised of our whereabouts."

"Yes, yes, I did not mean to lecture. My apologies, Fletcher. I am just curious about what you have done with John," Julianna laughed.

Fletcher laughed, too. "Oh, old Sober Sides had to report to the earl, then you were right, he planned to set off for Somerton to see his mama. Then, if I understand correctly, I am to be free of a tutor and be a man of the world, since Father has decided he has a new position to offer him." Fletcher ended this last bit of information with a definite note of pride in his voice.

Unfortunately, his aunt's inward reaction was not one of such joy as he continued. "Yes ma'am, I am planning on seeing the sights of London and taking in some of the Season. You need not worry so much, Aunty, I am going to help you keep an eye on my sister for a while."

Julianna realized her role would be expanded to keeping an eye on the two of them. Then she chided herself for her worrying ways. No doubt the young lord had gotten a fair bit of experience and polish during his travels about the continent. His tutor, old Sober Sides, as Fletch liked to call him on occasion, was a steady, serious young man who would have kept a close watch on his young charge and no doubt taught him to steer clear of dangers and trouble. And just last night she had been telling the earl she expected Fletcher to help watch out for his sister. She had just hoped that Fletcher's tutor would also be there to lend a hand. Julianna had been counting on the presence of the serious young man to lend some sobriety to the Season as well as to even out her numbers when necessary if they were entertaining. There was naught she could do about it now; she would just have to manage without him.

"Excellent news, Fletch, not that I worry about Dee getting into too much trouble. It is the gentlemen I worry about trying to lead her into trouble." Julianna laughed slightly trying to make light of her deepest fear.

"Have no fear on that count, Aunt Jules. No fellow is going to play fast and loose with my sister. They would have to go through me first." Even Fletcher looked surprised over this protective outburst.

Odelia herself lightened the mood at that moment. With a roll of her pretty blue eyes she declared, "Oh dear, what was the sense of even having a dancing lesson? With all of you "protecting" me, no gentleman will even be able to get close enough to me to be able to ask me to dance with him!"

After the laughter had died down Julianna stood, putting an end to the enjoyable interlude. "Odelia we should be off to make some morning calls soon. How much time will you need to get ready?"

"Oh, I just about forgot we were to go make calls this afternoon. I will need to change my gown and have my hair tidied. Could I have a half an hour?"

"That would be most acceptable, my dear. Let us meet in the foyer in thirty minutes."

Odelia turned on her heel and fled from the room without another word to either her brother or her aunt. With a good-natured smile, Julianna turned to bid farewell to her nephew who was regarding her quizzically.

"Why ever do they call them morning calls if you make them in the afternoon?" he demanded comically.

"That, my dear, is another mystery of life. There really is no rhyme or reason to most of the myriad of little rules followed by the *ton*." After a very brief pause and a slight laugh Julianna continued, "I guess I, too, ought to change and tidy myself before we go out. Enjoy your afternoon, Fletcher. Will you be here for the evening meal? Should I tell Cook to expect you?"

"Oh, I imagine so, Aunt Julianna. Tomorrow is time enough for me to start making merry now that my education has finally ended," Fletcher declared with a wicked chuckle, which sounded quite odd to his aunt who was still remembering him as a little boy.

Julianna managed to restrain herself from comment, merely lifting her eyebrow dubiously before kissing him on the cheek and exiting the room with rather more decorum than had Odelia mere moments earlier.

Chapter Five

The two Montgomery ladies enjoyed making the rounds visiting various friends for the requisite twenty minutes, meeting new people and furthering acquaintances they had met on previous days. Odelia was energetically absorbing every ritual of the Season and was skipping along beside her aunt as they were finally making their way to her friend's house for a longer visit before returning home.

"This is the most fun I have ever had," she declared with youthful vigor. "I can hardly believe you tasted this for just a few weeks and decided to give it all up! How could you ever stand staying at boring old Somerton when you could have been spending the Season here with all the glamour and elegance of the *ton?*"

After a momentary pause wherein Odelia contemplated all the aspects of the Season she was most enjoying, she continued, "I declare, I do not wish to choose a husband this Season. It is by far too diverting. I think I shall enjoy all the Season has to offer this year and return next year to choose a husband."

"Well, Dee, you are completely entitled to make that choice, but keep in mind that the Season has not even fully gotten underway. You might find that you shall meet some nice, handsome lord and decide that this would be a good year to get married. Or you might decide to wait a few years. The only problem is, many of the friends you are meeting right now will be making their choice this year and moving on with their lives, so it will not be the same next Season."

"Maybe so, but I do not want to give all this up any time soon!" Odelia declared vehemently.

On that note they arrived at Odelia's friend's house. "Thanks for walking with me, Aunty Jewel. Are you sure you shall not need Beth to walk with you on your errands?"

"No, it is best if the maid waits for you so you are not walking home alone. At my advanced age I can get away with walking about by myself a bit. I shall be stopping in at Lady Chorney's home on my way back to our house, but I will still probably be home before you. Have a lovely visit, Dee, and I shall see you later."

"Oh, how delightful! I do hope she will plan something truly exceptional!" she declared, clapping her hands with characteristic enthusiasm before continuing in more subdued tones. "That is, if you deem it appropriate." She then grinned merrily at her aunt. "Oh, you *are* going to let her host a party for me, aren't you, Jules? I do not know any girls that are getting to have two different hostesses this year!"

"You are still such a scamp, Dee, it is hard for me to believe your father and I ever decided it was a good time to let you out of the schoolroom!" laughed Julianna as she bade her niece farewell. "Now behave like the young lady you are supposed to be and let me get on with my calls. I shall see you at home later and I will then let you know what has been decided." Again Julianna laughed at the crestfallen look on her young niece's face as she set off at a jaunty pace back along the streets of Mayfair.

When she arrived at Lady Chorney's elegant townhouse Julianna took a deep, fortifying breath before she ascended the stairs and used the knocker. Instantly a well-trained footman was opening the door and ushering her inside. Noting the fine quality of her garments, he ushered her into the viscount's exquisitely appointed parlor and informed her he would see if milady was "at home" to visitors.

Within moments Catherine squealed in delight from the doorway. "I hardly thought to believe my ears when the footman informed me Lady Julianna Montgomery was waiting to see me! What a delightful surprise! Please sit down. He shall be bringing in a tea tray for us momentarily."

"You have a truly lovely home, Lady Chorney. Thank you for seeing me," Julianna murmured politely.

"No, no, no thanks at all expected! And please you must call me Cathy like you did when we were children."

Spontaneously Cathy pulled Julianna into a quick hug, appearing to surprise both of them by the impulsive act. Smiling somewhat sheepishly at her guest, Cathy excused, "I truly did miss you very much."

Julianna was unaccountably warmed by the affectionate gesture, realizing she too had missed her old friend. "I was absolutely delighted to see you so unexpectedly the other day at Gunther's. I was hoping we could catch each other up on all that has been going on in our lives of late."

Briefly interrupted by the servants arriving with the tea, once they were each settled with a steaming cup the conversation flowed freely.

"I have been married to Lord Chorney for almost five years now. I had a couple of offers during my first Season, but my parents did not apply any pressure on me to settle down, and I was having so much fun I wanted a second Season."

Julianna interrupted, "My niece has said the exact same thing just today and the Season has not even properly gotten under way!"

Cathy laughed. "A girl after my own heart." After another girlish giggle, she continued. "Unfortunately my second Season was cut short by the untimely death of my grandfather. We left town early since we had to go into mourning. By the time I came up with my sister for my third time, I was ready to accept an offer of marriage and was so fortunate as to catch my dear Robert's eye."

"Tell me about Lord Chorney. I do not recall if I have ever had the pleasure of making his acquaintance."

"No, you may not have met him. You really were not in Town for all that long, were you? And he is a fair bit older than us, so it is quite possible that you did not meet him. You may not have even had any friends in common. The first Lady Chorney died several years ago, and at first he did not think of finding himself another viscountess. But then he changed his mind, came up for the Season, and found me." Momentarily looking uncomfortable, Cathy paused before forcing out another, more strained, giggle. "It is quite fortunate for his line that he had a first wife since she gave him a couple of fine strapping sons and I have yet to bear any children."

Seeing that this obviously affected her old friend deeply Julianna struggled for something to say, but all she could do was squeeze Cathy's hand in sympathy. "Things often don't turn out quite how we had expected, do they?" she asked in quiet understatement.

"Oh, but my dear Robert is quite lovely. He says he does not mind not having more children. This way he can have me all to himself. And his sons Winston and Charles are such dear young men. Of course, they are off at Eton for now, but the house is certainly a different place when they come home for holidays. But a little girl would be such a blessing to our family," she continued wistfully. "Which is why I said I would love to host a party for your niece. I know it is a bit unconventional, but it would be such a delight to share in Odelia's debut. Please say you have at least given it some thought."

"Actually I have given it some thought, and I would be happy to accept your generous offer. What did you have in mind?"

Catherine clapped her hands girlishly. "Oh, how exciting! Well, I was actually thinking that although we have quite a lovely ballroom, it might not do for us to host a ball for her since she is not family, and, no doubt, you shall do that and, of course, I would not want to go into competition with you. I was thinking a rout would be quite lovely. We could have music here in the morning room, card tables set up in the library, and of course, supper served in the dining room. We have enough space to have quite a number of people, so we can discuss together a delightful guest list in order to allow Odelia to meet with a large group of people. What do you think?"

Julianna impulsively gave her friend another warm hug. "Thank you so much. That is quite a splendid plan. I had no idea you had given it so much thought."

"Well, Julie, my dear, I quite love to entertain so there actually was no effort required. I have had quite a number of balls and other entertainments over the years, but this shall be so exciting. There's nothing like a young lady's debut, is there?"

Julianna's smile dimmed slightly as she thought of her own debut but had to agree nonetheless. "Yes, it is a marvelous time to be sure. I know Dee is beside herself with excitement much of the time. She will be in raptures about your ideas, I must say."

Lady Chorney hesitated momentarily before broaching the sensitive topic. "Julianna, I wanted to ask if you might consider the idea of inviting Viscount Beaufort to any of the entertainments you shall be hosting."

Julianna could barely look her friend in the eye, so discomfited was she by this question. Catherine regretted the awkward topic but persisted despite her friend's obvious reluctance.

Squeezing her hand in sympathy, Catherine continued. "I am sorry to bring it up, my dear, but it really must be faced. Have you ever spoken to Ackerley since you left London those many years ago?"

"I did run into him very briefly on the street the other day, but we barely exchanged anything more than the merest pleasantries." Julianna paused briefly before continuing staunchly, "I must admit, in all honesty, that I am dreading any occasion on which I may have to face him. No doubt he has given little or no thought to me all these years, but it was so awful when I said goodbye to him that I had planned to never see him again in my life if that could be arranged. Do you know if he does the social rounds during the Season?"

"Yes, my dear, in past years he did socialize to a certain extent. Last year he was more visible than usual, and this Season the *on dit* is that he is finally hanging out for a wife, so he is expected to be showing up at many of the events of the Season. He is considered quite the catch, so you can imagine the number of invitations that are arriving at his door. He is friends with my husband, so I know he would come if I were to send him an invitation, but I have decided my first loyalty lies with you, so that is why I have taken it upon myself to ask you about it."

"Thank you, Cathy, it is kind of you to take my feelings into consideration, especially when you are being so generous as to have this rout for my dear Dee. If he is a particular friend of Lord Chorney then there is no doubt you must send him an invitation."

Julianna stopped and thought for a moment. "I just don't want my old disgrace to taint Odelia, and I am dreading the stares and whispers when the tabbies strain to ogle our first encounter." She gave a delicate shudder. "Having spectators for such an awkward meeting is not going to be pleasant."

"True enough, but anyone brought out in the household of the Dowager Duchess of Westerley has the backbone to pull it off," declared Catherine loyally. "But I do have an idea that could take away some of the stress and unpleasantness."

Julianna turned grateful and questioning eyes toward her hostess. "Go on. Tell me before I perish of curiosity."

"What do you think of me inviting the viscount for tea on an appointed day, and you showing up 'unexpectedly' and meeting him without a large audience?"

Julianna laughed with delight. "Oh, Catherine, you are a dear! That would be splendid. Awkward, no doubt, but a splendid idea nonetheless. When, do you suppose, would be a good day? But don't you think he will see right through the ruse?"

In a matter-of-fact tone Cathy pointed out reasonably, "It doesn't really matter if he does. Politeness dictates that he accepts whatever we tell him. You shall be dropping by to discuss the details of my upcoming rout for Lady Odelia. You could even bring her with you to lend countenance to the meeting, or bring just your maid if you do not want Dee to witness your first conversation with your old beau."

Lady Chorney paused momentarily with a twinkle in her eye. "I think it will be good for Lucius to see you again. He gets a little too haughty at times, so it shall be a good reminder that not everyone does exactly as he wishes."

Julianna started guiltily. "No, no, I do not want to be an instrument for his humility. I just want any awkwardness to be handled in private. We shall have to manage civility if we are to meet publicly and not cause a great scandal. Please do not read anything more into it."

"Do not trouble yourself, my dear. I will not do anything to put you to the blush," soothed Catherine. "I was merely jesting." She then changed the subject with deft skill. "Now, what do you think of 'dropping by' two days from now? I shall write a note to Lord Ackerley this afternoon and ask him to call on me."

"Thank you, Cathy, that would be lovely," Julianna answered not quite honestly, but very politely, causing Catherine to grin at her friend.

"And what say you to the rout being one week from today?"

"One week?" questioned Julianna in shocked surprise. "Do you truly think you can pull it all together in a week?"

"Of course," answered the viscountess with simple pride. "It is really quite easy when you have as good a staff as we do. The biggest job will be the invitations which I shall get Chorney's secretary to help with as soon as you and I agree on the list."

With that, the two ladies set their minds to deciding on the most congenial mix of people to attend a lively gathering in Lady Odelia's honor. After another thirty minutes, Julianna declared she had monopolized too much of her friend's time and politely took her leave with promises to return two days hence for the uncomfortable meeting with Viscount Beaufort.

Chapter Six

Julianna was shocked to see the day dawn bright and sunny. It seemed to her as though everything ought to be as grey as her thoughts. She had barely slept the past two nights since she was seized with dread over the upcoming encounter with her former fiancé, Lord Lucius Ackerley, Viscount Beaufort.

Gazing wearily into the mirror, she castigated herself for being such a hen-witted gabby over the viscount. "You are being entirely too foolish," she told her reflection with a sigh.

"I know you are dreading a terrible scene, but keep in mind that as a gentleman he should have sufficient poise not to put you to the blush too greatly." Seeing the quizzical look on her own face she acknowledged, "I know, I know, the last time you saw him seven years ago was uncomfortable, to say the least. Things were said that were not fit to come forth from a lady's mouth, but you have grown up since then."

With another heartfelt sigh, she recalled that time. Those had been the worst moments of her young life. She had truly believed they were a love match, despite the unpopularity of such sentiments amongst the *ton*. She had felt so betrayed that she had said many regrettable things during that final scene. Then she had refused to see him when he had come pounding on her grandmother's door. She had never set foot in London since and had thus avoided seeing Lord Ackerley for seven years.

Now here she was on the verge of seeing him for the first time in all those years, and she felt ill at the prospect. One could not count that time on the street a few days earlier as they barely exchanged any words. Standing in front of Catherine's elegant townhouse, Julianna paused before ascending the stairs. Unsure if he had already arrived, she did not want to bump into him in front of the house, but it was difficult to make herself climb up and knock on the door.

"Come along, Julianna. You are not well representing the houses of Somerton or Westerley at this moment. Just imagine what the duchess would have to say over such cowardly behavior."

That motivational speech did the trick of getting her moving. With an effort of will, Julianna finally made use of the brass knocker and was admitted by a footman immediately. He gave no indication of having seen her dither on the doorstep while he bowed her graciously into the viscountess' receiving room.

"Lady Julianna Montgomery to see you, milady," announced the footman before excusing himself and shutting the door on the flurry of activity that resulted.

Lady Chorney jumped up excitedly from her seat while Lord Ackerley took his time getting to his feet, stunned as he was by this sudden appearance.

Julianna made a graceful curtsy and finally managed to raise her eyelashes and survey the room. It was not playacting that caused her sudden intake of breath as she saw her old beau again. In fact, it took all the force of will she possessed to keep her reaction within bounds. At that first brief encounter, she had been too surprised to take in his splendour. No one had told her the viscount had grown even more handsome in the ensuing years, the strength of his jawline more pronounced, and just the very slightest of grey at the temples in his nearly ebony hair. Forcing her jaw not to drop open in shock, Julianna felt her stomach flutter with nerves as she gripped tightly to her friend's hand and tried not to cause an ill-bred scene in Catherine's parlor.

Observing the niceties, Catherine dragged her friend further into the room while she prattled on. "Julianna, you remember Beaufort. Lord Ackerley was just telling me about his work on his estates. Will you join us in a cup of tea my dear, Lady Julianna?"

With a gulp of air, Julianna smiled wanly at her former fiancé as he bent briefly over her outstretched hand. Almost forgetting what her friend had asked in the rush of heat she felt as his warm breath brushed over her knuckles for the briefest of seconds, Julianna blinked owlishly at Catherine.

"Oh, yes, tea. Yes, please," she stammered almost incoherently before dropping into a chair.

There was a moment of strained silence as Catherine rustled back to her seat and poured Julianna the offered refreshment. Lady Chorney then took pity on her two nervous visitors and began an inconsequential flow of breezy social chitchat. As she commented about the weather and the various balls she had attended that week, her two guests were visibly gathering their scattered wits. Slowly they joined in the conversation.

Despite knowing beforehand that she was going to see him that day, Julianna was unprepared for the effect the sight of Viscount Beaufort would have on her wits. Ever since she fled from London, she had prided herself on being a poised woman. But here she was acting like a complete ninny. She called herself to task for such missish behaviour, forced her disordered thoughts under control, and joined Catherine in making social small talk.

"Lord Ackerley, I apologize for my tardiness in expressing my sympathy on the loss of your mother. I know it has been some time now, but losing a parent is always a deep pain that never fully vanishes." Julianna saw the slight clench of his jaw and remembered belatedly that it had been a rather complicated relationship. "How are things on your estate? I trust all is well at

Beaufort?" she inquired tentatively, trying to put her roiling emotions behind her and make another try at polite conversation.

Somewhat relieved that she had finally broken her silence and surprised at her poise, the viscount struggled to contain his uncalled-for anger. Ackerley responded, "All is well on my estate, thank you for asking. And how is your family?"

Unsure which family he was referring to she replied vaguely at first. "Well, thank you." After a brief pause, she continued more informatively. "We are in Town for my niece's debut. Hart's daughter, Odelia, is making her first curtsey to Society, in fact, she has already been presented at court, so she is officially out now. I am to be her chaperone."

Luc was surprised to have a laugh burst from his lips. "It is hard to see you as a chaperone. How can you be her chaperone when you still need one for yourself?"

A light blush stained her cheeks as she replied dryly, "Hardly the truth, my lord, but it is kind of you to say so."

Happy to see her guests relaxing a little, Lady Chorney stepped in to direct things along her chosen path. "My husband and I will be hosting a rout with Lady Odelia as guest of honor next week. Do say you shall come, my lord."

Surprised that this invitation would be extended in front of her, Julianna froze for the briefest moment but then forced a polite smile to her now bloodless lips as she turned her startled eyes between her friend and her old beau.

Luc felt blindsided by the compassionately protective feeling sweeping over him at the sight of Julianna's pale face. He was impressed with her composure despite her obvious surprise at the turn of events. He admitted to himself that he had thought it was a set up when she arrived at the Chorneys' door while he had been invited for tea, but it was clear that she had not expected him to be invited to her niece's party. Luc did not want to feel compassion for the woman who had once torn his life apart.

Looking coldly at Julianna, Luc accepted politely, but hauteur was evident in his tone. "I would be delighted to attend. Send me the details, and I will be sure to put in an appearance."

Used to how cold and calculating the viscount could be with anyone he considered not his friend, Catherine was not completely shocked by Lord Ackerley's reaction, but she was somewhat taken aback by just how frigid he sounded since she considered herself to be one of his closest associates. She had counted on him to be nice but now was feeling bad that she was putting her dear Julianna through this experience.

Then Julianna surprised everyone present, including herself. "Do try to squeeze it in, my lord," she said in coolly composed tones. "I am certain Hart would be pleased to see you. Of course, with your, no doubt, busy schedule we would understand if you were unable to be present."

With a sardonically lifted eyebrow, Lucius acknowledged she had won this round. They were all happy when Lord Chorney suddenly entered the room at that moment. Despite his air of preoccupation, he was, as usual, dressed and groomed as though he had just left the gentle ministrations of his valet. A smile bloomed on Catherine's face as she admired his still handsome features despite the passage of time and the grey beginning to accumulate in his hair.

"Catherine, my dear, I did not realize we had guests, how remiss of me," he began calmly as he greeted his wife with a chaste kiss upon her cheek before turning to their guests politely.

"This is my dear friend, Lady Julianna Montgomery, the Earl of Somerton's sister," introduced the viscountess.

"It is my pleasure to meet you. I knew your brother fairly well before he retired to the country to raise his children. I am so sorry about your sister-in-law. It is such a tragedy to go so young." The viscount expressed sincere sympathy bringing an unexpected lump to Julianna's throat despite the years that had already passed.

"Thank you, my lord. I am very happy to make your acquaintance. It is generous of you and the viscountess to host a rout for my niece. My entire family is aquiver with nerves over her foray into Society. Now that court is behind us, it will be quite lovely for her to be able to get some experience in a smaller, congenial setting before she attends other, larger occasions, and of course, her own formal ball."

"No thanks needed. I should actually thank you. My wife dearly loves to entertain, so she is delighted for any excuse." The viscount smiled indulgently at his pretty wife before turning to their other guest.

"Luc, my boy," he boomed heartily. "What are you doing here eating such useless things our cook enjoys preparing for my wife's tea?"

Everyone laughed, and much of the tension that had been accumulating in the room dissipated.

"I really must be going," stated Julianna before anyone could resume their seats. "Thank you for the tea, Catherine, I shall catch up with you again soon. It was lovely to meet you, my lord. And a pleasure to see you again, Lord Ackerley," she concluded with as much sincerity as she could force into her voice, not quite meeting his eye as she hurriedly excused herself before anyone could dissuade her.

As the door shut on Julianna's quickly retreating form Lady Chorney turned on her other guest.

"How could you be so mean in front of my dear friend, Ackerley?" she demanded heatedly. "'I'll try to squeeze you into my busy schedule,'" she misquoted sardonically. "What was that supposed to mean? It is to be a rout for heaven's sake, not a ball. You cannot just drop by for a few moments, or it will be remarked upon. Either come or do not, but I will not allow you to cause a scene to darken this poor young woman's Season whatever your issues might be with her aunt. She is a sweet young girl and surely she is at enough of a disadvantage entering

Society without her mama at her side. She needs help and encouragement, not any of your highhanded set downs!"

Surprised by her vehemence and slightly ashamed as it was, Lucius tried to defend himself. "You do not know the entire story, Catherine. It is rather complicated."

"I do not give a flying fig how complicated it might be nor which details I may not be privy to. When you are in my drawing room, you will ensure that you have proper behavior toward any other guests I may have," she declared.

"Yes, my lady," he answered meekly with a twinkle finally appearing in his eye.

Robert had remained silent during this exchange, but at that final statement he burst out with a laugh. "Whatever did you do to earn such a tirade from my usually sweet wife?"

"Not much, Robert, I swear to you! I merely did not want to commit myself to attending your rout next week."

"Why ever not, my boy? You always come to my wife's entertainments," Robert stated with some confusion.

Luc hesitated momentarily before answering starkly. "I was once engaged to marry Lady Julianna, and the association did not end amicably. I cannot say I would look forward to an evening spent in her company."

Determined to be a loyal friend to Julianna despite her husband's close association with Lord Ackerley, Catherine plowed into the unknown waters despite a momentary hesitation. "Well, I do not know what you did to make her end the engagement, but you must be civil now. You must decide for yourself what you think is best for your own peace of mind, but I will not tolerate you making a scene at my party. You are usually a lovely guest to have. That is why I wanted you, but if you are going to put either Montgomery lady to the blush then I do not think I will welcome your presence."

Somewhat chastened but definitely amused by the uncharacteristic anger from his hostess, Luc finally agreed to attend. "And I promise I shall be on my very best behaviour. Have no fear, my lady."

Unconvinced, Catherine merely replied, "See that you do," with a slightly disgruntled harrumph.

Chapter Seven

"I think you have outdone yourself, Maizy. My hair looks perfectly glamorous. I hope you did an even better job with Odelia, since she is the one we are all working so hard for." Julianna couldn't help being delighted with her looks that evening. Despite her nerves, even she had to admit she was looking her best.

"I think you ought to quit worryin' yourself over that youngster, milady. She has been ready for her debut for years. She is looking pretty as a picture this evening, if I do say so meself. Despite her constant squealing I managed to get her hair just so. She could barely sit still she was that excited."

Sharing a conspiratorial grin with the maid, Julianna allowed a chuckle to escape. "We are all doing our best for our favorite young lady. This is going to be the first time all four of us have attended the same gathering. While our own formal ball will be Dee's official introduction to Society as a whole, this is going to be her first big event so it is very important that it go smoothly for her."

"You needn't worry so, milady. Your family are all perfect and lovely. It will be exactly as you wish. I'm certain of it."

Grateful for her maid's loyal enthusiasm, Julianna told her not to wait up and then quit the room.

Julianna was full of pride as she smiled at her family in the close confines of the carriage. Her brother and nephew looked less than pleased to be on this particular ride, but Odelia was grinning her delight. After settling into the carriage, Julianna looked everyone over critically. She noted they were all dressed in their best finery, not a single hair out of place. She smiled with satisfaction.

Their own ball was just a few days off, so this evening would be an excellent lead in for Odelia. It would set the tone for Odelia's Season and it appeared as though the night would be a huge success, provided, of course, that nothing went wrong. She knew her friend had put a great deal of effort into ensuring everything went smoothly. And the earl had finally realized his responsibilities and had been prevailed upon to attend. Julianna breathed an almost imperceptible sigh of relief for a moment before her nerves tightened once more as she thought of the coming evening to be possibly spent in Lucius' company. Dread and determination crept up her spine in equal measures.

The carriage drew to a stop. A footman handed the ladies down from the carriage, and then Hartford and Fletcher escorted them up the stairs to be announced. Squaring their shoulders, their aristocratic history sitting lightly on them, the Montgomerys looked around their surroundings almost haughtily, their blue blood very evident to all onlookers. Then Hart sheepishly bowed away, Fletch saw an old, school chum and broke into a boyish grin, and Julianna smiled lovingly at her niece and nephew, thus breaking the veneer of unapproachability that had momentarily surrounded the small family.

Catherine came forward to greet her guests of honor while eligible young men queued up behind her clamoring for an introduction to the pretty young lady.

"Welcome, ladies, it is so lovely to have you in our home. Odelia, my dear, you look absolutely ravishing this evening. I do declare you shall break hearts throughout the *ton* this Season.

And Julianna, I have never seen you look as good as you do this evening. I do think you shall be setting some hearts aquiver yourself."

Julianna and Odelia both blushed charmingly. Julianna maintained her composure, of course, and complimented their hostess on the results of her obvious efforts. "Everything looks wonderful, Catherine. You are clearly an expert. Thank you so much for hosting this evening."

"Please, do not even mention it. Entertaining is one of my greatest joys. Now, come and let me introduce the two of you to some of my other guests."

Thus began a swirl of activity for the next hour or so as Odelia and Julianna met and made conversation with a careful selection of the most fashionable and influential Society had to offer. Viscount Chorney was not one of the very wealthiest men of Society, but clearly he was comfortably well off. Their London house was a townhouse to be sure, but it was on the rather large side. Lady Chorney could actually boast a ballroom, albeit a small one, but for tonight's entertainment the ballroom was kept closed. She had decided a select group for conversation would be best to acquaint Odelia with the ways of the *ton*. So it was into the drawing room that she first ushered her guests. Catherine's piano and harp were set up in the room for the use of any of the guests who wished to demonstrate their skills. She also had a couple of musicians to provide entertainment until the guests got up the nerve to try their hand.

Tables had been set up in the morning room for any that wanted to try their skills at some genteel games of cards. On this rare occasion, the viscount had opened the doors of his library for any who wished to peruse his book collection or discuss various arts. And through the door into the dining room, Julianna could see that preparations were under way to serve a supper later.

All the guests were dressed in their finest evening attire. The ladies were a sea of colours while the gentlemen were almost uniformly dressed in the requisite knee breeches, elegantly dark. Odelia had to struggle to suppress a giggle over the sight of various ladies wearing peacock feathers in their headdresses.

In an effort at discretion, she leaned over and whispered into her aunt's ear. "I just hope none of those ladies get too close to the candles. That would indeed be a distraction no one was prepared for!"

With a reproving glance, Julianna swallowed the giggle struggling to escape at the mental picture painted by Odelia's words. "You behave yourself, young lady."

"Always, dearest Aunty," Dee answered with a dimpled grin.

Finally, satisfied that Odelia could hold her own, Julianna slipped away for a quiet moment to gather her thoughts and refresh herself with a drink offered to her by an attentive footman.

"It's much more exhausting when you are no longer seventeen, is it not?"

Julianna started in surprise, blushing as she met Lucius' quizzing gaze. But she held her own despite how flustered the viscount made her feel.

"Has no one mentioned to you it is very bad *ton* to remind a lady that she is no longer a youngster, my lord?" she demanded pertly.

Lord Ackerley was surprised by the bubble of laughter coming from his own lips. He was determined to be polite for the sake of their hosts. He just never would have expected to enjoy an evening spent in Julianna's presence.

Julianna smiled disarmingly to show she truly had not taken offence. She continued after heaving a heartfelt sigh. "Unfortunately, you are not mistaken. During my own short Season, I thought everyone I encountered was lovely and kind and meant well toward me. I could dance until dawn, sleep for a couple hours, then spend the day shopping and gadding about Town before getting ready to dance until dawn once more. The

Season has barely gotten under way, and I am near exhaustion just from the preparations."

She paused again before looking out at the guests and spying her dear niece. "But when I see how much fun she is having, it makes it all worthwhile."

Lord Ackerley followed her fond gaze and took an assessing look at his companion's charge. She really was a pretty young woman, if not quite in his taste. "It is quite obvious your work has paid off. She looks like she will have a very successful Season." Turning back to Julianna he continued, "It's strange for me to see you in this role of doting mama, but it seems to suit you."

"You never thought I would be a mother?" she asked incredulously before blushing fiery red at the implications brought to mind by her question. Trying to regain her composure, her quick wit swiftly moved her tongue into safer conversational channels. "Well, I can never fill the shoes of their own dear mother, but I have taken great joy in helping Hart raise his children. I shudder to think where we would have all been without each other at that terrible time."

Wishing he could bite off his own tongue for being such a muttonhead, Luc tried to lighten the tone. "Well, they seem to have turned out rather well. You have reason to be proud of your contributions in that regard."

"Thank you, I actually do take an inordinate amount of pride in how they have both grown up. Poor Hart was so distraught over losing his dear wife that he left much of their care to me. I really had no idea what I was doing at first, but I quickly found myself mimicking whatever my own parents had done. I would like to think Hart and I turned out to be fairly decent people, so I figured it would work well. There were, of course, times I would have loved to walk away or at least have someone else to advise me – remembering things my parents had said is not the same as knowing *why* they had said it. But we have all muddled through, and here they are – mostly grown up — and I must admit that I quite like them, so at least I did not bungle the job too terribly for all my inexperience."

Julianna was unsure why she was confiding all this to the viscount she had previously vowed to avoid, but at times he seemed so easy to talk to. That had been one of the things she had loved about him and the one thing she had missed the most when she had terminated the relationship. During the first days and weeks after going back home, she had lost count of the number of times she wished she could talk things over with him, as ridiculous at that thought was after all that had happened.

Striving for a light tone the viscount said, "Now all you have left to do is marry them off."

He instantly realized this was somehow the exact wrong thing to say. Julianna's face had been so animated, open, and confiding as she spoke of her struggles with raising her brother's children, but now, while she maintained a polite smile, her face was shuttered, and the smile no longer reached her eyes.

"It has been a pleasure reminiscing with you, my lord, but now I must bid you adieu," Julianna managed to remain socially correct as she extracted herself from the awkward situation and once again found herself practically fleeing from her former fiancé.

Lucius watched in dismay as Julianna walked away with her back ramrod straight and her head held at a proud angle. He wondered why he always seemed to make the lady leave. It was far from his proudest moment. He had actually been enjoying his conversation with her, much to his surprise. She truly had matured into the potential he had seen in her seven years ago. *She would have made a good viscountess,* he thought with a pang of regret despite all that had transpired between them.

With a slight sigh, he watched her circulate politely through the crowd before realizing he was making a cake of himself. He ought to be circulating as well, not mooning over an old flame like a lovesick youngster. With a wry smile, he went off in search of his hostess to get her to introduce him to some of the eligible young ladies present.

Catherine was understandably hesitant when she saw Luc approaching her with purposeful strides, but she was delighted by his request to be introduced to a few of the ladies. She had chosen her guest list with care, and while she had Odelia and Julianna in mind as the guests of honor, there were several eligible young misses at the rout. Lord Ackerley was one of the most eligible bachelors of the *ton* so it would be quite the coup if she could boast that she was the one who introduced him to his future bride.

Unfortunately for Catherine's plans for him, Luc could not quite work up any enthusiasm for the ladies she was introducing him to, despite his intentions. He was, of course, perfectly polite and charming, and none of the ladies felt the least bit slighted in his attentions, but his heart just was not in it. He kept finding himself comparing each girl to Julianna and finding them lacking, much to his chagrin. At the back of his mind, he kept an ear out for where she was in the room and whom she was talking to. It was most frustrating!

Luc could not help but be relieved when enough time had finally passed for him to take his leave without causing offense or unnecessary gossip. He politely said his farewells to his friends, Catherine and Robert, and headed for the door. On his way to collect his outerwear from the butler he again encountered Julianna.

"Are you leaving already, my lord?" she asked.

"Yes, I am promised elsewhere," he answered less than truthfully hoping she would not press for more information and surprised she had even spoken to him at all considering how their last conversation ended.

"Have a good night, then," Julianna replied in soft tones as she started to turn away.

Lucius could not help himself. He impetuously reached for her hand and gallantly pressed a brief kiss to her wrist. Seeing the bemused look in her eyes, he quickly let her go and departed with the softly spoken words, "Until next time. Good night."

Julianna was disgruntled to find the spot where his lips had pressed still tingled warmly. It took a supreme effort of will not to scrub at it with her free hand, not wanting to draw undue attention to herself. Plastering on a politely sociable smile, she again turned to mingle but somehow inexplicably with Luc's departure, some of the sparkle had gone out of the evening.

Chapter Eight

Julianna and Odelia had been presented to Lady Caroline Fielding, the Dowager Countess of Hearst, and her sweet young daughter, Lady Abigail Fielding. Abigail too was fresh from the country for her first season and was trying to acquire a bit of Town polish before the Season began in earnest.

Being basically of equal rank, all four ladies curtsied to one another. Dispensing with the formalities, Odelia and Abigail quickly settled into an earnest conversation about all they had already seen and done in the big city. This discussion was frequently punctuated with happy giggles making all in the vicinity smile indulgently.

"Oh, to be so young," declared Lady Caroline longingly, looking at Julianna as though they were of a similar age. "I remember my own Season was most diverting. Of course, much has changed since then has it not, my dear?"

Realizing the lady was speaking to her as though they had shared a Season, Julianna was unsure how to answer. She did not actually want to draw any attention to her own disastrous Season, but neither did she wish to own up to years she had not yet lived. Julianna was aware that helping her brother raise his children had no doubt aged her, but she took leave to presume she did not actually look old enough to be their parent. The high road of diplomacy was the only way to handle the awkward situation.

"No doubt much has changed, my lady, but let us hope these young ladies enjoy themselves just as much as you did."

"At least we are not faced with the daunting task of finding a husband. I just wish my poor dearly departed was here to help dear Abigail pick out her future lord. Her brother, the current earl, is of no use in this case. He is too busy setting up his nursery. I ask you, do I look old enough to become a grandmother?"

Once again Julianna mustered up a diplomatic answer. "Not at all, my lady, but isn't it so much fun to play with the babies without any of the responsibilities that come with raising small children?"

"Well, you do have a good point there, my dear." Lady Hearst finally looked carefully at Julianna for the first time. "What was your name again?" she asked with a somewhat altered tone.

"Lady Julianna Montgomery. My brother is the Earl of Somerton."

"And your grandmother is the Dowager Duchess of Westerley." Lady Hearst now looked at her with slight sympathy. "I remember your debut into Society. You were a beautiful young lady. You are Lady Odelia's aunt, not her mother. I apologize for assuming otherwise."

"Please, do not apologize. I do not mind the comparison. I have been helping my brother raise his children for the past several years, so I do feel like her parent right now with all the complications that brings with it," she concluded with a self-deprecating laugh.

Lady Hearst looked at Julianna shrewdly. "You are not actually terribly old, my lady. Are you hanging out for a husband for yourself as well? I saw you speaking for quite some time to that handsome Viscount Beaufort."

Again Julianna laughed, although this time it was a bit more forced. "No, no, my lady. This is Odelia's time, not mine. I put all that behind me seven years ago. And Lord Ackerley is just an old acquaintance," she prevaricated.

Not wishing to prolong the awkward encounter, Julianna finally extricated herself from the conversation. "It was a pleasure meeting you, Lady Caroline. No doubt we will be seeing each other in the coming weeks. I hope you enjoy the rest of your evening."

"And you, Lady Julianna."

For what felt like the millionth time, Julianna wished fervently that there was nothing of note in her past and hoped fiercely that it would have no effect upon Odelia's Season. As she thought about her dear young niece, Julianna looked across the room and saw her in animated conversation with Abigail and a couple of young men with whom she was not acquainted. Julianna decided to investigate.

"Odelia, Abigail, are you having a nice time?" she asked with pointed emphasis.

Odelia turned her charming smile upon her aunt. "Oh, yes, Aunt Jules, we are having a lovely evening, thank you. Are you acquainted with these gentlemen? Lady Chorney introduced us."

Turning to her new friends with a pretty smile, Odelia performed the introductions. "This is my dear aunt, Lady Julianna Montgomery. Aunty, this is Mr. Kenneth Landon and this is Mr. Tom Jackes. They went to school together, and they were just telling us the funniest story about a prank they pulled on their schoolmaster. It is most diverting," she concluded with a gurgle of laughter.

Unable to resist her niece's enjoyment, Julianna looked at the young men with an encouraging smile that almost perfectly matched her niece's.

Mr. Jackes suffered from an unfortunate speech impediment and was quite overcome by the attentions of both Montgomery ladies. He dissolved into a stuttering heap of nerves.

His old friend, used to Tom's suffering, showed no sympathy. Landon smacked him on the back forcefully.

"Breathe, man, breathe." With a good-natured chuckle, he looked at Julianna. "Tom's a great fellow but he's not very good around such pretty ladies." This caused Mr. Jackes' condition to worsen making Odelia's soft heart melt toward the unfortunate young man.

"Do not pay him any mind, Mr. Jackes. I was greatly enjoying your story. You had just gotten to the part where the schoolmaster found your little gift. Then what happened?" Julianna found one more reason to be proud of her niece, she was so kind when dealing with people and making them feel comfortable. The young man was able to continue with his story, haltingly at first, but then he got into the rhythm of his tale.

While Tom regaled the younger ladies with adventures, Kenneth looked at Julianna with chagrin. "I apologize, my lady. I should have known better than to tease him in front of ladies. It angers me so when others make merry of his condition, and here I am doing it myself."

"Well, it is not really me to whom you should apologize." Kenneth flushed to his roots at this mild rebuke, so Julianna took mercy on him. "But it appears that no harm was done. It sounds as though the two of you have had a colourful time while away at school."

The young man grinned. "Without a doubt, we have enjoyed ourselves immensely," he agreed.

"Mr. Landon, I think I am acquainted distantly with your family. I was sorry to hear of your father's ill health. Has there been any improvement?"

"Thank you for your kind inquiry. He has improved slightly, but unfortunately, none of the doctors my mother has hired have been able to hold out much hope of a full recovery."

"I am sorry to hear that, my lord."

Landon smiled sheepishly. "We aren't really all that close, but I do hope the old gentleman pulls through. It is cursed unpleasant being the heir to a viscountcy during the London

Season. I think I might have to retire to the country until the situation blows over."

Julianna could not help the gurgle of laughter that escaped her as the young man looked furtively at the matchmaking mamas eyeing him with avid interest. He again flushed bright red as he realized the vulgarity of what he had just said.

"Not to say I don't like the attention of the ladies, my lady, it is just that I'm not quite sure if I am ready to be leg-shackled at this time."

"No need to explain. I am quite sure I understand perfectly. In either case, you have my sympathies," Julianna answered kindly as she excused herself to return to Lady Chorney's side.

By the end of the evening, it was obvious that Odelia and Abigail were bound to be dear friends for years to come. They promised to spend the morning shopping on Bond Street before attending the 'at home' together, provided, of course, that Odelia could prevail upon Julianna to accompany them.

The Montgomery ladies decided to remain with their host and hostess until the last of the guests had been waved off; however, Hart and Fletch could not be convinced that they, too, should remain to the end. "I am not the debutante, why should I stay?" was Fletcher's succinct declaration on the topic, which his father wholeheartedly supported.

"Besides, Jules, would you not agree that our dear Odelia will be somewhat more popular with the young men if her father and big brother are not around to glare at potential suitors?"

There really was no arguing with Hart's reasoning, so with a good-natured laugh Julianna waved them off to their club while she remained to oversee the rest of Odelia's evening. Despite her earlier hesitance about appearing amongst the *ton* for the first time in seven years, she was enjoying herself considerably. She could not really say that she loved gossiping, but it was pleasant to catch up on all the news of the fashionable Society. Julianna was interested to know who had married and started a family since her own debut Season. And meeting new people had always been a fascination for her, so she really was in her element.

After the ladies waved off all the guests, Catherine told the servants they could finish cleaning up the next day. After a footman brought Catherine, Julianna, and Odelia piping hot cups of tea, they were left alone. All three ladies finally felt they were all talked out, so they sat in companionable silence while they sipped their tea. After a few contemplative moments, Julianna finally broke the silence.

"We really cannot thank you enough for your generous hospitality, Catherine. The evening was a success, and I am certain Delia is now quite prepared to face the *ton* at all the fashionable gatherings she is bound to be invited to after this."

"Julianna, please, think nothing of it. I had a grand evening and was delighted to throw a bit of a party. I am just happy to have a small part in her debut. And it really wasn't all that much extra work for my staff since your brother sent over a couple of footmen to assist and he promised they would be back in the morning. It has been a pleasure catching up with you over these past days. Hopefully, we shall stay in better touch after this."

"You have my word on it, my dear friend. Now, I can see this young lady should be off to her bed." On those words, Julianna roused her tired niece, and they bade their hostess farewell.

Chapter Nine

The next morning began much later than usual for the Montgomery ladies. Odelia wrapped herself in a dressing robe and slid into her aunt's room as her morning chocolate was delivered by their lady's maid.

"Good morning, Aunty Jules," she chirped cheerfully as she helped herself to a sip of Julianna's chocolate.

Julianna groaned as Delia threw open the drapes. "How can you possibly be so cheerful and awake this morning, imp?" she demanded with incredulity.

"I'm young, what can I say?" Odelia answered cheekily. "Now, are you getting up? We should hurry if we are going to meet up with Abigail."

Julianna groaned again as she peeked at her niece. She then screeched in mock outrage. "How can you drink my chocolate *and* expect me to get up right now and go shopping of all things?" She shuddered with a degree of disgust.

"Come on Aunty Jewel, you cannot hate shopping! What kind of a girl are you?" Odelia laughed as she handed the steaming mug to her aunt. "But you are right. It is outrageous for me to steal your chocolate. It is scrumptious! And look what a delightful day it is going to be. Now, do not be a slug-a-bed. The maid shall return shortly to help you dress. I shall meet you in the morning room momentarily." Odelia fled the room as Julianna hurled one of her pillows in her direction.

Being the doting aunt that she was, Julianna did make haste to prepare for the shopping expedition despite her lack of enthusiasm. Within a short time, the two Montgomery ladies were on their way to collect Abigail and then headed for the shops that the young girls wished to frequent.

Julianna was heartily bored. She had never enjoyed junketing about the shops overly much but felt now that after the weeks of preparation for the Season she would gladly wait several years before she set foot inside them again. But seeing how much pleasure the two young girls were taking from it, she struggled for patience. While Odelia and Abigail giggled and dithered over ribbons, Julianna decided she had had enough. The shop they were in was respectable and the girls would be fine for a while with the footman waiting upon them.

"Girls, I am going to dash across the street to the circulating library to see if I can find something of interest. If you are finished before I am, have James escort you to Gunther's and bespeak a table for us. We shall have a small nuncheon before we head back to the Fieldings' for the afternoon."

"Oh yes, Lady Julianna, that would be lovely," was Lady Abigail's polite reply. "We shan't be too much longer. It is just so hard to decide," she concluded with a giggle.

"I am sure it is," responded Julianna kindly, managing not to roll her eyes. "I will see you both in a few minutes."

Julianna made good her escape and almost fled from the store. She heaved a heartfelt sigh of relief as she slipped into the hushed quiet of the library without realizing she was being followed. Julianna took a deep, appreciative sniff of the air, enjoying the scent of old paper and leather. Barely managing to stifle a squeal as she felt a large hand descend upon her shoulder, she whirled to confront whoever had accosted her.

"Oh my, Lord Ackerley. You startled the wits right out of me!" she declared as she clutched her chest dramatically.

Lucius chuckled at her theatrics. "I am so sorry to have scared you, Lady Julianna. I should have realized you were distracted when it was so clear you were enjoying a moment of appreciation for your surroundings," he teased her with customary charm.

Julianna shot him a sheepish grin. "I am supposed to be escorting Odelia and Lady Abigail on a shopping expedition. I decided to see if the library had anything new that would be of interest."

Lucius eyed her knowingly. "I remember how much you disliked shopping. It was most unnatural of you."

Julianna let out a gurgle of laughter despite the quiet of the room. "Yes, it is terribly strange, I know. But a few moments amongst the books should fortify me to continue through the day," she concluded with a droll tilt of her finely arched eyebrows.

"Do you really think you will have time to be reading at the height of the Season?" Luc asked with some surprise.

"There is always time for a good book, my lord," was her definite answer as she proceeded to peruse the shelves. "Whatever are *you* doing here, if you think there is no time to read?" she asked after a moment.

It was now Luc's turn to look sheepish. "I was on my way to my club when I saw you exiting the frippery store. You had such a look about you that I just had to investigate."

Again Julianna burst out with a cheerful laugh prompting other patrons to look at them with censor. Luc looked at the woman before him with delight as she gazed back at him with chagrin. He took her arm and escorted her outside to the sidewalk.

"I apologize, my lady. I should have left well enough alone when I saw you exit that shop. I would never want to get you banned from the circulating library." Luc laughed as Julianna grinned good-naturedly at him.

"Pay it no mind, my lord. I am sure I shall be able to convince them to allow me to return. Surely they are not so stuffy as to black list someone for a fit of laughter."

"Well, I would not put it past them from the looks they were throwing our way, but as long as you are sure." Luc let the subject drop. "Now where might I escort you?"

Julianna made to object but he pre-empted her.

"It is the least I can do since I interrupted your brief escape from the torture of shopping." Luc laughed down at her. "What kind of gentleman would I be if I left you to fend for your helpless self?" he teased knowing what a capable young woman she was.

"Very well, my lord. You may make yourself useful. I need to make the terribly long trek over to Gunther's to meet up with Odelia and Abigail. If you feel so obliged, you may interrupt your trip to your club long enough to escort me safely up the street," Julianna declared with sham snobbery.

The viscount flourished a courtly bow all the while looking at her with a twinkling eye before extending his bent elbow for her to take his arm.

"Might I have the pleasure of treating you and the other young ladies to Gunther's famous treats?" Luc offered with gallantry.

"Oh, no, my lord. I am sure you would much prefer not listening to those two silly gigglers," Julianna struggled to imagine the elegant lord sitting through a session with the two young women despite the fact that he had escorted her to that establishment on numerous occasions when she was about their age.

"Come now, it shall be like old times," declared Lord Ackerley as though reading her mind. "I feel I owe it to you after running out on Catherine's rout last night."

"Did you run out on us, my lord?" she asked questioningly with an arrested expression upon her face. "I thought you said you had an appointment."

Luc coloured slightly. "Well, yes, I did, but still, in the interest of supporting Odelia's Season, we all must play our part."

Julianna smiled good-naturedly and allowed the subject to drop despite the almost irresistible urge to demand what possible role he thought he needed to play in Dee's Season.

The young ladies were delighted by the viscount's appearance. They were determined to practice their feminine wiles on him, and he was gracious enough to allow it without leading them too far astray. Julianna found it highly entertaining to watch the girls trying to appear sophisticated despite their obvious inexperience. She was oddly touched by Luc's patience with their silly giddiness as she fought the urge to roll her eyes in derision at their antics.

As their tea and crumpets were served, Julianna and Luc's eyes met and they smiled conspiratorially to one another. Julianna was surprised by the rare sensation of feeling at one with the viscount. It was exceedingly strange after the years and conflict that had passed since they had been friends, but it could not be denied.

She enjoyed the moment but was wary of putting too much stock in it. Clearly Lord Ackerley was a very experienced ladies' man, and she would do well to guard her heart carefully. Her own experience with him in the past should have taught her that lesson resoundingly. She gave herself a shake for being so foolish as to need a reminder. *Should I even allow the womanizer to spend time with my innocent young niece?* she questioned, filled with guilt and indecision.

After their treat had been consumed, the viscount tried to excuse himself. However, he was not able to extricate himself from the younger ladies before they had managed to extract a promise from him to share at least one dance with each of them at the next dance they all attended. As he was bowing over her hand in farewell, his eyes twinkled up at Julianna.

"And what about you, Lady Julianna? Will you save a dance for me?"

"If you actually show up at the assembly rooms I will be nearly overcome by the shock so I doubt that I shall be in any position to dance with you," was her teasing reply.

"Touché, my dear, touché," he had to agree since he was nearly notorious for avoiding the overtly obvious Marriage Mart. "However, in my own defense, I must point out that I have been known to attend at times in the past."

"True, but from what I have been told, those occasions are few and far between," she parried.

"Are you making a habit of listening to gossip about me, my lady? I find I am flattered at the thought," he teased.

Julianna coloured delicately but could not deny his charge. She was momentarily at a loss for words, which caused the viscount to laugh and tweak her nose before he gave a cheery wave to all three ladies and strode briskly from the establishment.

"Isn't he just the most divinely handsome man you have ever laid your eyes upon, Lady Julianna?" Abigail was nearly swooning in her admiration, which Julianna could not help but find slightly nauseating. Maybe it was her chagrin over his cavalier departure or maybe it was her own swoony feeling inside, but she suddenly felt rather waspish with regards to the handsome viscount.

"No, Abigail, I must say I find the Duke of Carlisle to be far more divinely handsome, although it is true that Lord Ackerley is passably good looking."

Abigail gasped in shock over this outrage to the object of her youthful crush and began to sputter in defense of the viscount. Odelia saved her friend from causing a scene by interrupting bracingly. "Yes, but Abigail, you must admit that the Duke of Carlisle *is* devastatingly handsome. That really cannot be argued against."

It was a true fact, and Abigail calmed down. Julianna had instantly regretted her uncharacteristic, grumpy attitude and made an effort to completely restore the situation by reminding the girls of their afternoon plans.

"Now girls, we really must be running along if we are not to be late for Lady Hearst's 'at home' this afternoon. Lady Abigail, your mama will frown fiercely at us if we are not on time, I am sure. And no doubt you both shall wish to run a comb through your hair before the guests arrive."

That was just the right thing to say to distract the giddy young girl as Abigail squealed once more. "Oh, no, Lady Julianna, do I look a fright? Let's hurry."

Julianna stifled a giggle of her own as they set off to the Fieldings' elegant town home. Young girls really were terribly predictable, she thought to herself with amusement.

Chapter Ten

L ater that afternoon Odelia was delighted to see her grandmother, the baroness, Lady Ashwood, who stopped in briefly to see Lady Hearst. Surprised to see her relatives there, the baroness quickly extracted a promise from Julianna to bring her dearest Dee to see her the next day.

"Lady Julianna, you really must bring the dear girl to see her grandparents. We would so enjoy hearing all her plans for the Season. Perhaps his lordship and I could make a few suggestions toward her success."

Despite Lady Ashwood's condescension, Julianna was quick to agree to the summons as she stifled her dismay over her own negligence. They ought to have called on the older woman as soon as they had arrived in town. Of course, Hart's in-laws had not kept very close touch with their grandchildren, but still it was socially backward of her not to have called previously. Julianna could only hope the older lady didn't ring a peal over them the following afternoon.

As soon as the Montgomery ladies arrived home, Julianna asked a footman if her brother was home. She was quickly informed that he was busy in his library, and she hurried to find him.

After a quick knock on his door, Julianna briskly entered her brother's very masculine place of work. She never ceased to admire the handsome room and even today, despite the turmoil of her mind, she was brought up short by her visceral reaction to the room. Julianna gave her head a quick shake and strode over to her brother's desk.

"I think I got myself into a quagmire with Dee's grandmother, Hart, and you are going to have to extricate me," she began without preamble.

The earl, having been deep in thought prior to her bursting into his room, was understandably unsure what to make of his sister's declaration. He blinked at her blankly for a moment before demanding, "Whatever are you on about, Jules? I am in the middle of some paperwork. Can this not wait until later?"

Julianna sat herself down in one of the wing-backed chairs placed strategically in front of his desk, clearly making herself comfortable. "I am afraid not, my dearest brother. I forgot to let Lucretia's parents know we were coming to Town for Odelia to make her curtsy into Society, and it would appear you did not do so either. We ran into your mother-in-law at Lady Hearst's this afternoon."

At the sight of his upraised eyebrows she hastened to add, "She managed not to make a scene, but she wants to see us tomorrow. I am not ashamed to admit to you that I am afraid of her and would rather not face her on my own. Nor do I want Odelia to have to do so. So, since in all reality it should have been your responsibility to let them know, I think you have to come with us to take tea with her on the morrow."

"Oh dear," Hart said in clear understatement. "You are right, Jules, we should have let them know. It is just that they have paid so little attention to the children through the years, even before Lucretia died, that I did not even think about it. I must admit that I have pretty much forgotten about them entirely. But they have always been sticklers for appearances, so they would not appreciate finding out about our presence in Town this way." Hart looked at his sister with an appearance of almost trepidation. "Do you suppose I ought to go on my own to present my apologies and smooth things over?"

Julianna finally found it in her to laugh over the situation. "As much as I would rather that, no, I do not think we need to sacrifice you in such a way. Let us brazen it out. You are right. The Ashwoods are more concerned about appearances than anything else. We shall all go for tea. Perhaps you can prevail upon Fletcher to accompany us, and we will all just go as though it is normal for us to be calling upon them." After a moment of reflection Julianna added, "I even forgot to send them an invitation to Dee's ball, so we might as well deliver one in person while we are there."

Hart looked at Julianna dubiously while he mulled over her suggestion. "Well, it is as good a plan as any."

As early as was socially acceptable the next day the four Montgomery's stood on the street in front of a large stone house in one of the most exclusively fashionable neighborhoods of London, just kitty corner to Hyde Park. It was beautifully elegant and unassuming despite its size. Fletcher voiced what they were all thinking:

"Are you *sure* we have the right place, Aunt Jules?"

How typical, Julianna thought with some asperity. *I am not even related to these people. Why did I have to give the directions to the coachman?*

Out loud she replied, "Ask your father, Fletch. Surely he has been here at least a time or two."

"You have a good point, Aunt Jules. Why have *we* never been here before?" Odelia inquired reasonably.

The earl was at a loss as to what to tell his children. Their mother had been happy to get away from her parents, and the Ashwoods had not paid much heed to Dee or Fletch while their daughter was alive, much less after her death. "Well, children, I must admit I do not think your grandparents had much interest in either babies or young people. No doubt now that you are older they would like to develop a relationship with you," he concluded diplomatically.

Julianna could not bear for her beloved niece and nephew to think anyone in their family did not love them as she and their father did. "I know for certain that now that they are going to get to know you, they shall want to pursue that acquaintance further. Now come along. Let us not dither here on the street. The servants will chatter about us." With those bracing words she strode up the stairs to the door.

Sure enough, the servants were watching. Before she could even reach for the knocker, the door was swept wide open by a footman, and the butler stood in preparation to take the ladies' wraps and the gentlemen's hats.

"My lady is expecting you. Please, follow me," intoned the butler so formally that the entire family was struck uncharacteristically dumb as they followed him down the short hallway to what was obviously the formal receiving room. It was exceedingly strange for the earl and his family to be so intimidated by the aristocratic display since they themselves were from the highest echelons of society. Nonetheless, most of their lives they had been sheltered from such overt displays, and they worried for their reception.

"Your guests have arrived, my lady," announced the butler before he disappeared from the room as discreetly as he had arrived.

Lord Ashwood stood at formal attention while his wife remained seated as befit her station. All six occupants of the room gazed uncertainly at one another, at a loss as to what to make of each other, until Fletcher broke the silence.

Striding forward with an outstretched hand and a friendly smile on his youthful, lean face he approached his grandfather. "Lord Ashwood, it is a pleasure to see you. I hope it is not an imposition that my father and I joined the ladies in dropping by this morning. Our aunt thought it best that we all come and greet you."

His grandfather could not help but return his relaxed grin with a smile of his own. It was impossible to remain too starchy in the face of Fletch's infectious *joie de vivre*. "Not at all, Fletcher. It is our pleasure to finally have you in our home." Turning to

Odelia, he continued, "Odelia, my dear granddaughter! How you have grown since last we saw you. You look so much like your lovely mother that it brings a pang to my chest."

Poor Odelia was at a loss how to answer this since it had been years since she had seen her grandparents. Obviously she would have grown, she thought with uncharacteristic sarcasm. Unsure what to say in response to his questionable statement, she merely dropped an elegantly deep curtsy and refrained from any comment.

This must have been the correct response as Lady Ashwood finally broke her silence. "Please come in, all of you, and be seated. Parker, our butler, shall shortly be bringing in the tea service. We have a few moments to get reacquainted before he returns."

There was a pause filled with the rustle of skirts while everyone found a place to sit. None of the furniture was really made for comfort, but the Montgomerys managed to settle themselves politely.

Again they glanced about at one another. Julianna felt compelled to speak to cover over the awkwardness but worried that it was not her place as the Ashwoods really were no relation of hers. Relief filled her as their hostess resumed speaking.

"It is lovely that you all could come. It is so hard for us to believe that Odelia is actually ready to have her first Season! Would you mind sharing with us what you have planned for the coming weeks?" Despite their formality and obvious discomfort, it was exactly the right thing for the grandmother to say.

Odelia began to speak with enthusiasm about all she wished to see and do while in the city. Within minutes Fletcher chimed in and they were soon vying with each other to regale their grandparents with stories of what they had already done and what they hoped to accomplish. Interspersed in their stories were also details of the ball they were planning that was to be held in a couple of days, and the invitation was extended. The reception to their invitation was lukewarm, but it did not overly dampen the visit.

The earl and his sister smiled warmly at the youngsters and allowed themselves to relax marginally. Perhaps they had worried for nothing.

"Lady Julianna, it is nice to see you have finally returned to Town," began Lady Ashwood.

Unsure of the lady's intent, Julianna merely replied in soft tones, "Thank you, my lady, I am enjoying being here with Lady Odelia."

"I would think it would be difficult for you after your own aborted Season so long ago," continued the older woman with just a hint of malice in her seemingly concerned tone of voice.

Finally understanding Lady Ashwood's implication, Julianna's voice took on hints of steel. "It is never difficult to be with my darling niece, Lady Ashwood, but thank you for your concern. Will we be seeing much of you and Lord Ashwood throughout the Season, or do you find the rigours of the social rounds to be too daunting?"

Julianna feared she had gone too far with her question, but they were all surprised when Lord Ashwood chuckled in his deep voice. "That was a great parry, Lady Julianna. Ah, here is the tea. Such impeccable timing, Parker. I think my lady is not too old to manage the pouring, are you my dear?"

Lady Ashwood shot a quick glare at her husband but stood to pour the tea for their guests. It was almost laughable to see Fletcher trying to balance the delicate cup in his large hand. Julianna regretted that she had not seen fit to train him more in the art of taking tea, but it was difficult to get the athletic young man to sit still for something he viewed as completely silly. She was happy to see he was managing not to spill anything on her ladyship's light-coloured furniture.

Having gotten nowhere with Julianna, Lady Ashwood turned her veiled venom onto more likely prey. "What have you been keeping yourself so busy with lately, Hartford? We have not seen you in years."

Hart was not going to take full ownership of this particular problem since the road to London can be travelled in both directions. "It is true. It has been much too long since we have seen you at Somerton."

The Ashwoods had the grace to look guilty momentarily. The earl had mercy on them and continued speaking. "I have actually become quite involved with the politics of the nation over the last few years. I am involved in several things presently with the Earl of Westfield. Are you acquainted with him and his new wife? I understand we are invited to a large ball they shall be hosting soon. Perhaps we shall see you there."

"We do not often attend very large gatherings as you can never be certain who else shall be attending. I understand the earl and his wife are rather loose in their standards when they are throwing larger gatherings and invite almost anyone involved with politics at times, which nowadays could include anyone from the lower orders, couldn't it?" Lady Ashwood barely suppressed a shudder at the thought of sharing a ballroom with anyone not carrying the bluest blood in their veins.

Regretting the conversational path he had chosen, Hart made an effort for diplomacy as befitted his political leanings. "Well, such events are rather educational if nothing else."

"Not the kind of education I require," declared Lady Ashwood with marked snobbery.

Surprisingly, Fletcher managed to extricate his family gracefully from the visit. The requisite amount of time had passed, and they had not been invited to remain longer. Despite being family, it was obvious the Ashwoods would not invite familiarity so Fletcher stood, managing not to knock anything over with his gangly long arms.

"Thank you, Lady Ashwood, for the refreshments, those cakes were quite tasty. I believe the time has come that we must take our leave. It was a pleasure to see you again. No doubt we shall see you around Town over the next weeks while we gad about with Delia." He again shook hands with his grandparents as the rest of the Montgomerys stood and politely made their farewells as well.

In short order they were being handed into their carriage and were on their way with sighs of relief all around.

"Well, that was interesting," observed Odelia, her tone dry. "I guess we know now why we have never seen much of the Ashwoods. We are not high enough in the instep for them despite being Montgomerys of Somerton and the family of the Duke of Westerley." She laughed. "How did they ever allow mama to marry you?" she teased her father.

"An excellent question, imp," he teased back. "Now where shall we drop everybody? I must attend a session of the House of Lords shortly and have a meeting with Westfield beforehand so I have to be quick."

"I am for Gentleman Jack's," declared Fletcher nonchalantly as his sister looked at him with eyes round with surprise.

"How did you gain access to such a place? You have only just arrived in Town!" she demanded with the requisite lack of respect of a younger sibling.

"I know people," he was defensive but obviously reluctant to go into any detail.

Julianna interrupted the emerging argument. "Good then, Hart, you can drop us all off on your way to the House. Odelia and I have some calls to make this afternoon. We can manage on foot or if need be we shall call a hackney before we return home. Should we expect you for supper tonight? Odelia and I will be dining early as we have accepted a couple of invitations for the evening. You will be eating with us, won't you, Fletcher?"

"Probably," was his unhelpful reply.

"I cannot promise anything, Jules, I am sorry to say. The sessions may run late today, as there is much to debate. Do not wait for me. The staff can easily set a place for me if I do make it in time. If I do not see you, have a lovely evening, my dear."

Used to not seeing much of their father, Odelia and Fletcher didn't seem much put out by his being so busy. As the carriage drew to a stop at a busy corner, they hurried to get down and set off about their errands.

"Goodbye, Papa, have a nice argument," was Odelia's cheeky farewell.

Before she stepped down, Julianna asked her brother in some concern. "You do seem a bit more preoccupied than usual. Is everything all right?"

"Yes, yes, all is well. Never you mind your pretty head about it. Although, I may need you to host a small party for me sometime soon, come to think of it. I will have my secretary discuss the details with you."

He already seemed elsewhere but Julianna couldn't help her teasing. "Trying to turn someone up sweet, are you?"

Hart laughed despite his seriousness. "Something like that. Now do hurry along, dear Jules. I must be on my way."

With a huff of resigned indignation, she allowed herself to be handed down, standing and watching as the carriage horses trotted briskly off down the street. Julianna was momentarily nonplussed as to what to do next but she blinked away her indecision and prepared to take leave of Fletcher. He surprised her with some gallantry.

"Should I escort you two ladies somewhere? You didn't say what calls you were making. Perhaps I should leave off my own appointment and make sure you two are looked after."

Julianna laughed delightedly. "Oh Fletcher, you are growing up to be quite a nice gentleman. But no, do not worry about us. We shall be perfectly all right. We aren't even planning on doing any shopping, so we shall not have anything that needs to be carried. We will meet you back at the house in a few hours."

After their visits were done, the two ladies decided that the day was fine enough to walk home. Julianna was relieved that Dee had agreed to the walk. She was finding the city rather confining when compared to their usual active lifestyle. Of course, here they were always on the go, which she actually found somewhat exhausting, but back home there was so much more activity – walking about the estate or visiting with some of the tenants. And today London was actually enjoying some fine weather for once, and the ladies were happy to take advantage of it.

Once again, though, Julianna found herself trying to explain the Ashwoods' strange attitude. "Odelia, I am certain you have noticed there are many amongst the *ton* for whom titles and position are everything. You can comfortably take it for granted since your father is an earl and his mother's father was a duke and you have been surrounded by wealth and privilege your entire life."

"Titles don't really mean all that much, Aunt Jules. It just means that your great-great-somebody did something nice for the king," countered Odelia matter of factly.

"Well, that is a bit of an oversimplification. It is easy for us to think that way. In our case, as Montgomerys we have had titles on both sides of our families for several generations. But your mama did not. Your grandfather is only the second Baron Ashwood. From some people's perspective, they are barely landed gentry. His grandfather made a monstrously large fortune in trade and managed to buy into the gentry. Your grandmother was from a fine old family. I think her father was an earl, but they were on the verge of collapse financially so they married one another for reasons far different than love."

"I think that is very common in our world. It does not explain their attitude toward me and Fletch. In fact, since we are the offspring of earls and dukes, shouldn't they be all the more interested in cultivating the connection if that is how they feel about our family's titles?" asked Odelia still trying to understand.

"You would think so, wouldn't you? But unfortunately, I think they just cannot get beyond their own insecurities to care about anyone else. Not their own children and certainly not their grandchildren. Since appearances are so all important to them and children are often messy creatures, they never had much time for them. I remember your mother's determination that you and Fletcher were not to be left with nannies or governesses. She was absolutely resolved to lavish all her love upon you herself, not leaving it to someone else to love and raise you." Julianna paused with a catch in her throat thinking about the fact that her poor sister-in-law ended up having to leave it to someone else to finish what she had started with her children after all.

Odelia too must have been thinking along the same lines since she was uncharacteristically quiet for a moment before she squeezed her aunt's arm and answered her. "She got her wish. She did not leave us to a governess. She left us to you. And I must say I think you did quite a lovely job of it. Well at least with me, maybe not so much with Fletch," she concluded with a twinkle in her eye.

"Now speaking of strange grandparents, your great grandmother, the Duchess of Westerley has summoned us for a dinner she wishes to hold for you," Julianna began in a somewhat worried tone that dissolved into a gurgle of laughter as Odelia turned eyes round with delighted surprise upon her.

"Truly, Aunty? I can barely credit it! We are to have dinner with the Dowager Duchess? All of us, including Fletch? Who else do you think she shall invite? How perfectly exciting! My Season shall be set now for sure if the Duchess vouches for me!" Odelia could barely contain her glee at the materialistic privilege being offered to her, momentarily imitating her Ashwood relatives. "What do you suppose has made her take an interest? I didn't think she cared too much about us either."

"Perhaps she heard your other grandparents had invited us and she could not be outdone," Julianna speculated cynically. "It does not really matter what prompted it, you can be sure she will not stint once she has made up her mind to do it. And, of course, the duchess is a stickler about who she spends her time with, so you can be sure it will be the most elevated of company."

After a pause while she reminisced, Julianna continued, "Actually, she always had a knack for inviting the most interesting selection of guests to her dinner parties. I remember I quite enjoyed the couple she had while I was staying with her during my own Season. I am quite sure you will be delighted by her efforts."

Julianna was surprised to find herself looking forward to the event her grandmother was planning. She was starting to feel that perhaps Hart was right, maybe she should be considering this a Season for herself as well. She would have to give it some more thought as she had promised him she would.

She was only giving half a mind to her niece as Odelia chattered on excitedly about all the gossip she had heard during their visits that afternoon as well as her anticipation for the various invitations they had accepted for the coming days. She had yet to run out of giggles and words by the time they arrived at their own elegant home. Julianna's indulgent smile had begun to fray a bit about the edges, and a headache was pushing to the front of her forehead by the time the footman opened the door for them. She resolved to lie down for a few minutes before she prepared for dinner.

"I apologize for cutting you off, Dee, but I must go have a wee rest before the evening rounds. Please excuse me. I'll see you at dinner." With that Julianna swept up the staircase swiftly making for her room.

Chapter Eleven

A few days passed in which the ladies were involved in swirls of activity going from afternoon visits to dinners, balls, or routs. They even had the promised tickets to Almack's, which were highly coveted despite the insipid entertainment on offer. Julianna had quite enjoyed escorting her niece to the various ladies' homes for tea and gossip. It was such fun to watch the interplay of conversations as Odelia found her own place in Society. It seemed she was a natural at the social niceties and collected friends wherever she went. Julianna was rather more serious and did not make friends nearly as easily as her niece, but she was finding her own space amongst the ton as they made their rounds.

The evening they spent at Almack's had been quite remarkable despite its reputation for being rather mediocre entertainment. It had started out on the right foot.

"You look amazingly beautiful this evening, Aunt Julianna," praised Odelia as she gazed appreciatively at her dearest relative.

"Why thank you, Dee. You look quite lovely yourself. Have you requested the carriage to be brought around?"

"Yes, Hartley has seen to it. It's rather exciting to be just the two of us going out for the evening and to have a carriage at our disposal. It so rarely happens for some odd reason. It seems Papa always wants to drop us off somewhere. By the way, what is the earl up to this evening that was so serious that it got him out of escorting us to Almack's?"

Julianna laughed with good humour. "In all reality, Dee, I did not really care what he was occupied with this evening. I decided we would be better off without him. His presence at other events of late has been somewhat off-putting, has it not? Whether he is growling at us to hurry up and get ready to go home or glaring at any or all of your potential dance partners, I thought he would be a bit too much for us this evening."

"Great choice," Odelia congratulated her aunt as she did a little dance of glee over the prospect of the evening before them.

The ladies gracefully descended the stairs and were handed into their waiting carriage when the footman announced its arrival. Both girls struggled to contain their excitement over the evening.

While Odelia's excitement was evident and obvious, Julianna's was much more complex. She had enjoyed her evenings at Almack's when she was a younger girl. She remembered them as uncomplicated evenings of fun. The only activities were dancing and gossiping. One never counted the eating since there was little or no food. The punch was reported to be watered down, and the lemonade was merely passable. Despite that, Almack's was *the* place to be for the Marriage Mart. Every debutante wanted to be there, and every chaperone or matchmaking mama did whatever was necessary to procure vouchers from the patronesses who controlled the invitation list. If your name was not on the list, you could not enter those hallowed halls on King Street.

Julianna's memories of dancing at Almack's were, for the most part, pleasant and uncomplicated. She had spent several evenings there with Luc, but fortunately, those memories were untainted by the ugliness that ended their relationship. Julianna's feet began an involuntary tapping at the thought of the evening of music and dancing ahead.

Julianna and Odelia were filled with anticipation as they got out of the carriage and entered the rooms. Both were gratified to be acknowledged by the doorkeeper, Mr. Willis, since that austere gentleman was known to be a stickler of snobbery. After he checked their vouchers and waved them through to the rooms, Odelia looked around with something akin to awe etched on her pretty face.

The rooms had been cleverly designed with thought given to not wasting any space. The orchestra was placed on a balcony elevated above the dancing couples.

"It feels like the music is floating down to entrance the audience," Odelia declared with whimsy.

Julianna merely smiled in return. She could not help but agree with her niece despite how fanciful it sounded.

The evening passed in a blur of activity as the two ladies whirled about the room in the arms of a different gentleman for each number. There were times during the evening that Julianna felt as though her feet were not even touching the ground, like she was floating in a beautiful dream.

Lord Ackerley had bowed over her hand already twice, any more would surely be remarked upon. So when he came around a third time, Julianna shook her head with almost bashful hesitation.

Luc knew he was making a cake of himself but he could not resist the pull of her warmth and beauty. Despite how their relationship had ended with such harsh words seven years ago, he couldn't seem to keep away from her. Or maybe it was because of the words that had been said. The accusations she had made that night had never made sense to him. Perhaps he was subconsciously drawn to her in an effort to prove her wrong. Gritting his teeth to refrain from colourful language he extended a different invitation.

"If my lady is weary of dancing, could I have the pleasure of escorting you to the other room to procure a glass of punch?"

Turning twinkling eyes up to his face, Julianna glanced at the viscount through her lashes. She felt aglow with warmth and possibilities and could not refuse his invitation. Placing her hand in the crook of his elbow they proceeded from the room.

"Only for a few moments, though, my lord. I must return and keep an eye out for Odelia."

"I understand."

At the back of her mind, Julianna knew spending this amount of time with the viscount was bound to be a mistake, but she could not resist for this evening. It was as though a spell had been cast over them for this one night stolen from history. Julianna felt like a young girl once more, in love with her prince charming. She knew not to believe in fairy tales, but for this one beautiful night she allowed the fantasy to hold sway. Reality could wait until morning.

Sure enough, after a few minutes of friendly banter while they sipped the rather tasteless punch, the viscount escorted Julianna back to her original place. He bowed formally over her hand before bidding her adieu. Julianna felt a shiver go up her spine at the final sound of his goodbye. She shoved that thought to the back of her mind along with all the other unwanted thoughts she had determined to deal with later. For tonight, she would allow herself to feel like a princess waiting for her knight.

Julianna continued to dance and laugh with various gentlemen, always keeping a watchful eye upon her niece. Despite having a lovely time for the rest of the night, to her, it felt like some of the enjoyment dimmed when Lord Ackerley left the rooms after saying goodbye to her. She refused to accept such a ridiculous notion and ignored the sensation.

Not too much time had passed before Catherine approached. "Whatever did you say to Lucius, my dear?"

"Nothing of import, why do you ask?" Julianna was made curious by her friend's question.

"Well, it seems to me that he left pretty much immediately after bowing over your hand."

"Please, do not read overmuch into that. I assure you we are getting along very well and without controversy. I promise I said nothing to overset his sensitive feelings." Julianna allowed a note of sarcasm to seep into her voice.

Catherine responded with a ripple of laughter. "That was not what concerned me. In fact, the exact opposite. I was worried that the two of you may have inadvertently worked yourselves up to warmer feelings than you expected."

Julianna felt her face heating with colour but refused to acknowledge the possibility that her friend could be right. "You need have no fear in that regard either, my dear friend. His lordship and I are acquaintances of long standing and did enjoy a couple of dances this evening. That is all. I cannot comment on when or why he left. He said nothing of his plans for the evening to me."

Catherine continued to eye her friend speculatively for another moment before allowing the subject to change to a juicy tidbit of gossip she had heard earlier that evening. Julianna breathed a little easier as the conversation turned to a more comfortable subject.

Late into the night Julianna finally had the carriage brought around and escorted her niece home to bed. It had been a lovely night.

The next couple of days continued to pass quickly as the ladies went about the various activities of the Season. They shopped on St. James Street, went to Piccadilly to visit Bullock's Museum, got some books to peruse at Hookham's circulating library despite Odelia's adamance that they would surely not have the time to enjoy them, and even spent an evening at Vauxhall. Odelia was very satisfied with how her Season was progressing.

Finally, the evening of the Duchess' dinner invitation arrived. It promised to be an interesting event.

Odelia, filled with far more excitement than the rest of her family, was amazingly the first to be ready and waited impatiently at the bottom of the stairs for everyone else. Pacing with a measure of uncharacteristic irritation, she complained to the butler.

"What do you suppose is keeping everyone, Hartley?"

"Well, my lady, I suspect they are just endeavoring to ensure they look nearly as lovely as you tonight," he surmised diplomatically.

"You cannot distract me with your flummery, Hartley, but thank you for the kind compliment. I am ever so anxious about getting there. Do they not realize how the dowager duchess will react if we are late?" Odelia fretted.

"I am sure they are aware. Never fear, Lady Odelia, you are just early. No doubt the rest will be along shortly. Do you wish me to send a footman to knock on their doors?"

"Yes, thank you, Hartley," Odelia agreed before thinking better of this plan. "No, wait, if someone goes and knocks it will just distract them and they will be even later. Let us wait and see. We should give them each a couple more minutes before we send someone to check on them."

Odelia resumed her impatient pacing. Finally, she was relieved to see her father descending the staircase. She released an unladylike whistle in reaction to his handsome appearance.

"Papa, you sure look nice this evening," she complimented. "I am impressed. Your valet has outdone himself."

"Thank you, my dear," answered Lord Montgomery. "You look exceptionally lovely yourself this evening. Although your colour is rather high, are you running a fever? You have not gone and painted yourself, have you?" he demanded with growing concern.

"No, I have not painted myself, Father!" declared Odelia, aghast at the suggestion. "I am merely impatient to be off to Great Grandmother's house for the evening. I have to admit, despite everything Julianna has tried to teach me about decorum and grace, I have been pacing, which no doubt explains any heightened colour. Do I truly look fevered?" Odelia's vanity was disturbed by the thought, and she ran to the mirror hanging just down the hall.

"No, no, never fear, Dee. You look marvelous. Now come get your wrap on. Here comes Julianna and Fletcher."

"Finally!" Odelia declared with vehemence. "I was beginning to fear you would never be ready."

Julianna gazed in assessment at her niece wondering what was behind her unusually prompt behaviour while she allowed the butler to assist her with her wrap. "Is there a reason for your obsession with our timing this evening, my dear?" she inquired. "It is usually the other way around. We are most often made to stand here with impatience while it is you that dithers in her preparations. On this occasion, I think you should have someone check your clock since your impatience is for naught. According to that clock on the mantle, we are exactly on time. We shall arrive at your great grandmother's house just when we should, perhaps even with some moments to spare. Is there anything you wish to share with the rest of us?"

Odelia's colour deepened under her aunt's scrutiny. "No," she declared with a degree of defensiveness. "I just do not wish to keep Great Grandmother waiting," she stated, trying to sound prim.

Julianna looked unconvinced but refrained from further comment as the footman announced their carriage was ready and the family departed. She determined to keep a close eye on her niece that evening to see what could have gotten into the girl. *Most likely she has developed a* tendre *for one of the gentlemen and has discovered that he will be attending this evening. This should be interesting,* mused Julianna as she made herself comfortable and arranged her skirts to avoid wrinkles on the short ride to her grandmother's fine home.

Upon arrival, they were greeted by the duchess's aging, but perfectly proper, butler. He greeted Julianna with restrained affection and warmly welcomed the rest of the Montgomerys. After they had given their wraps, hats, and gloves to the waiting footmen, they were escorted to the morning room. The dowager duchess was receiving her guests and a footman was serving drinks while they waited for all the guests to arrive before adjourning to the dining room.

"Lord Hartford Montgomery, the Earl of Somerton, Lady Julianna Montgomery, Lord Fletcher Montgomery, Baron Hanford, and Lady Odelia Montgomery," the butler intoned formally as he ushered them through the door and before he returned to his post to await the next guests.

At the butler's announcement, there was a brief lull in conversations as the previously arrived guests turned to observe the newest arrivals.

"Welcome, my dears," greeted the Dowager Duchess of Westerley with somewhat uncharacteristic cheerfulness, allowing Hart and Fletch to kiss her dry cheeks and accepting graciously as Odelia dipped into an elegant, respectfully deep curtsy.

Turning to Julianna, the dowager duchess granted her approval. "You have done well with the girl. She looks like she'll do." It would seem to be faint praise to an outsider, but Julianna, knowing her grandmother well, was gratified by the praise of her efforts at raising the younger Montgomery generation. She stepped forward, and grasping her grandmother's hand tightly, gave her an affectionate kiss on her papery cheek, wishing she could hug her but knowing the older woman would not welcome such a public display.

Nodding curtly, the dowager duchess turned back to her other guests and led her newest arrivals into the room. Turning to Odelia, she inquired kindly, "Do you know everyone present, my dear, or should I perform some introductions?"

Odelia glanced around the room with a becomingly hesitant smile upon her pretty face, examining who all was present. It appeared that she was already familiar with those who had already arrived. She was delighted to see that some of her friends were there, and after another moment of brief conversation with her great grandmother she skipped off to join the young people clustered in one corner.

Lady Abigail, Odelia's new young friend, was there standing in conversation with Mr. Landon. The young baron was looking slightly harried by the girl's giggling conversation, and despite Odelia's propensity toward giggles as well, he looked relieved to have her join them. Julianna, seeing the interaction, wondered momentarily if she should somehow intervene, but thought better of it. *Very little harm could come to any of them in this company*, she thought with comfort as she looked around at the group assembled by her grandmother.

Instead of joining Odelia's group, she opted instead to approach Abigail's brother, the Earl of Hearst. She had known him only distantly during her Season, but if she remembered correctly he had married a girl she had gone to school with. It would behoove her to widen her circle of friends, especially if Hart made good on his intent to find himself a wife. Maybe Julianna could give him a push toward someone she would enjoy having as a new sister-in-law.

"Lady Julianna?" questioned the Countess of Hearst somewhat gushingly. "I could barely credit it when we received the invitation from the dowager duchess! How *are* you? I know it is hardly the convention but I really must give you a hug."

With that announcement, she made good on it and enveloped Julianna in a soft, warm embrace. Lady Eliza Fielding's ample bosom made for a comfortable hug and Julianna found herself transported back to the youthful joys of the few years she had spent at finishing school. Eliza, along with Catherine, had been her closest friends, and Julianna again berated herself for allowing her old friendships to deteriorate. Not wanting to allow any negativity, she shook the thoughts from her head and smiled warmly at her old friend.

"Eliza, my dear. Or rather I should say, Lady Hearst, it has been much too long! You look well. It is a delight to see you. I know it has been a few years, but let me congratulate you on your marriage."

"Oh, Lady Julianna, we received your lovely letter when we got home from our marriage trip. I owe you a heartfelt apology for not responding. I was so distracted by the pending arrival of my lord's heir that I could think of very little else," excused the young countess blushingly.

"Well, then, multiple congratulations are in order it sounds like," replied Julianna with a soft laugh.

"Multiple indeed. We have not been idle. There are now three young Fieldings toddling around our estate — the heir, a spare, and our darling daughter. So I declared a halt. I was determined to see some of the Season especially as this is little Abigail's debut. No more babies, at least not this year." The countess prattled in such friendly terms that Julianna was entranced.

"Three young children, what a blessing for you! I would dearly love to meet your little ones," enthused Julianna.

"Would you really?" questioned her friend wonderingly. "I must say when I was single I had absolutely no desire to see youngsters until they were out of short coats, but I do dote on my own darlings, so I would love to introduce them to you. We left them on the estate with the governess and nurses, but I am longing to see them already." Hitting on an idea she continued with enthusiasm, "If you are serious, perhaps we could ride out to the estate one day to see them together."

"Of course I am serious, you silly gabby. I always loved children. Sometimes I think the smaller the better, although I must say Fletcher and Odelia became even more interesting with age. It would be such fun to ride out to your estate and meet your babies. We could catch up on all that you have been up to in the past seven years."

On those words, the earl broke into the conversation. "If that is the case, Lady Julianna, I will be sure not to accompany the two of you," he began with a warm teasing look at his plump and smiling wife. "It would be lovely for Eliza to have a female friend to visit with, and she has been pestering me to take her to see the children all week, but I have been much too busy in the House to take her myself. You would be doing your country a great service if you go with her, leaving me free to carry on with the business of governing."

Julianna couldn't help herself from bursting into laughter at this supercilious statement. "I believe you must be cut from the same cloth as my brother. Hartford has much the same opinion of the serious importance of his position in the House of Lords. While I'm sure the king and the country could manage for a day or two without either of you, I would be delighted to go into the countryside with Eliza. All this gadding about with Odelia is a daunting task, and I am no longer used to being in the city for such long stretches. It would be a delight to see trees and fields and livestock." Then turning back to Eliza she concluded, "We are having Dee's ball in two days. I have to admit, until that is over I cannot think of anything else. And, of course, I will have to ensure Odelia would be properly cared for while we are away." She paused for a moment and saw that her friend was looking disappointed. She hurried to add, "I promise you, as soon as my niece's ball is out of the way, I will call on you and we will make arrangements."

On an impulse, Eliza gave her another friendly hug. "I am so happy to be reacquainted with you, Julianna! It will be highly diverting!"

Feeling an obligation to circulate amongst all the guests, since the hostess was her grandmother, Julianna politely extricated herself from the Fieldings and turned to see who else was in attendance.

As expected, her cousin, the current Duke of Westerley and his wife, were in attendance. Since the Duke was much closer to Hart's age Julianna had never played with him when they were children. It was disloyal of her but she had never much cared for the duke and duchess since they were a rather cold and imposing couple. Julianna excused herself with the thought since they had never made any effort to be kind to the Montgomerys despite their many tragedies. However, family was family and Julianna braced herself to at least be polite.

"Damian, how pleasant to see you. And Gretchen, you are looking well. How are the children? Are they at Westerley or did you bring them to London with you?" she asked kindly imagining the parents would be happy to speak of their offspring.

"Of course they are at Westerley, Julianna. They are too old to be clinging to their mama, and much too young to leave the schoolroom behind, even for a short time. Jonathan, our heir, is just about ready to leave for Eton so he must have his nose in the books in preparation," was the duchess' somewhat snide answer.

"Eton already? My how the time flies. I didn't think he was much older than nine or ten."

"He shall be turning ten in about eight weeks. His entrance exams are in six months. He was coddled a little too much when he was little, so now he has to make up for lost time by studying as much as possible. We have a tutor for him besides his governess." Seeing the look of incredulity upon Julianna's face, she hastened to explain. "There is so much involved in running the dukedom, he must be as prepared as possible, you know. I often wonder how Fletcher will manage since Hartford chose not to send him to school. Although, of course, Somerton is no doubt, much less involved than Westerley."

Julianna struggled to suppress her amusement at the Templetons' supercilious attitude. Their contemptuous superiority was so extensive that she couldn't help but see the humour in it. "It is true he was sadly neglected in his education. We must just trust that his beloved cousin will be kind enough to steer him in the right direction if he flounders too awfully after we have passed."

Unaccustomed to anyone speaking to them with anything other than full deference, the duke and duchess did not catch Julianna's sarcasm. "Well, young Jonathan will be very busy but of course he will recognize his family obligations."

"Speaking of family obligations, if you will excuse me," Julianna made good her escape fervently hoping the dowager duchess had had the kindness to ensure she was seated far from her cousins. As she turned away, she was surprised to see how full the room was becoming. *Grandmother seems to be trying to outdo herself this evening,* Julianna thought with some wonder.

Feeling a bout of shyness overtake her momentarily, Julianna sought out the familiar presence of her brother. Seeing him in conversation with an elegant-looking young couple she was unfamiliar with, she hesitated briefly before stepping across the room to meet them.

Seeing her approach, Hart paused in his conversation to welcome her into it. "Lord and Lady Westfield, let me introduce you to my little sister. Julianna, this is the Earl and Countess of Westfield. I believe we are promised to attend their ball sometime this week. Justin and I are involved in a few things together politically."

Julianna dipped down into an elegant curtsy. "It is a pleasure to make your acquaintance. And might I say congratulations on your recent marriage. I know it has been a little while now, but you get to be newlyweds for a year, do you not?" she asked with a little laugh.

Ever gracious, Beth, the young countess, took Julianna's hand warmly and pulled her up from her curtsy. "Thank you, Lady Julianna, it is a pleasure to meet you. And you are mostly correct." With a twinkling smile to her husband before turning back to Julianna, Beth continued, "Except that we plan to be newlyweds for longer than a year."

Despite having a few more years than the earl's young wife, Julianna couldn't help but admire her instinctive poise, wishing she could appear so calm and unaffected by the bustle of highborn Society all around her. Drawing a deep breath, she made a deliberate attempt to block everything else out and concentrate on the conversation at hand.

"This is your first Season in London, is it not Lady Westfield? How are you enjoying it thus far?" she asked politely just barely catching the shimmer of emotion that crossed the countess' porcelain-like face.

"Thank you for asking, Lady Julianna. Yes, this is my first Season, just like the young debutantes," she laughed. "I am enjoying it very much. I think doing it for the first time as a married lady has its advantages. I need not worry about garnering proposals at the very least," she concluded with another teasing glance at the earl. "What about you? I understand you had your own Season a while ago and you are now here accompanying your niece," she concluded this last statement with a slightly questioning note in her voice which caused Julianna to raise her eyebrows in enquiry.

Beth hastened to add, "I mean, you look so young. I would think it was your Season as well."

Now it was Julianna's turn to laugh. "Believe me, my lady, looks can definitely be deceiving. My season was seven years ago."

"Seven years ago?" Beth repeated. "Were you even out of the school room seven years ago?"

"You are a flatterer, Lady Westfield, I do believe you shall be quite popular amongst the *ton*," declared Julianna with delight. "I was definitely out of the school room. Our hostess this evening, my grandmother, the Dowager Duchess of Westerley, brought me out in fine style. It was not terribly long after our parents had died. Perhaps it would have been best for me to wait another year, and I did not enjoy it overly much. So when my brother's wife died leaving him with two young children, I was happy to head back to the country and be with them." Turning to survey the crowd, looking for her niece, she continued, "Now it is Odelia's turn to make her curtsy to Society."

There was much Julianna left out in her explanation but Beth didn't pry, merely answering politely, "Well, she looks like a lovely young lady. I hope the two of you enjoy her first Season together. We shall look forward to having you at our ball."

Chapter Twelve

Feeling like she had been elegantly excused, Julianna again turned to survey the room. Despite her efforts to concentrate on her conversation with the countess, she had felt the hairs on the back of her neck quiver in recognition. Before her eyes settled on him, Julianna knew Viscount Beaufort had arrived.

Julianna could not believe her grandmother's audacity, nor could she believe her own perverse reaction to the situation. *Why do I have to be so aware of him?* she demanded of herself. While she was momentarily alone, she did her best to appear unaffected as Lucius crossed the room to her side.

"We keep meeting up in the most unlikely places," she began on a light note. Despite how much she enjoyed his company each time she encountered him, she could not forget how their relationship had ended in the past, and why. Nor could she help questioning why he would persist in attempting to spend time with her. *Could he perhaps be looking for some form of revenge? Trying to make me have feelings for him in order to hurt me?*

"Unlikely for you, maybe, but I cannot say that I'm shocked to find you at your grandmother's house," Luc replied reasonably, waiting to see how she would react.

"I suppose that is reasonable, but I can be shocked by it. I did not know you were close with the dowager duchess." Julianna knew she was being contrary but she felt like picking a fight with the man standing before her in all his smug self-assurance.

"Not exactly close, but we have stayed in touch over the years. If you will recall, she did favor my pursuit of a relationship with you in the past." As the words were leaving his mouth, the viscount wanted to recall them immediately. Whatever could he be thinking to tease her like this in public?

Maintaining her composure by a thread, Julianna coolly replied. "How good of you to attend this evening. If you would excuse me, I must see to some matters."

Wishing it were otherwise, there was nothing he could do to prevent her, and he watched rather helplessly as Julianna again walked away from him. Clearly it was becoming a habit over the past couple weeks. Or rather, something she had learned seven years prior. While he stood there feeling momentarily at a loss he was surprised to be joined by Lord Hartford Montgomery.

"Ackerley, I have not set eyes on you in years. How are you? Why do you never take your seat in the House?" Hart began the conversation from his own vantage point.

"I leave such things to those best equipped. I have appointed someone I trust to conduct the business for my seat quite efficiently, Lord Montgomery. I do not think you have cause to complain," Luc hedged.

"No, you are correct. That young lad you appointed actually does represent you creditably. Nonetheless, it would be good to see you doing your duty," continued Hart.

"I feel I am doing my duty by allowing Mr. Dale, who is far more competent than me, to carry on as he sees fit, my lord. And as you have agreed that he is doing the job creditably, you have no room to say I am not attending to my duties."

Hart was impressed that the viscount wasn't backing down and granted him a reprieve, on that subject at least. "I could not help but notice my sister did not look overly happy to see you, my lord. Are you going to cause her some upset this evening?"

"Not if I can help it, my lord. I have nothing but the utmost respect for your lovely sister and would never want to cause her to be discomfited. Your grandmother's generous hospitality is legendary. I am merely here to enjoy the exceptional skills of her kitchen staff." Despite his denials of having any political aspirations, the viscount managed to extricate himself from the sticky conversation with Hartford with practiced diplomacy.

For all his lack of attention, Hart Montgomery really did love his sister and wanted her to be happy. Unfortunately, he had no comprehension of what was best for her, so he was unsure how to deal with Lord Ackerley. "I must tell you, my lord, I feel I failed my sister in the past and no doubt continue to do so, but I want the best for her. I want her to be happy. I do not want you disturbing her."

"I understand, my lord," soothed Luc. "Never fear. I will do my best as a gentleman not to disturb any member of your family. However, as it appears your grandmother is about to lead us into dinner, it would cause a bigger scene if I were to depart at this point. Shall we trust that she exercised wisdom while planning her seating arrangements and wish each other a pleasant evening?"

Hart could not argue with the logic of his words. And really he had never found fault with the younger man. It was only his sense of loyalty to Julianna that made him bristle toward the viscount. He was hungry and really didn't want to cause a scene.

"Enjoy your evening, Ackerley," Hart responded stiffly before walking away to offer his elbow to the lady indicated by his grandmother's lifted eyebrow.

After Julianna had walked away from Luc, she again sought familiarity and found herself drifting toward her nephew. Fletcher appeared to be enthralled by the conversation of Odelia's young friend, Lady Abigail Fielding. Julianna could barely restrain herself from rolling her eyes in amused dismay at the slightly smitten look on the young man's face as he listened in rapt attention while she rattled on ceaselessly.

Abigail was a sweet young debutante, but emphasis in her education had most definitely not been placed on developing the ability to converse on any subject of note other than fashion or gossip, it would appear. Of course, she did manage to accompany each statement with an almost endearing tinkle of laughter and a question designed to appeal to the ego of whichever manly gentleman was listening. It seemed to work to an interesting effect on several young lords in her vicinity, but Julianna trusted that her nephew's burgeoning sense of responsibility would prompt him to see he required more in a potential mate than a pretty decoration for his arm.

Hoping her brother would notice since she was unsure how she, as merely an aunt, could steer her nephew away from such a misalliance, Julianna looked around to see if she could catch Hart's eye. She was almost shocked to see him looking so sternly at Viscount Beaufort. If her eyes did not deceive her, it would appear that Hart was lecturing the viscount right here in her grandmother's receiving room!

With eyes wide, a sense of the ridiculous overcame Julianna, and she struggled to keep from bursting out in laughter. She just managed to reign in any giggles, but her eyes were still dancing with amusement as the viscount happened to glance in her direction. A frisson of awareness snaked up her spine as Luc held her eye and almost imperceptibly lowered one eyelid in a semblance of a wink. Julianna was cheered by the shared joke of the always-preoccupied Earl of Somerton giving a lecture to a young peer of the realm.

Despite the lecture he had just received from the Earl, Luc could not resist the impulse pushing him toward Lady Julianna. "Might I have the honor of escorting you into dinner, Lady Julianna?" he asked, formally polite.

Unbearably nervous all of a sudden, Julianna could not voice a reply, merely nodding in answer, taking his arm delicately, and proceeding to the dining room along with the rest of the duchess' guests. She expected her grandmother would ensure they were at opposite sides of the table, so she felt a jolt of surprise to see his name next to hers at the place seating. The Earl of Westfield was seated across from her, and Mr. Landon was to her right. It was going to be an interesting evening. She only hoped her nerves were up to the task she faced.

After everyone was seated and the first course was being served, the guests began to converse with their neighbors. The earl seemed to be deep in a discussion with the lady to his right about some sort of an issue in the House. Julianna fleetingly wished Hart were there since he took such an interest in those things. She glanced across at the earl's wife to see how she was dealing with her husband's inattention, but she appeared to be amused by it and was engaging the guest on her other side in polite conversation.

Odelia had been seated on the other side of Mr. Landon and she was busily monopolizing his attention. That left Julianna with the viscount. Social etiquette dictated that she must converse with him. She had a choice — make polite social chatter such as she has been trained from the cradle or take control of the situation, speak her mind, and stop being a ninny about it.

Julianna was tired of always doing the "correct" thing. She was sick of the façade of politeness Society put up to hide all the ugliness they secretly condoned. While she did not want to make a scene in her grandmother's dining room, she also wanted to begin to carve out an independent life for herself. So she decided to take the bull by the horns so to speak. Of course, her training since birth would rear its head, and she did so as politely as possible.

"So, my lord, it appeared my brother was ringing a peal over you. Whatever could that have been about?"

Luc paused for the briefest moment in the act of bringing his soup spoon to his mouth as he heard her question. Julianna was always so proper and never caused a ripple of discomfort. Even as a very young lady that had been one of the qualities that predominated her personality. It was one of the reasons he had thought she would have made a perfect wife at the time. But it was also one of the reasons he had not fought harder to keep their engagement in force. He had thought a perfect wife would be a perfectly boring mate. Now she was asking a question that clearly indicated she was about to cross a line. She was leaving the confines of the strictest propriety. And he was intrigued.

"What makes you ask, my lady?" Luc blandly replied, curious to see if she would retreat back into perfect respectability or if she would pursue the topic.

She pursued, in low enough tones that no one else could hear. "I have been on the receiving end a time or two and have witnessed his lectures more times than I can count," she began with a laugh in her voice. "I know what it looks like."

Luc continued to look at her in silence with his eyebrow raised in question, waiting to see if she would continue with her inquiries.

A becoming, rosy blush touched her cheekbones but Julianna persisted with her questions. "Since he spoke to you almost immediately after we had been speaking, I was concerned his discussion with you might have had something to do with me — thus my inquisition."

Luc smiled and decided to tease her a little. Now was certainly not the time or place to pursue his own pressing questions. "He was actually lecturing me about my lack of attention or attendance in the House of Lords. Your brother feels quite strongly about a peer's responsibility toward our fellow countrymen, it would seem."

Julianna was embarrassed that she had thought otherwise but managed to maintain her composure. "Yes, he can be quite eloquent and fierce on the subject to be sure. I suppose I must apologize on his behalf. Sometimes his enthusiasm gets the better of him. However, in his defense, he truly does care about these issues and wants to effect changes for the better."

The viscount admired her attitude. She recognized her brother's faults and his better qualities with a surprisingly clear eye. He decided to be truthful with her and see how she reacted. "But you were actually correct, after he lectured me for my lack of political aspirations he proceeded to warn me that he would have to take action if I were to ever cause you any sort of discomfort or pain."

Julianna could not help herself, she burst out with a hearty guffaw of laughter, quickly stifled, of course, when she felt all eyes upon her, especially those of her very exacting grandmother. Blushing to the roots of her hair, she turned glittering eyes up to the viscount's face, endeavoring to gage the degree of his seriousness.

He smiled benignly, waiting to see what she would say, enjoying the fact that she again saw the humour in the situation.

"I find I must ask, what was the threat?" she asked in her sweet tones.

It was Luc's turn to stifle laughter, surprised at her curiosity over the matter. "He was rather vague on that aspect of the matter. I believe he was leaving it to my imagination. Since he had already mentioned the strength of his authority within the government, perhaps I was to infer I would have to face the wrath of Parliament if I had the audacity to cause discomfort to the sister of the Earl of Somerton."

Julianna smiled in genuine amusement at Lucius' words. "Perhaps you are correct. I must admit it is in keeping with my brother's personality that he would enjoy allowing you to think that. Although I must say I am surprised he thought to warn you away from me. He is most often rather oblivious to what is going on in his own home." This last statement was made in such a tone, a mixture of wistfulness and worry that it caused the viscount to look at her with intense, watchful eyes for a brief moment.

Not wanting to draw undue attention to their conversation, he did not look long, but in that momentary glance he managed to catch the worried crease between her eyebrows before she gained control over her features. Once more she was the perfect-looking young woman she wanted the *ton* to see, no trace of concern upon her face. But he had seen it, and it tugged at his midsection.

For a fleeting moment Lucius wondered in a temporary fit of anger why the Dowager Duchess had seated them beside each other. He did not want to have any feelings toward this woman. She had ripped apart his life seven years prior. He had no reason to trust she would not do it again if given a chance. He had worked through his anger and attained a neutrality that was quickly slipping away. It was being replaced with warm feelings he did not wish to have toward Lady Julianna Montgomery. But against his better judgment he found himself inquiring in a barely audible voice, "What is it, Julianna? What has troubled you about what is going on in the earl's house? Is it Odelia?"

At his question, her eyes flew toward his face, then flickered ever so briefly to Fletcher, then back to the viscount.

"Or is it Fletcher?" The viscount, ever aware, had caught the tell-tale glance and exerted a supreme effort of will to prevent his own eyes from straying toward the young baron to see what could have his aunt so concerned.

Despite her resistance, gratified by his pursuit of what her concerns might be, Julianna didn't know how to proceed. He was hardly an appropriate confidante. But she longed to share her worries with someone. Even just to talk it through and get another perspective would be of benefit. But confide in Lord Ackerley? It was no doubt the farthest thing from appropriate. Julianna shook her head in denial.

"My lady," the viscount began with an almost wheedling tone to his voice. "You can trust me to keep your secrets."

"My lord," she began with repressive tones and a stern look, maintaining the use of formalities. "This is hardly a subject for me to discuss with you, nor is this the place for such a conversation."

She was blind to the fact that she had revealed much in that statement. Lucius realized he was correct; she was worried about something. Stubborn and determined, he persisted.

"Then ride with me in the park tomorrow. In my phaeton, we can be public and private all at once. Perfectly appropriate and above reproach." Luc's tone was all that was reasonable.

Julianna gave a cross between a laugh and a sigh. "You are incorrigible, my lord. How can I go for a ride with you in this private but public manner? I must watch over Odelia."

Not to be dissuaded, the viscount persisted. "Surely, as such a popular young lady, Odelia shall also be going riding? It would appear that the young baron would be delighted to escort her if the idea was placed in his mind ever so correctly."

Julianna could no longer resist, but she refused to drop the formalities. "Very well, my lord. If you can arrange it that you both arrive at the same time, she and I can be ready to accompany you."

"Julianna, it will be fun. I pray you, do not sound as though I have just convinced you to visit the guillotine," he chided with a twinkle in his eye. "I shall ensure the baron is on his best behavior and is punctual as well."

Unsure of the viscount in this mood, Julianna offered a rather benign smile before turning to address Lord Westfield, across from her, determined to resist the nearly irresistible but nonsensical pull exerted by Lucius. Besides, it was impolite to monopolize one dinner companion while ignoring others.

Feeling dismissed ever so politely, Luc turned to speak with the lady to his right feeling he had accomplished all he could manage for now. He would try again before the ladies left the gentlemen to their port.

Sure enough, before the end of the meal, as one course was being changed to the other, Luc again tried to engage Julianna in conversation. As polite as always, Julianna did converse with him, but resisted any efforts to be drawn into anything overly personal or confide any secrets. But she did not take back her promise to ride with him the next day, and with that he had to be content.

After the ladies excused themselves, leaving to take tea in another room while the gentlemen drank their port, Luc engaged Mr. Landon in conversation.

"I noticed you speaking with young Lady Odelia. She seems to be a charming young woman." Luc tried to be nonchalant but it did not prevent the young baron's nervous reaction.

"Yes, Lord Ackerley, she is quite charming," Mr. Landon managed to stammer in obvious distress. "I have no intentions in that direction, my lord, if that is your concern."

"No, no, rest assured, I have none either. I just saw you two talking," soothed Luc with reassurance. "Just making conversation," he laughed as he jovially slapped the other man on the back.

Still unsure but gratified at the attention of the older, more sophisticated viscount, the young baron relaxed incrementally. "Well, if you're just making conversation, my lord, then I'll admit to you she is a funny little thing. Great fun to talk with since you don't have to actually do much talking, but she doesn't giggle as much as her friend Lady Abigail, so it isn't nearly as irritating." Mr. Landon grinned at this statement. "And, even more importantly, she doesn't seem to be nearly as desperate to find a husband as many of the other young debs seem to be. Maybe she's just better at hiding it." The baron paused for a moment to worry about that possibility.

"No, you are probably right. She is quite young, and there are not the usual reasons in her case that other young ladies face with a need to marry in their first Season. As the earl's only daughter, no doubt she does not face any pressure to make up her mind quickly. She seems like a sensible enough chit to want to see more of the *ton* before she ties herself up." The viscount eyed up the younger gentleman before him to see how he was taking his opinion.

Kenneth Landon wasn't the very brightest student ever to have graduated from Eton, but he was far from slow. He recognized the wisdom behind what the viscount was saying but realized there had to be a reason for this conversation. Since as far as he could recall he had never had any discussion with Lord Ackerley before, other than the briefest of greetings as they crossed paths on occasion, he had reason to be suspicious.

He eyed the viscount with curiosity. "I still find myself wondering why we are discussing this," Landon said with a questioning lift to his tone. "If you aren't after the younger Montgomery lady, perhaps it's the older one. But with what I've heard whispered about your past, why would you even look in that direction?" Landon thought rather highly of Lady Julianna, but he had heard that she had broken her engagement with this very lord. It was difficult for him to fathom any continued interest from the viscount.

"Never you mind any whispers about Lady Julianna," Luc started with a vehemence that surprised even him. Forcing his tone into a more reasonable frame, he continued with the truth. "To be honest, I do want to take Lady Julianna to the park in my phaeton, but she refused my invitation as she feels she has an obligation to remain at Lady Odelia's side at all times." His frustration still shone slightly through his voice.

After a moment of thinking about the viscount's statement, light finally dawned on the young baron. "I get it — you want me to entertain the young Lady Montgomery so that the aunt is free to be with you."

Resisting the urge to roll his eyes, Luc smiled at the younger gentleman. "What a great idea. Maybe you should take her for a ride around the park tomorrow afternoon."

Mr. Landon smiled at the viscount in the utmost good nature. "I certainly have no objection to extending the invitation. But you must understand, she's a terribly popular young lady and she may already be engaged."

Luc had to be satisfied with that. "If you would be so kind as to let me know how it goes before the end of the evening, it would be most appreciated." He was disgusted to find himself close to growling at the affable young baron.

Luc was relieved when the Duke, who was standing in as host while his grandmother was with the ladies, stood to signal it was time to join the women. Contrary to all logic, he wanted to see Julianna again. He found it almost distressful how eager he felt. It made no sense whatsoever considering their history, especially when one considered the vast number of eligible young ladies available this Season. Coupled with her resistance to his attempts at informality, it really was ridiculous for him to pursue the acquaintance any further. And yet he found himself drawn to her warm presence as soon as he entered the room.

As soon as the gentlemen entered the room, Julianna felt an odd tingle creeping up her spine. She knew it was because of *him*. Why did he have to have this effect on her, she demanded of herself for what felt like the umpteenth time. It was quite odd when one gave it thought, which of course, she did as she struggled to display no reaction, keeping her attention glued to the best of her ability upon whatever the Duchess of Westerley was saying. It took a supreme amount of effort since Julianna was rarely ever interested in what her cousin's wife had to say at the best of times, let alone when she was struggling to remain indifferent to a handsome viscount.

As the duke's wife droned on about her brilliant children and their accomplishments, Julianna wondered with terrible uncertainty why Lucius could be taking an interest in her concerns. Was he searching for a way to hurt her in an attempt at seeking revenge for the social wrong she had done to him those many years ago? Surely he couldn't still care. She hadn't even been sure if he had cared back then. Cared about her, Julianna, that is. Of course he had cared about the embarrassment of the broken engagement. But all the shame had been piled upon her; he had faced no consequences whatsoever. So really he had no reason to seek revenge.

But why had he remained single all these years? He would have had his pick of any eligible young lady, with his fortune and his title, especially after his father died and he came into his full inheritance. *Many young ladies are willing to overlook a tendency toward infidelity,* she thought with a hint of scorn, feeling her face take on a waspish look before the duchess recalled her to the conversation.

"Would you not agree, Julianna?" Gretchen, the duke's wife, asked with condescension dripping from each word.

Proving her good breeding was ever present, Julianna's distraction did not prevent her from replying. "Of course, your grace, the roses on your estate have always been the most beautiful I have ever seen. I am delighted you have continued to care for them so diligently since my grandmother moved to the dower house."

The duchess could not help being surprised by how effortlessly Julianna deflected any comment thrown at her, and she felt a degree of respect being born in her heart for her husband's cousin. In more sincere tones than she had ever used toward Julianna in the past, the duchess invited, "You should come see me at one of my 'at homes' while we are in London, Julianna. We will not be in Town for too long, but it would be pleasant to get to know each other a bit better. Since each of our families have spent so much time at our estates over the past several years, we have not really gotten to know each other. We should rectify that."

Somewhat taken aback by the unprecedented invitation, Julianna smiled kindly at the duchess. "Thank you, your grace, for the invitation. I shall look forward to it," she accepted graciously without actually making a commitment.

The duchess acknowledged her skillful evasion with a dip of her head while Julianna excused herself. Wry amusement shined in the duchess' eyes, but Julianna kept her face impassive as she turned away.

Rising from her spot on the settee beside the duchess, Julianna attempted to search out Odelia while also avoiding making eye contact with the viscount. She was distracted by her awareness of his presence in the room. As she scanned the assembled guests she could see that, once again, her brother was engrossed in some sort of in-depth discussion, which ruled out him keeping an eye on either of his children.

Spotting Odelia in animated conversation with Kenneth Landon, Julianna couldn't help but smile warmly at her beloved niece's antics as she began to make her way through the milling guests toward the duo.

Guests were beginning to take their leave of the dowager duchess. Tonight's invitation had been for dinner only, and many had engagements at various balls or other events also being held that evening. There was much movement as the milling guests circulated to say their goodbyes.

"Aunty Jules, Mr. Landon has just asked if I would accompany him around the park tomorrow afternoon. Please say I may. It shall be delightful. He has a lovely pair of horses he wishes to show me, and he promises to bring a phaeton," Odelia enthused with excitement, obviously delighted by this prospect.

Julianna could not resist allowing her eyes to seek out the viscount who was by now not far away. Their eyes met for the briefest moment in acknowledgement. Julianna forced her attention back to her niece.

"How lovely," she managed to reply with mustered up sincerity. Lucius had managed to orchestrate it somehow, and she found herself impressed with his managing ways. "Of course you may ride with Mr. Landon, provided he has a groom riding along and you make sure you are back within an hour. What time do you plan to come by?" she asked, turning to the young baron.

Kenneth almost quaked under the pressure of both Lady Julianna and Lord Ackerley looking at him with expectation. He began to stammer. "Would four o'clock be convenient, my lady?"

Lady Odelia clapped her hands with delight causing Julianna to smile her approval. "It would appear it is an excellent and convenient time, my lord," she replied with a small tinkling laugh as she looked to Mr. Landon for confirmation before turning to Lord Ackerley.

As the viscount stepped toward her, she turned ever so slightly so they had a modicum of privacy in the busy room. "I am impressed, my lord. I cannot say how you managed it, but I reckon if the invitation is still open, I am available to go riding with you tomorrow afternoon at four."

Grinning down into her smiling, upturned face Lucius Ackerley felt like a white knight from an old fairy tale, wanting to slay all his lady's dragons. His smile turned rueful at his fancifulness as well as the danger he courted with this woman.

"Excellent, my lady. Of a certainty, the invitation remains open. I promise to be prompt," he finished with a teasing smile.

"As shall I, my lord," Julianna answered with a twinkle in her eye, anticipating their outing with a heady mixture of delight and trepidation.

Chapter Thirteen

It was a good moment for an interruption so Julianna was happy to see her brother approaching, for once not distracted by his political manoeuvrings. Or maybe he was, as Julianna was reminded by what he was about to say.

"Julianna, Odelia, are you two ready to go? I believe we are promised to the Roxboroughs' later this evening. We really must be going as I have promised to meet up with someone there, and it is rather urgent that I speak with him. I have already said goodbye to the dowager duchess and I am going to go call for the carriage. Please be quick about your own goodbyes." After those words he spun on his heel with barely a glance at either of the gentlemen, expecting that the ladies would respond to his bidding without question.

There was a moment of silence left in his wake in which Odelia looked crestfallen and Julianna appeared dazed as she blinked away her surprise. She quickly recovered. "Gentlemen, it has been a pleasure dining with you. If you will excuse us, Lady Odelia and I must pay our respects to our hostess before we depart." With a pleasant smile, she gently but firmly pulled Odelia away as she smiled and waved to the gentlemen.

"I wonder what bee is in Papa's bonnet this evening," Odelia wondered to her aunt in a murmur as they made their way toward the dowager duchess.

"Mind your manners, my dear, he *is* your father," Julianna rebuked mildly.

"I'm sorry, you are right. It's just that he was *so* abrupt! Are these social events not supposed to be fun? They are not political meetings," argued Odelia trying to express what she considered to be a reasonable point of view.

"Dee, my darling, you are being just a wee bit naïve if you believe that. For this evening, let us shelve this discussion and enjoy ourselves, but we have a lot to talk about tomorrow." Julianna gave herself a mental to-do list of what she would need to discuss with the younger woman. Odelia needed to understand how social activities, and by extension marriages, worked in their world, and how all of that was intertwined with the politics of the day.

They had arrived at the dowager duchess so no further discussion was possible. Both girls made elegant curtsies to their highborn relative and thanked her for a lovely evening before leaving swiftly to meet up with the Earl of Somerton.

"Fletcher has begged off. Said he had other things to do and did not want to dance attendance on anymore debutantes," Hartford informed them as they climbed into the carriage with the assistance of the waiting groom.

"Did he say where he was going?" asked Julianna with a worried look and tone.

Her brother didn't notice due to his own preoccupation. "No. Just said not to wait up for him and he would see us on the morrow." He remained absorbed in his own thoughts while Julianna chewed her lip in consternation.

"That was quite lovely, wasn't it, Aunty Jules? Great Grandmother sure knows how to throw a dinner party, doesn't she? I am not normally partial to fish, but whatever her cook did with it this evening really could make me a convert," Odelia enthused, ready to chatter and gossip about the pleasant evening.

With a smile of endearment, Julianna turned her attention to her niece bidding herself not to worry over much. Fletcher was practically an adult. "Yes, Dee, the dowager duchess certainly knows everything there is to know about entertaining. And hiring good staff, for that matter. I wonder if her cook would be willing to share the recipe with ours if you enjoyed it so much. I shall mention it when I send around our note of thanks."

"Oh, that would be so good of you, Aunty, thanks. Although, when you think about it, what are the chances of the cook being willing to share?" Odelia asked with doubt in her voice. "Think about how jealously our cook guards his secrets."

"True enough, but there is no harm in asking. Besides, Grandmother and her cook will be flattered by the request if nothing else."

"Did you see what the duke's wife was wearing?" asked Odelia, ready to change the subject to a much more gossipy one. "What ever could she have been thinking to wear that colour with her complexion?"

Julianna just smiled and allowed the young girl's chatter to wash over her. Odelia didn't really require a response, and Julianna allowed her mind to drift to thoughts of how the evening had thus far gone for her. For a moment she allowed herself to push worries about her niece and nephew far from her mind and indulged in a frivolous daydream in which she was a carefree young miss being courted by a ruggedly handsome viscount.

After a moment, with a sigh but with determination, she pushed those thoughts back down into the hidden places of her heart. She wasn't sure what Lord Lucius Ackerley had in mind, and while she was almost certain he was enough of a gentleman not to intentionally hurt her, she did not trust that she would come to no harm in his company. She must guard her mind and heart well because if she let him get too near it, this time she doubted they would survive intact.

With renewed determination to resist any fantasizing about a future with the viscount, Julianna squared her shoulders as she descended from the carriage in front of the beautiful stone façade of the house in which they would be dancing until dawn. She reminded herself that she was about to enter the very same ballroom in which her future with Viscount Beaufort had fallen apart. It had been during the Roxborough ball that she had terminated her engagement exactly seven years before. She suppressed a shudder at the memory. Behind her, Odelia let out a little squeal of excitement.

"This is going to be so much fun, isn't it?" the young lady enthused as they climbed the grand staircase, trying to keep up with the earl as he hurried to enter the elegant building.

"Hart, wait for us," hissed Julianna with a hint of asperity, not wanting to cause a scene. But really, if they ran into the house, surely that would cause a bigger scene, she reasoned.

Checking his haste, the earl turned a sheepish face to his sister and daughter. "Sorry, ladies. I forgot for a moment that you were with me. Would either of you like my elbow?" He tried for a degree of gallantry.

Exasperated with her brother's one tracked mind, Julianna took one arm while Odelia took his other. Trying to mask her impatience with him, Julianna took a deep breath, expelling it slowly before turning to him with a smile.

"You must understand, brother dear, that we cannot run in gowns like these. Of course, according to Grandmother, it is not seemly for a young lady to ever run. So you mustn't mind our slow pace. We shall get there soon enough."

She paused for a moment before chiding him. "You really should make an effort not to forget your companions. And, just a quick tip — if you do find you have forgotten them, please do not tell them so. It is most off-putting."

Hart laughed at his sister's rebuke. "You are quite right. Hopefully, if you two were real ladies I would not be such a buffoon."

Both ladies gasped in outrage. "What do you mean by such an outrageous remark, Father?" demanded Odelia, shocked to the depths by her father's callous statement.

"Ouch," declared the earl with a sheepish face. "That was poorly said. I merely meant that you are not ladies I would court, so I have no need of impressing you."

Odelia was shocked into silence by his explanation, as she had never thought of her father pursuing a courtship. Julianna, having been previously prepared, did not allow his statement to distract her outrage. "But Hart, you are supposed to love us, and never, ever forget about us!"

"I do love you both ever so much, surely you know that. Oh, I am making a muddle of this evening, aren't I? Please, just forgive me and enjoy your evening. We are here now. We should go in and have a lovely time, right?" The earl was determined to meet up with his mystery appointment.

Still simmering with a degree of resentment, Julianna spoke with an uncharacteristic level of waspishness. "I certainly hope for your sake that your *rendezvous* is not with a lady, since clearly you have a long way to go in that department."

Not to be deterred by sisterly recriminations, the earl tweaked his sister's nose playfully, and then kissed his daughter's cheek in passing before he swept away into the crowd.

Both Montgomery ladies stood for a moment with matching looks of perplexity before they looked at each other and burst out laughing. "Your father is truly incorrigible!" declared Julianna while shaking her head. "Of what use is he to us this Season?" She asked the rhetorical question as she helped Odelia shake out her skirts to more advantage before they were officially announced by the master of the evening.

Since they were latecomers the ballroom was already overcrowded and it was a bit overwhelming to the country-bred ladies to descend the grand staircase into the sea of people. They presented quite a picture. Julianna's brunette hair offset Odealia's blonde, so opposite and yet with such a striking family resemblance.

When their names were called, many in the throng turned to watch their descent. Always elegant, Julianna turned several heads as her contained, maturing beauty caught the eye of many a connoisseur. Meanwhile, Odelia's youthful vigor and pretty face and form were looked on with favor by a completely different set. As soon as they reached the bottom, there was a queue forming of eligible men looking to secure a place on their dance cards.

The night passed quickly in a swirl of colour and light as the ladies were handed off to partner after partner. Julianna was ever vigilant in keeping an eye on her charge, but she still managed to garner immense pleasure from the evening's entertainments. It was with sore feet but light hearts that the ladies were finally handed into their carriage just a short while before dawn lightened the sky.

The earl had made sure not to forget his ladies again and had waited with a false show of patience as the girls enjoyed the evening long after he had concluded his business and was ready to leave.

"I guess I should not have let Fletcher go off on his own tonight. He could have escorted you two home," he growled in an irritable mood.

Not to be deterred, Odelia smiled at her father with full charity and reasonableness. "You should have told us if there was a certain time you wished to leave. I had a wonderful night and enjoyed nearly every moment of it. But I must admit, I am dearly looking forward to falling onto my bed as soon as possible."

"Did your meeting not go well, Hart?" Julianna asked with kindness.

Hart was chagrined by his own churlishness especially in view of the ladies' attempts to be understanding. "No, no, my dear. It actually went very well, better than I had expected or even hoped. I am just so single-minded that once my business was concluded, I was ready to go home, but you two were still having fun. I did not have the heart to tell you we had to go before you were ready, but I was wholeheartedly bored."

Turning to his daughter, he continued with uncharacteristic emotion. "Your mother would be so happy to see you, Dee. You are so beautiful and you seem to be making a nice little splash amongst the *ton*. I am terribly sorry she is not here to share this with you."

Julianna looked away with a catch in her throat. Odelia, though, caught her hand and squeezed it. "It is true. It would be quite lovely if Mama had never died, but I must say Aunty Jules is doing a bang up job of watching over me. Sometimes I think she is more diligent about it than Mama would have been." Her fake petulance caused the other occupants of the carriage to laugh, glossing over the emotional moment.

Chapter Fourteen

Despite the late night, Julianna awoke feeling fresh and ready to face the day, bounding from the bed when her maid scratched on the door before carrying in her morning's chocolate.

"Good morning, Maizy, isn't it a beautiful day?" Julianna nearly danced before the surprised maid but then winced when her feet protested the abuse.

"You seem right chipper this mornin', milady, despite your sore feet." The amused maid handed Julianna her steaming cup of chocolate before pulling open the wardrobe doors to decide what her lady should wear that day.

"I must admit, my feet are a wee bit tender, but we had so much fun last night, Maizy! Odelia was ever so popular."

"Seems to me you must've been popular too, milady, if your feet are tender. You must've had your share of dances, too." Maizy puttered around straightening the room as she spoke.

Julianna blushed and smiled in reminiscence. "It is true. I did do my fair share of dancing." After taking a glance at the clock on the mantle she gasped. "Nearly noon! Maizy, why did you ever let me sleep so late? There is so much to be done today! It is nearly the day for our own ball, and there are many things I need to attend to."

The reasonable maid clucked her tongue at her lady's signs of panic. "You don't have any appointments today, milady, nor are you expecting any guests. I didn't think you needed to do any more shopping, and you were out late last night. I figured you needed the rest more than anything else. No doubt you'll be out late again tonight, so sleeping a little later than usual isn't going to do you any harm. And milady Odelia is still abed, so there was nothin' for you to worry your pretty head about. I know you have your lists all written out, and almost everything is scratched off, so you need your rest more than anything, if you don't mind my sayin' so milady."

"I guess you are right. Although Odelia and I do each have an appointment to go out riding in the park later this afternoon, we haven't many commitments for today, so it is a good time to take a break. Thank you, Maizy. I think you are wiser than I am."

The loyal maid blushed at this praise. "Get on with you, milady. Now, what would you like to wear today? Should you dress now in your riding clothes or change later?"

"Since I shall be lazing about for a couple hours, perhaps I shall just put on a dressing coat to run down for some breakfast then remain above stairs until it is time to get ready to go out. If you have other things to do, please go about them and you could return to help me and Odelia around three. I believe we shall both be riding in carriages of sorts so we shall not require riding habits."

Thus dismissed, the maid bobbed a curtsy and went about her business. Julianna ran down to the dining room to see what had been left over from the morning meal. Delighted to see the array that had been kept warm in preparation for her and Odelia, Julianna tucked into a generous serving, feeling rather ravenous after the evening's exertions.

Odelia bounced into the room, as cheerful as always. "Good morning, my dearest Aunt! How are you? Did the boys leave us much food? We were dreadful slug-a-beds today, were we not?"

With a cheerful smile of her own, Julianna had to agree. "The servants were kind enough to anticipate our late arrival and kept everything warm for us. You will see that there is plenty to fill you up."

They sat in companionable silence for a few moments while they both savoured their meal. Julianna broke the silence.

"Remember last night you made the comment that the Season is all about fun and has nothing to do with politics?"

Odelia paused with a fork halfway to her mouth. "You aren't about to shatter my illusion of fun, are you, Jules?"

Julianna laughed. "So you already realize it is an illusion?"

"Not exactly," Odelia hedged. "But I guess when you think about the girls that are relying on a good marriage to secure their future and often even the future of younger sisters, there is a certain politics to it. Or the impoverished gentlemen with respectable titles that are looking for an heiress to marry. They might not be having nearly as much fun as I am during the Season. But Papa doesn't fit either of those categories, so why does he have to make every event about business or politics? Why can he not just escort us somewhere and watch us have fun? Or better yet, he could try to have a good time himself."

"I am glad you see there's more to this than having fun for many. But, Odelia, my dear, even for you this is a very serious matter. While you are in far different circumstances and really a lot of it *is* about fun, one day you *will* marry, and that is a very serious decision to make. You need to look far beyond fun in order to make a decision that will affect the rest of your life."

Odelia looked at her aunt and set her chin at a stubborn angle. "You never married."

"True enough. And I have loved nearly every moment of my life on the estate with the rest of you, but it has often been far from fun."

Odelia never enjoyed being serious for long and tried to divert her aunt with some teasing. "Nearly every moment? Which moments did you not like?"

Julianna laughed but would not be dissuaded. "Never you mind. The fact is, your father loves his work in the House of Lords, and it really is important to all of us. Somebody has to do it. He has accepted the responsibility, and we should support him as much as we can. It would be good for you to give it some thought since one day, when you are a wife, you will need to support whatever is important to your husband."

"Will he need to support what is important to me?"

"I hope you choose a husband that will support you in whatever you would like to pursue. You should look for a partner for your life." Julianna was treading on slippery territory. She knew there were women's movements being promoted amongst the bourgeois and even many aristocratic ladies had taken up the cause. She didn't know enough about it to take a firm stand one way or the other, but she felt quite fiercely that it *should* work both ways and wished that quite adamantly for her beloved niece.

Odelia pondered for a few moments. "Well then, I would say it is definitely a good thing that I want to enjoy at least one more Season before I settle down, isn't it? This way I can have all the fun I want this year. After the Season is over, I can go home to Somerton and think it all over at my leisure. Next year is very much soon enough for any heavy thinking."

With a little shrug and a small laugh, Julianna had to agree. "I guess you are right, Dee. Let us enjoy ourselves. But do give thought to how you could support your father. Maybe you should ask him about what he is trying to accomplish and see if there is anything we can do to help. I am certain he would appreciate the offer. After all, he is making all this fun possible for you."

Odelia wrinkled her nose as she thought about her aunt's words. With reluctance she admitted, "I guess you are right, as always. But if I ask him, he'll probably go on and on, and my mind will wander and I'll be no further ahead."

Julianna couldn't help her amusement over the truthfulness of her niece's statement. "Warn him in advance to think before he speaks. He needs to express it in layman's terms for ladies. It will be good practice for you both." With a firm nod, Julianna was about to get up. "I must say I am glad you can see the reasonableness of this. It is a relief that you are nowhere near as silly as your friend Abigail."

Odelia was surprised by her aunt's choice of words. "I am not sure where to begin with what you just said. Did you think I was silly? Maybe you and Papa should have let me go away to school. You only have yourselves to blame. And actually, Abigail isn't all that silly either."

"I'm sorry, Dee. I did not mean you any insult. I can truthfully tell you I have never questioned your intelligence, but even you must admit you can be a little silly at times. Wouldn't you say it's a part of the fun?"

Odelia's face turned sheepish. "I guess you are right. I do enjoy being silly sometimes. But Abigail is a great girl, even if her silly moments are longer than mine."

"She seems to be a nice, sweet, young lady, and I am glad you have found a companion to share your Season with. But she truly does not strike me as being all that bright." Julianna's worry over Fletcher's interest in the girl was shading her judgment. She really had no objection to Odelia being friends with her. Then she wondered if that was somehow a double standard. She sighed in exasperation at her own silliness.

"Never mind, Odelia. What will you be doing today while you wait for the baron to come for you?" Julianna knew just how to distract a young lady.

"Isn't it exciting, Aunty Jules? I hope he brings a curricle, or maybe a high perch phaeton! It will be just the thing to be seen riding in either of those."

Julianna sat back and enjoyed her niece's chatter for a few moments, content that the girl was concerned about the social aspects and truly seemed to have no romantic interest in

Kenneth Landon. Then she thought of the need to continue her niece's education.

"Would you like to write the thank you notes for last evening, or should I?" Julianna broke into Odelia's stream of conversation.

Odelia blinked in surprise. "You would allow me to do it?"

Julianna tried for a casual shrug. "Absolutely, somebody has to. We need to write notes to the duchess and Lady Roxborough. You could do both or choose one and I will do the other."

"What a great idea! Let's split it. I think Great Grandmother's note requires a higher degree of finesse than I am prepared for. You do her and I shall write to Lady Roxborough. Am I representing all Montgomerys or just you and I?"

"Well, Fletcher did not attend, so not him for sure. I doubt your father will do one of his own, so it would be nice to mention him somehow in your note as well as the two of us."

The two ladies finally left the breakfast room, allowing the footmen to clear away the remnants of the meal. Julianna and Odelia adjourned to an upstairs parlour where they set themselves to their writing.

After a comfortable interlude of relaxing pursuits, when the time arrived to go to the park, Julianna and Odelia were waiting with far different outward appearances.

"I can barely stand the wait," Odelia declared as she paced.

"Odelia, my dear, Great Grandmother Templeton would have much to say about your lack of decorum just now."

Odelia looked somewhat sheepish as she sank gracefully into a nearby settee. "I know, Aunty Jules, but I so hate to wait. You do realize, don't you, that this shall be my first time to go riding at the fashionable hour?"

"I know, Dee, but sit still and allow your cheeks to cool. You do not want to *appear* impatient at any rate." Julianna laughed, knowing it would be impossible to get the younger girl to actually quell her impatience. At this point, appearances were the best she could expect.

Julianna herself was unsure how she felt about her upcoming expedition. She had a ridiculous longing to see Luc again, which was utterly mortifying. Nothing good could come of this afternoon, and she was wondering why she had agreed to it.

Odelia wiggled on her seat. In an effort to distract herself, she started a conversation with her aunt. "So you are going riding too, right? With Viscount Beaufort? That's exciting! I thought you did not wish to be friends with the handsome lord. You told Abigail he was not to be trusted."

"Therefore it is hardly exciting, is it?" Julianna denied all of her feelings in that statement. "But I must admit it shall be quite lovely to ride in the park this afternoon."

Odelia agreed. "We shall be the talk of the *ton*!" Despite her glee, she managed not to be distracted away from her earlier thoughts. "But why are you going with the viscount if you do not wish to? You seem very capable of saying no."

With a laugh Julianna had to agree with her niece. "'Tis true. I have had much practice with you and your brother, haven't I?"

Dee's eyes turned shrewd. "Stop prevaricating, Aunty. You do not have feelings for Lord Ackerley do you?"

"Don't be silly, Odelia," she hedged. "It is merely a carriage ride, not a declaration of any sort."

"But rumor has it the viscount is looking about for a wife, so why would he be taking you to the park at the fashionable hour instead of one of the debutantes?"

Deciding she had had enough of the unanswerable questions, Julianna put an end to the questioning with one of her own. "With reasoning like that, should I be expecting a declaration from Mr. Landon?"

Odelia released a tinkle of laughter, acknowledging her aunt's reasoning. "I should think not. Poor Mr. Landon wishes to enjoy himself even longer than I do. I believe he sees me as a safe companion since I am not setting my cap at him."

Chapter Fifteen

After a momentary pause, the ladies heard the knocker sounding. Odelia leapt up from her chair then subsided before the quelling look she received from her aunt.

"You must wait while he is announced, my dear. It is always best to make him wait for at least a couple seconds," Julianna explained with slightly dry sarcasm.

Then the butler was there announcing that both gentlemen had arrived. Odelia ran from the room with Julianna following at a more sedate pace, ordering her own cheeks to resist the flush rising up.

As Lord Ackerley handed Julianna into the phaeton, he could not help admiring her elegant beauty. "You look lovely this afternoon, my lady."

Her cheeks warmed at the compliment. "Thank you, my lord. What beautiful horses. Are they a new acquisition?"

Luc laughed at her turn of the subject but allowed her to lead for the moment. "Yes, fairly new. I got them at Tattersall's a couple of months ago. Very sweet goers, but they get anxious if they don't get taken out every day. I did not use them yesterday, so I had to take the long way to get here in order to work out their fidgets. They should do well now that they have blown off some of their steam. Has your brother set up much of his stables here while you are all in Town?"

"Unfortunately no. He is not too much of an enthusiast for sports of any sort other than the verbal sparring he seems to enjoy so much. We, of course, have a couple of carriages for our use while we are in Town, but our riding horses were left at home. And of course we have nothing to compare to these two."

Catching the wistful note in her voice, Luc offered generously, "I have brought up several lovely mounts to my stables here. Just say the word, and you could have the use of one of them."

"Oh, no, my lord, that is far too generous." Julianna was firm in her declaration.

"Not really. It will save the grooms from having to exercise them. I may have overestimated how many horses I would need for my personal use. Now they are just eating themselves to fatness since we cannot turn them out to any fields. The grooms do their best, but the poor things could use a proper ride, I assure you. You would actually be doing me a favour."

Julianna looked sceptical for a moment, but she dearly loved to ride and could not resist the offer. With a shy smile at the viscount she accepted graciously. "Perhaps it is wrong of me, but thank you, I would love to go riding."

"Excellent. After a couple passes through the park, let us swing by my stables on the way back to your house, and I will introduce you to my head groom. Then whenever you feel like riding you can just have one of your servants bring him a note, and he will have a horse made ready for you." He thought for a moment then gave her a stern warning. "But promise me you will never ride without a groom. You are no doubt still used to country ways. It would not do for you to go out alone."

Somewhat taken aback by his tone, her eyes flew to his face, searching for the cause. Seeing only concern for her safety she acquiesced. "I promise, never fear. And thank you so much for your kind offer. I have been wishing I had thought to bring my own sweet Sophie to Town. It would be such fun to ride her in the mornings. There is nothing like a good gallop to blow the cobwebs from your brain after a late night of dancing."

The viscount agreed wholeheartedly and resolved to ride with her at the earliest opportunity. He allowed a few moments of silence while she looked around at the beauty of the park and the bustle of others before pursuing the line of questioning for which he had brought her out that day.

"So, Julianna, what has been troubling you?"

Julianna was startled by his abrupt question and blushed rosily. Despite trying to prepare, she hadn't really expected him to pursue his questions from the previous evening thinking it was merely an idle, passing thought.

"Whatever do you mean, my lord?" She was determined to remain formal with the viscount.

"Come on, Julianna," he chided. "We are as private as you said you wanted to be. Surely you can drop the formalities. We were once very dear friends. Can't you call me Luc?"

"That was a long time ago," she replied with stiff lips.

"Not so very long," Luc answered with a warm, soft voice causing Julianna to turn her eyes to his face searchingly. "Tell me what's troubling you. Is it the children?"

Julianna could no longer resist. She nodded in affirmation. Biting her lip to keep it from trembling, she took a deep breath before beginning.

"It isn't so much Odelia, although I cannot help worrying about her, too. A girl's first Season is full of so many possible pitfalls. But she seems to be handling herself quite maturely despite her penchant for giggling at everything."

The viscount chuckled at her description causing a tremulous smile to touch Julianna's lips before she continued.

"I actually worry more about Fletcher. My brother is so caught up in his politics that he leaves everything at home in my hands. That was mostly all right when they were small. It no doubt would have been better for him to be more involved, but I could handle frogs and dogs and whatever little boy pranks he got up to. Now Fletcher is pretty much a man, and I have no experience with that." Julianna laughed with self-deprecation still wondering how she came to be confiding in Luc about this.

Luc could barely stand to watch her wring her hands with anxiety. "*Ne t'enquiete pas, ma petite,*" he said while reaching out and clasping her cold hands.

Julianna was almost undone by his softly murmured words. It somehow sounded so much more intimate when said in another language. 'Don't worry' is so innocuous when said normally. Then the endearment – 'little one'. But he had made it all the more personal by saying '*my* little one.' She felt altogether flustered by the combination and felt like further unburdening herself in this unfamiliar environment of warm acceptance.

Clutching his hand tightly in both of hers, Julianna felt unexpected tears welling in her eyes. Looking at the viscount with her beautiful blue eyes swimming in unshed tears, she exclaimed, "Oh, Luc, I should not be burdening you with all of this, but I just do not know what to do about Fletcher. I worry that he's going to fall in love with some completely inappropriate young lady like maybe Lady Abigail Fielding. And he has started to stay out until dawn or even later doing who knows what because he is not with us."

"But what is it about this that is troubling you? He seems to be a reasonably steady young man, and these sound like the usual antics young men like himself get up to at his age." Luc hated to see her in distress and struggled to understand wherein her worries lay. Julianna was not usually the sort to give in to fits of mawkishness. Except that one time, of course.

"Perhaps it is usual antics, but unless a mature gentleman explains certain things to him or even takes him about a bit, I am afraid he shall easily get in over his head. I know, Luc, I am probably being silly. But it seems just last week he was a little boy. Now he is getting into things that I cannot clean up after him, and it weighs on me. The worst thing about it is that his father, the earl, seems to pay even less attention to him now than he did when he truly was a little boy, and I feel it should be the opposite. Now is when he needs a bit of fatherly attention."

A single tear finally broke over her lashes, sliding down her cheek unchecked, and Luc was undone.

"Let me see about him. Perhaps I can steer him through the quagmire of his young manhood."

Julianna offered a tight smile and shook her head. "I don't think so, Lucius Ackerley. From what I have seen and heard, you are a rake. I do not think I want my sweet young nephew being steered by the likes of you."

Startled by the vehemence in her tone, Luc stared at her in surprise; this was the second time she had said something similar. "What have you seen and heard about me?"

Blushing to the roots of her hair, Julianna again shook her head. "Never mind that. Thank you for your offer, but I really don't see how you could help with Fletcher. You aren't even a relative."

Deciding for the moment to set aside his offence, he stuck to the subject at hand. "At the very least I could engage him in conversation and pry a little." This offer finally brought a sweet smile back to Julianna's lips and Luc was gratified. "Then I could see what he has gotten himself into and determine whether or not you have reason to be concerned."

Julianna cocked her head in question. "That is such a thoughtful suggestion, Luc. Although I expect prying will be a bit of a challenge for you as a man. Why are you bothering with my worries at all?"

Now it was Luc's turn to blush a little. Not having a coherent answer for her, he merely shrugged and replied flippantly. "A gentleman never allows a lady to worry overmuch."

Unconvinced but grateful nonetheless, Julianna accepted his offer. "When will you talk to him? And do you promise to tell me whatever you might find out, even if a gentleman is not supposed to allow a lady to worry?"

Laughing at her sarcasm, the viscount agreed. "I think your niece mentioned you would be at the Westfields' grand event tomorrow evening. I will endeavour to strike up a conversation with him there. If you promise to go riding with me the next morning, I will tell you whatever I managed to find out."

Julianna searched Lucius' face while he struggled to keep any emotions other than benign interest from his countenance. "I still wonder why you would go to any bother for us, but I find that I am desperate." Realizing that could be construed as churlish, she continued with full honesty. "But in all reality, I think you would be better at perceiving his intentions than his father would be, so I shall accept your offer. Thank you for trying. And thank you for making me tell you about it. Strangely enough, I feel a little relieved just from confiding in someone."

After a moment of silence fraught with emotional tension, Julianna turned the subject to one far less personal. Realizing she was still clutching his hand, she cleared her throat with slight embarrassment and let go of his hand rather hastily and asked, "Have you been to any entertainments hosted by the Countess of Westfield?"

"A few. She is an accomplished hostess. When they were newly married she struggled a little, I think, but she seems to have really found her footing amongst the *ton*. She is now considered one of the leading ladies of Society much to her amusement."

"They seemed to be quite pleasant. I look forward to the event. Odelia's grandparents seemed to have an interesting opinion about it, but I am sure they are mistaken."

Luc raised an eyebrow in question at her statement causing Julianna to explain. "Fletcher, Odelia, Hartford, and I visited the Ashwoods a couple of days ago. They are rather high in the instep, if you aren't well acquainted with them. They said they could never attend an entertainment hosted by the Westfields since the earl and his wife are far too lax in their standards and allow even those of less noble birth to attend their larger gatherings. It would have been funny if it were not so sad."

The viscount had to agree. "I have a very slight acquaintance with Ashwoods. I think they were friends with my parents when they were alive. I would have to agree with your assessment of them – they did seem to be terribly proud and unbending the few occasions I have spent any amount of time with them. In a way, I suppose you can be glad they have not spent much time with Odelia and Fletcher since it would have been a stifling environment for them as children."

"That is certainly looking on the bright side." Julianna laughed. "There were many times that I wished Lucretia's family had paid more attention to her children, but you are quite right, that is not a quality she would have wanted them to adopt."

"Of course, with your own parents being gone, no doubt you would have been happy for some adult supervision to help you with them after their mother died." Luc had not given any thought to what troubles she had faced at the time and was just now realizing what a challenge it would have been for her.

With a sigh and a small smile, Julianna acknowledged the truth of his comments. "The dowager duchess was no longer speaking to me, and Hartford was nearly prostrate with grief. I was all the children had, and I deeply longed for someone to guide me." Realizing she was indulging in a serious bout of self-pity that was far from attractive, she tried to turn the subject to something more positive. "It wasn't all bad, though. Children adapt remarkably well. And what truly saved us was the housekeeper. Mrs. Parks has been the housekeeper at Somerton most of my life, and she had witnessed how my mother raised Hart and me. Whenever I was in doubt on anything I would turn to her to talk things through."

"Those two were certainly lucky to have you," the viscount commented with admiration clearly evident in his voice.

Julianna shook her head in denial. "It was more like I was lucky to have them. It was a rather dark time in my life, and I have to tell you it is pretty much impossible to be depressed for long when in the presence of lively youngsters."

Not wanting to continue conversing in this vein, Julianna again turned the subject. "We somehow got off the topic. Now tell me what should Odelia and I expect tomorrow evening when we attend the Westfields' entertainment?"

Realizing what she was about and admiring her all the more, Luc allowed the change of subject. "Well, I have to admit, the Ashwoods are correct. When the earl and his wife have an evening of the arts, as they like to call it, they do invite quite a variety of company. No one terribly low class or unacceptable, of course, but not the usuals you would find at Almack's, let us say. They enjoy hearing multiple sides to any story, so they invite some with strong opinions outside the perfectly accepted realm. For example, you could come across a few suffragists as well as various political writers from some of the papers. There will be musicians of all sorts, too, I am sure."

"It sounds like it shall be a truly fascinating evening. Dee often complains about not being allowed to go away to school, so it will be an interesting education for her."

Luc was pleased that she was not turning up her pert little nose at the prospect of rubbing elbows with those less fortunate than herself. He was looking forward to introducing her to his brother and hoped she would be able to accept him with equal aplomb.

Julianna gave a little bounce on the seat beside him. Turning to him with a grin she demanded, "All right, my lord, enough strutting about the park, let us go introduce me to your horses."

Luc found her irresistible and grinned right back at her as he deftly turned his phaeton around and guided them skilfully out of the park towards the mews behind his elegant townhouse.

"Jeeves, this is Lady Julianna Montgomery. She will be making herself comfortable here in our stables. She will be taking out some of the horses for exercise periodically. Would you be so good as to show her around for a couple of minutes? She would like to see which horses might be to her taste."

Jeeves stared intently at his master for a couple of seconds but he was well enough trained not to reveal the shock he was feeling at that moment. He recovered quickly.

"It would be my earnest pleasure to show you around our humble quarters, milady," he declared with a flourishing bow.

Offering the crook of his elbow, Jeeves took Julianna over to a series of stalls. "Pardon me for saying so, milady, but you must take care when you ride out on any of Beaufort's mounts. The viscount isn't known for choosing sedate horses to ride."

Julianna released a tinkling laugh. "Never you worry about me, Mr. Jeeves. I have been riding since before I could walk. The viscount has promised me some spirited mounts, and I look forward to setting them through their paces."

Julianna was then thoroughly entranced by the beautiful horses stabled there. The two men stood back and admired as she quickly brought the horses under her spell. The usually skittish stallions were soon eating from her hand and allowing her to pat them gently through the railings of their stalls.

Turning back to the men with an enchanting smile of gratitude, Julianna was gracious in her thanks. "Thank you, Mr. Jeeves, for taking the time to show me around. I look forward to seeing you again very soon." Then turning to Luc she continued, "I do believe, my lord, it is time I should be getting home. No doubt Odelia will already be there and will be wondering what has become of me."

Luc bowed in acknowledgement, turned, and helped her back into his high phaeton. Jeeves stood with a couple of grooms watching them drive away.

"If you had told me this morning that his lordship would be instructing me to allow a woman into his stables I would have told you you'd had too much to drink. Never in all my days would I think to see the likes of that!" Jeeves declared with vehemence.

One of the grooms grunted in agreement while the other was even more upset. "I had to work here a full year before he'd let me drive any of his matched teams! And he's going to let that little chit come and go however she pleases? If that don't beat all, I don't know what does!"

Jeeves figured he knew what was in store. "Just you wait and see. Must be looking to get leg-shackled."

The groom wasn't so convinced. "Nah, she seemed a little long in the tooth for that, wouldn't you say?"

Jeeves wouldn't be swayed. "She wasn't so old as that. And really there's no other explanation for him letting her into his stables. He's trying to turn her up sweet. Mark my words, he has to be moonstruck to be bringing a female to my stables."

The grooms couldn't disagree with Jeeves' logic and merely grunted their agreement as they turned to continue their work about the stables.

"Thank you so much for a lovely afternoon, my lord." At his censorious look Julianna quickly substituted. "I mean, Lucius." Quick to move on, she continued. "Thank you for offering to check on Fletcher for me. And for offering me the use of your horses. I really appreciate it."

Luc instinctively wanted to reject her gratitude but didn't know how to respond, so he just hopped down and hurried around his carriage to assist her to alight.

"If I do not see you sooner, I shall see you tomorrow evening."

A thrill shivered up Julianna's spine as the viscount leaned over her hand and placed a warm kiss upon her wrist. With haste, she snatched her hand back before he could sense her melting emotions. Silently cursing her own crumbling defenses, Julianna gracefully hurried up the stairs while a footman held the door open for her. She paused momentarily on the threshold to turn and wave casually while the viscount watched from the street.

Julianna kept her smile in place as she ran up to her room, only allowing it to waver as soon as she had closed the door behind her. She almost slammed it but caught herself in time, not wanting to draw any undue attention to herself until she had managed to get her roiling emotions back under her control.

Pressing her back to the closed door she slid down in a pool of fabric as she allowed the tears to flow down her cheeks unchecked.

Why is he being so nice to me? Can I trust him? He very nearly broke my heart seven years ago. Why am I taking such a risk? But he seems so kind, generous, and mature! Maybe it is time I forgive him and give him a chance. She paused as her thoughts ran wild. *Can I turn a blind eye to such behaviour?*

Still unresolved, but more optimistic than ever about her future, Julianna stood up, dried her tears, straightened her skirts, and left her room in search of Odelia.

Odelia had so much to relate with enthusiasm about her own afternoon out riding with Mr. Landon she barely seemed to notice her aunt's distraction as she discussed at length whom she had seen and how everyone had looked.

"Are you quite all right, Aunt Julianna? You have barely uttered a word in the last ten minutes."

With a start, Julianna realized it was true. Forcing her tumultuous thoughts back under control, she smiled warmly at her niece. "I am perfectly fine, my dear. I'm glad you had such a nice time with the baron. Does it seem likely that he shall come around to take you riding again?"

"I knew you weren't listening!" Odelia declared with surprise. "I just told you five minutes ago that he is taking me out again tomorrow."

"Really? Are you sure?" Julianna blushed to her roots at the evidence of her lack of wits. But then she thought of something much more important. "Tomorrow? He wants to take you out again so soon? Are you sure that's wise, my dear? You told me yourself that neither of you are serious about any relationship with each other. If you go out riding with him two days in a row you are sure to set tongues to wagging about your behaviour."

"I thought of that, but we had such fun together so we agreed on a solution. He's going to bring a landau, and Mr. Jackes and Abigail will also join us so there will be less to remark upon by any old biddies who wish to gossip about me."

"That was shrewd thinking, but please have a care about your own feelings as well as Mr. Landon's. At this moment you both think you don't have feelings for each other and you each profess not to want to pursue serious relationships at this time. But from what I have witnessed these things can change quite quickly."

"I am sure you're right, Jules, but I am equally sure that it will not happen to me, at least not with Mr. Landon. He feels much like a brother to me, except that he never insults me. He is, in fact, the perfect companion for a Season in which I don't want to accept any offers."

"Just be careful, Dee. You aren't a child anymore. And I noticed that once again I'm not invited along upon this excursion. Is that by design?" she asked with a teasing lilt to her voice.

"Perhaps," Dee teased back.

"Well, I may not be along on every excursion, but I will be keeping an eye on you."

Odelia ran to her aunt and gave her a swift, warm hug. "I know, Aunty. That is the best part. I do try to be careful, but I feel like you are my safety net. You will catch me if I start falling into too much trouble. Thank you for being here with me."

"I would not want to be anywhere else," Julianna answered with feeling as she returned her niece's warm clasp.

Chapter Sixteen

Julianna had felt like a schoolgirl as she and Odelia giggled their way through their preparations for the evening the next day. She had gone to visit the viscount's stables early that morning. She had been too keyed up to sleep late even though she knew she would pay for it the next morning. The stable hands had raised their eyebrows at her presence but it hadn't taken her too much cajoling to get them to saddle up one of Ackerley's horses for her. One of the grooms had insisted on accompanying her on her ride. She was disappointed not to have the ride completely to herself, but she had to acknowledge that she had given her word to the viscount.

They had enjoyed an exhilarating gallop, and Julianna returned home feeling more happy and positive than she could remember feeling for a very long time, at least since they had come to Town. She was giddy with excitement over seeing Viscount Beaufort again. And she was looking forward to whatever interesting amusements were to be on offer at the Westfields' that evening.

She was keenly aware of the rustle of her skirts as she descended the staircase. It felt like all her senses were much more sensitive than usual and she was glad to be wearing gloves. This evening it was Julianna's turn to impatiently wait for the rest of her family in the front hall.

But she didn't have to wait over long. As prompt as usual when it came to anything touching on politics, Hartford strode with purpose down the same stairs seemingly preoccupied with his own thoughts. Until his eyes fell upon his sister. A low whistle came from his mouth.

"Lady Julianna Montgomery. You certainly are a sight this evening."

"A sight?" she asked in horror. "Whatever do you mean?"

The earl laughed with genuine amusement. "I truly am a backward oaf. I apologize profusely, Jules. I meant that in a good way, truly. You will be the most elegantly beautiful woman there this evening, I promise you. Seeing as you are my sister, I almost never think of you in that way, but I have a feeling I will soon be fielding requests for your hand."

Gratified by her brother's clumsy compliments, Julianna blushed a little as she laughed along with him. Then they both turned to watch as Odelia and Fletcher descended the staircase together.

Fletcher was again in a gentlemanly mood and he had waited at the top to offer his elbow to his sister. They made a remarkably handsome pair as they slowly descended. Odelia was in her looks that evening and would surely be that night.

In fine spirits and in charity with one another, the family waved to the footmen and were whisked away in their carriage for the short ride to the Westfields'.

Impatient as always, Odelia complained. "We should have walked since it's only a couple of streets away. Now we have to wait for this entire line up to move so we can get down in front of the house. It truly is silly."

Fletcher was also fidgety, but he answered her with reason. "I have to agree that it seems silly, but it really wouldn't do to be seen walking. You have to arrive with your slippers in pristine condition. Besides, when it's time to go home, even though it's only a couple of streets over there is no way you could walk there safely."

Odelia could not argue with the truth of his statements so she merely harrumphed in her corner, tapping her toe in impatience as they slowly inched forward.

Finally it was their turn to descend from the carriage. The four Montgomerys made an elegant, stately entrance as they climbed the stairs to the Westfields' elaborate home and were announced to their hosts.

Despite her slightly hectic colour from excitement, Odelia managed to keep herself contained, Julianna was proud to see as they made their bows and curtsies to the earl and countess. They only had time to say, "hello" before the next guests were announced and they had to move on into the overflowing rooms.

The four family members quickly separated pursing their own personal interests, although Julianna made every effort to remain close to Odelia throughout the evening. The two ladies made their way to the ballroom since the youngest Montgomery loved to dance and had already promised her hand to several gentlemen before they had even arrived.

As Odelia was swept onto the dance floor by her first partner, Julianna responded to the imperious wave of Lady Hearst.

"There you are, my dear. It has been several days since we have seen each other. How are you?"

"I am well, Lady Hearst, thank you for asking. And might I ask how you are feeling? We were sorry to hear you were under the weather on the evening of my grandmother's dinner party," Julianna responded with something less than the full truth.

Lady Hearst answered with sadness. "I was so disappointed to miss the Duchess' dinner, let me tell you. But I was glad that my son and daughter-in-law were able to take Abigail with them so she did not have to miss out despite my inconvenience. My darling daughter did such a good job describing everything that I feel almost like I was there. Although, I must say, her description of all that the duchess served to her guests made me hungry for days."

Julianna couldn't help but laugh at the older woman's words. "It is true. The food was delicious. The duchess never scrimps when it comes to what to serve to her guests."

"You are looking quite lovely this evening, my dear. If I hadn't heard you say otherwise, I would believe you were setting your cap for some gentleman. Have you changed your mind about searching for a husband at this late date?"

Julianna gritted her teeth at the older woman's rude observation. She knew she was obviously older than the debutants, but she was surely far from her dotage. Despite her irritation she managed to keep a smile on her face and after some politely inane conversation excused herself without causing an ill-bred scene. As an "older" single woman, despite the place her birth gave her, Society would not look kindly on her expressing her true feelings to such women as Lady Hearst.

Quickly cheered by the attentions of several kind gentlemen Julianna was able to push her irritation from her mind, at least for now. The early part of the evening passed in a happy blur as Julianna alternated between dancing with attentive and handsome lords to visiting with her lady friends. Her active mind managed to enjoy the attentions while also keeping a close eye on Odelia's progress through the evening, as well as watching out for the arrival of Viscount Beaufort.

Despite her vigilance she was momentarily distracted by a conversation with her dear friend Catherine when she looked up and spotted Luc in the crowd. Her cheeks warmed as he caught her eye upon him. Smiling more rakishly than usual, he turned in her direction after tossing some words over his shoulder.

Turning back to Catherine so as to finish their conversation and not to appear overly forward, Julianna did not realize there were two gentlemen approaching her.

"Malcolm, what a delight to see you here," greeted Lady Chorney with joy.

Julianna turned around at the low response, a smile of welcome touching her pretty face. She was stunned with a moment of confusion, but she then felt all the blood drain from her face at the sight of the two nearly identical looking men standing before her.

Lord Lucius Ackerley was smiling warmly at Julianna, but his look quickly turned to puzzlement as he noticed her moment of distress. She, of course, quickly recovered and appeared to be her usual composed self, if perhaps a bit stiffer than was her wont.

"Lady Julianna, might I present to you my half-brother Mr. Malcolm Mansfield? Mac, this is Lady Julianna Montgomery."

Malcolm bent over Lady Julianna's cold hand with a rakish flourish, pressing a smacking kiss upon its back. He gazed at her shrewdly through slightly narrowed eyes, worried about his brother's renewed interest in his former fiancé. Determined to ascertain her worthiness of his beloved brother, Malcolm endeavoured to engage her in conversation.

"It is a pleasure to make your acquaintance, Lady Julianna. How are you enjoying the Season thus far?" Malcolm began with a seemingly innocent question.

Holding tight to her composure and refusing to look at the viscount, Julianna answered through tight lips. "It has been quite lovely so far, thank you for asking."

"I understand you have been in the country for several years and have only recently returned to the pleasures the *ton* has to offer."

Julianna's distracted gaze sharpened at his suggestive wording, but she remained composed and polite. "I am here as a chaperone to my niece who is making her debut this Season. We are enjoying the pleasure of attending various dinners and balls and are looking forward to seeing more of the city as the Season progresses."

Luc could see what his brother was doing, and while he appreciated the concern that motivated it, as a grown man he could look after himself. He was surprised to see the distress well hidden in Julianna's eyes and hoped it was not disgust over his brother's obvious lack of nobility.

Hoping to ascertain the reasons for her distress, Luc tried to engage Julianna in conversation.

"How are you enjoying your evening thus far, my lady?"

"It is quite lovely, thank you, my lord. It was a pleasure to meet you, Mr. Mansfield. Lady Chorney, if you will excuse me, I must find my niece. Good evening." Before they could stop her, Julianna had turned on her heel and disappeared into the crowd.

Luc turned to Catherine for an explanation. "What happened to her, Lady Chorney? We had made such progress in our friendship over the past week or so. Now she looked like she could barely tolerate the thought of my presence."

Malcolm stepped into the conversation with angry words and a tight voice. "No doubt it is my baseborn presence which unsettled the earl's sister. I know the Earl of Somerton has trouble with me being included in certain political conversations."

Dismissing his brother's comments Luc teased Malcolm despite his concern about Julianna. "The earl objects to your politics, not to who your mother was. I don't think the earl has even noticed we are brothers. But it did seem Lady Julianna was troubled by you in some way."

It was now Malcolm's turn to tease. "Perhaps she found me irresistibly handsome and was unsure how to handle such hot emotions."

Catherine stepped into the conversation at this point after laughing at Malcolm's comments. "I see you are as humble as ever Malcolm. I have known Lady Julianna for years, and she is one of the least arrogant members of the aristocracy you are ever going to meet. It is one of her most appealing qualities as a friend when you are not connected to earls and dukes. Of course, I am sure she has never been fellow guests with the likes of you, but

I don't think it was that. If you two will excuse me, I think it best if I go find her."

When Luc made to protest his own desire to search for her, Catherine waved him to silence. "If you go there is a greater chance of a scene, or at least, of some unwanted gossip. If it is something completely unrelated to you, she will search you out later and apologize. Otherwise, you can call on her tomorrow and ascertain for yourself what is going on."

Luc could not fault the wisdom of her words despite the fact that his own instincts were pushing him to dash off into the crowd to make all things right for her. Then he remembered they were supposed to go riding in the morning and he had an assignment to fulfill on the lady's behalf. After watching Catherine walk away, Luc bade farewell to his brother and set out purposefully into the crowd to find Fletcher.

Julianna fled to the ladies' retiring room, slipping behind a curtain murmuring something incomprehensible about a torn flounce. She managed to keep her sobs silent as the tears flowed freely down her cheeks.

Lucius has a brother! How did I not know he has a brother? Julianna's mind raced over all the possible implications that had occurred to her as she had looked up in the ballroom to behold what appeared to be two Lord Ackereleys. She had managed to rein in her rioting thoughts at that moment, but now they held sway as she wept. *Did I make the most awful mistake seven years ago? How can I live with this?*

No one must ever know! With that last vehement thought ringing in her mind, Julianna brushed the last of the tears from her cheeks. After checking to make sure she was alone, she stepped out from behind the curtain and grabbed a moistened towel to wipe the evidence from her face.

Looking in the mirror, she could see she did not look quite right, but she was almost certain no one would be able to tell that the bottom had dropped out of her world that evening, and for that she was grateful. It was time to go check on Odelia and endure the rest of this night. She pasted a smile on her face, and although it didn't quite reach her eyes, most at the gathering would never look deep enough to realize.

Looking as serene and composed as she could manage, Julianna emerged from the retiring room feeling like she was a different woman than the carefree one who had arrived that evening. Everything hurt, and she had to struggle not to wince at the noise being generated by the throng of people crowded into the Earl of Westfield's house. Not thirty minutes prior she had thought the sounds invigorating, now they hurt her ears.

Pulling back her shoulders and lifting her head high, Julianna strode forward. All her aristocratic breeding and training came to her aid that evening as she smiled politely to the various acquaintances she encountered as she made her way through the crowds in search of Odelia.

"There you are, my dear. I have been searching for you everywhere."

Odelia turned a surprised face to look at her aunt. "Why were you searching for me? I have been here in the ballroom all evening."

With a shaky, distracted laugh Julianna explained. "I tore my flounce and had to retire for a moment, and then when I came out I couldn't see you. With all the crowds, you were a bit hard to find. Are you almost ready to go home?"

Now Odelia was shocked. "Go home? Why would I ever want to go home? Look around. The night is obviously still young, since there are such crowds here. I can even hear the major-domo announcing names, so people are still arriving. We could not possibly leave now!"

With a somewhat wan smile Julianna replied, "No, of course not, never mind me. I shall be about if you need me."

Finally taking notice of someone other than herself, Odelia asked with some concern, "Are you alright, Aunty? You sound a little strange."

Bolstering her slipping smile, Julianna answered in a firmer tone. "Of course, I am fine. I shall just go and find some of my own friends and check in with you in a little while. Perhaps we can go in to the late supper together."

About an hour later when Odelia went to collect her aunt in order to go into the dining room together she was surprised to find her sitting along the wall with the older ladies and the wallflowers. However, since her aunt was deep in conversation with a woman Odelia didn't know, it seemed to her Julianna was enjoying herself.

When Odelia caught her eye, Julianna excused herself from the older lady she was talking with and went to join her niece. "Are you all danced out?"

"Never!" declared Odelia with joy. "But I am a wee bit hungry. You had mentioned we ought to go into supper together, so I came to find you. Was I interrupting, or is now a good time?"

"Now would be perfect," Julianna lied with a straight face. Food was the furthest thing from her mind, and she wondered if she would be able to force anything past her dry mouth.

"Are you having a nice evening?" Julianna asked, making conversation as they found seats after they had filled their plates.

"Oh yes, I am having a grand time! I have danced every dance and have met some lovely people. Lady Westfield came to me with a couple of young gentlemen who had requested an introduction. Is that not just so droll?"

"Oh, yes," Julianna agreed with as much enthusiasm as she could muster as she pushed around the food on her plate.

"What about you? Are you having a good time?" Odelia thought to ask.

"I too have met some lovely people. Did you notice the young lady I was speaking to when you approached us? Her name is Lady Isabella Hetherington. She is quite a lovely young woman despite some unfortunate circumstances. She is terribly shy, so these large social occasions are quite difficult for her.

Several years ago she had a bad fall while out riding and has a limp, so she does not enjoy dancing."

"Then why would she sit in the ballroom? There are other places to be this evening. There are crowds of people in other rooms here."

Julianna acknowledged Odelia's logic but explained, "The poor dear loves music, so she wanted to sit in the ballroom for a time and just rest her foot. In the other rooms it is often standing room only. She doesn't want to draw attention to her infirmity so she does not always ask for a chair. I should have introduced you to her – you would be a great friend for her since you do not seem to have a shy bone in your body."

Odelia laughed. "It's true. I think I got my father's gift for talking to anyone. Too bad ladies cannot go into politics. Of course, I would have to care about all those things to be a good politician anyway."

Julianna smiled in genuine amusement at her niece's words, feeling like her face was about to crack since it had been so stiff for half the evening.

"Speaking of your father, I wonder where he is," Julianna mused.

"Knee deep in politics, I am sure. There is such an interesting array of guests here tonight, I'm sure he is having a grand time."

"No doubt you are quite right. Have you seen Fletcher by any chance?" asked Julianna.

"Not for some time. He was in the ballroom for a while, but then I saw your friend bearing him out of the room."

"Which friend was that?"

"Lord Ackerley, Viscount Beaufort," Odelia answered with a flourish.

In her distress, Julianna had forgotten about his promise to speak to Fletcher, and her promise to go out riding in the morning to see what he had found out. There was no way she was going to be keeping that particular promise, unfortunately. Just the mention of the viscount made her nerves jittery, and Julianna could no longer sit still.

Seeing that Odelia's plate was empty, Julianna stood up. "Shall we return to the ballroom?"

"But you did not finish your supper," Odelia protested.

"That is quite all right, I wasn't really hungry anyway."

"Well, if you are sure, I would love to return to the ballroom. Lead the way, Lady Julianna." Odelia bowed with mock formality to her aunt.

Odelia danced the night away, and Julianna managed not to draw any attention to herself, for which she was grateful. The crowds had noticeably thinned, and finally it was time to leave. Fletcher was nowhere to be found, but Hart came in search of the Montgomery ladies after asking a servant to summon their carriage.

"Ladies, might I see you home safely?" asked the earl with an elegant bow.

"Yes, please," answered Julianna with heartfelt relief.

Odelia pouted a little. "Must we really? I am having so much fun."

"I know, pumpkin, but the poor countess cannot go to bed while there are ladies still in her home, and we are amongst the last to still be here. It is definitely time to take our leave. You would never want to be known as someone who overstays their welcome, would you?" Her father hit on just the right argument.

"Of course not. You are right, as always, ever the diplomat. Take me home to my bed where I can dream that I still dance," Odelia decided with dramatic flair.

After taking their leave of the earl and countess, Julianna and Odelia were handed up into the carriage with much different sentiments.

"That was the best night yet," Odelia declared with enthusiasm. "I do believe I have danced a hole right through my slippers. I had so much fun tonight."

While she elaborated to her father, Julianna struggled with her own feelings. For her, it had been the worst night ever. It was hard to imagine that they could have been at the same event but had such vastly differing experiences.

With relief, Julianna finally found her bed that night and was able to allow all her woes to flood onto her pillow. Despite her worries about Fletcher, she resolved not to go riding with the viscount the next morning. She just could not face him with these feelings so raw. Julianna questioned whether she could ever face him and wondered how she could endure the remainder of the Season. Repairing to their country estate was her keenest desire. Odelia and Hart would have to be consulted on when they thought would be a good time to do so. No date they suggested would be soon enough.

Chapter Seventeen

T he next day Julianna was sitting in the morning room staring sightlessly at a list she was supposed to be compiling when the butler arrived.

"Lord Ackerley, Viscount Beaufort, has called to see you, my lady. Should I show him in?"

"No!" Julianna declared with vehemence before she thought better of it, a sense of déjà vu flooding over her. After pressing her lips together to stem the tide of declarations that clamoured to be released, Julianna took a deep breath and continued in much calmer accents. "I am not feeling at all the thing, Hartley. Would you be so kind as to tell the viscount I am not at home to company this afternoon? I believe I shall retire to my chamber to have a rest. Thank you, Hartley."

On those words she made good her escape, leaving the butler to deal with her mess. Julianna was relieved that Odelia was not there to witness her distress over the viscount's visit. With any luck Dee would have such a lovely afternoon out with her friends, she would have too much to talk about to notice her aunt's distraction.

Hartley was surprised by his mistress' request since she was always so kind and hospitable. In all his years with the family he had never seen Julianna turn away a guest. But he had to admit she did look pale and piqued today, so it was possible the Season

153

was proving to be too much for his much-loved mistress. And actually, this viscount requesting a meeting with the lady was none other than her former fiancé. No doubt the poor lady had her good reasons for refusing to see the cad.

The butler was colder than usual in his dismissal of the viscount. "My lady is not home to visitors this afternoon, my lord. If you would like to leave your card, you may do so on your way out."

The viscount had been disappointed when Julianna had not shown up at their appointed meeting to ride that morning. He had much to tell her after his interview with Fletcher the night before. But when he considered how late the ladies had no doubt stayed at the ball the night before and how early they had agreed to meet, he had simply surmised that she had overslept.

Now the butler was telling him she was 'not at home to visitors.' That was a far cry from 'not at home,' and Luc felt rebuffed. He thought he had come to know her much better over the past couple of weeks and would have sworn it was unlike her to behave in such a way. But given their history, he should probably not be surprised. Clearly, the lady had problems. He slammed out of the house in disgust vowing never to return.

Just as he was swinging up onto the seat of his phaeton, Luc glanced back at the house. For a split of a second, he locked eyes with Julianna, who was peering out from an upper floor window. She hastily stepped away allowing the curtain to fall back into place, but the viscount had seen enough to know she was not coldly dismissing him. Her pretty face had been deeply imprinted with misery, and tears were streaming down her cheeks. Luc's instinctive reaction was to dash back up the stairs and demand to be allowed to see her, and he jumped back out of the phaeton. But with his foot on the bottom stair, he checked himself.

He had no right to make any demands of her. She had barely given him permission to use her given name, let alone granting him access to her personal feelings. She had refused to see him. Clearly she was miserable, but there was little evidence to show he was the cause or that he could help her with her problems. For now, he would have to respect her privacy. He resolved to seek her out that evening.

The only trouble was he had failed to ask the butler where the ladies were promised that evening. He should have asked to see Odelia. Luc again thought to dash back up the stairs but thought better of it once more. He was making a cake of himself standing there for so long in front of their house. If anyone noticed his conduct, it would be an *on dit* before the dinner hour.

With determination, he forced himself back into his phaeton. He decided to head to the park to see if Odelia could be found there. It was his only option besides going to every social event he had been invited to that evening looking for them. He would do that as a last resort. Luc knew, even as that thought formed in his mind, that he was about to make a fool of himself over the Montgomery chit once more but could not find the energy to care.

Luc was relieved not to have to ride around for too long before he spotted Odelia and her three companions. They had gotten out of their carriage and were strolling in the gardens. The viscount quickly pulled off the road and jumped down from his phaeton while his tiger scrambled to catch the horses leads.

"I shall return momentarily. Walk them if you have to. On second thought, could you please turn them for me? As soon as I get the information I am looking for I shall be leaving the park."

He strode with determined speed over to Odelia and her friends hailing them as he neared. Odelia heard him first and turned with a smile.

"Lord Ackerley, what a pleasure to see you here today. You know my friends, Lady Abigail Fielding, Mr. Kenneth Landon, and Mr. Tom Jackes, do you not?"

"Yes, of course. It is a pleasure to see you all again. What a lovely afternoon for a stroll in the park." By this point, the viscount was beginning to realize he had been rather hasty in his dash to the park and was unsure how to broach the subject he wished to discuss. Luck was on his side. With Lady Odelia, you just had to wait for the information to flow.

"Is my aunt with you, my lord?" Odelia asked as she peered past the viscount's shoulder.

"No, I actually stopped by to invite her to come riding with me, but she was not at home to visitors," he explained.

"Oh, no! Did Hartley say what was wrong with her? I hope she is not getting sick. We are supposed to be going to the Duke of York's grand ball tonight," Odelia exclaimed as Abigail chimed in.

"You absolutely must be there, Odelia. It is to be the event of the Season. It would definitely not be the same without you!"

Satisfied with the information he received, Lord Ackerley tried to defuse the young girls' worries. "Perhaps she is merely tired. Did you speak with her today?"

"Yes, actually she seemed perfectly fine before I left, even though she was, as you said, a bit tired." Odelia thought, her usually smooth brow wrinkled for a moment before continuing. "Perhaps you misunderstood our butler. My aunt may have had some errands to run and merely stepped out for a few minutes."

"Perhaps," agreed the viscount with a soothing tone to his voice.

Thus relieved, the four young people resumed their enthusiastic discussion of the upcoming ball.

As the viscount was taking his leave Odelia asked, "Will we see you there this evening, my lord?"

Fearing he had already revealed far too much of his personal affairs, the viscount hedged. "Perhaps. I am uncertain of which commitments I have made for the evening. Will you dance with me if I show up?"

Odelia was slowly becoming familiar with the ways of the *ton* and managed to put on a simulated mask of indifference. "Perhaps if you arrive in time for there to be any spaces left on my dance card, my lord. I cannot make any promises on the subject."

The viscount laughed at her antics, and Odelia grinned back at him.

After he had left, Odelia turned to her friends. "I think I should return home and check on my aunt. It strikes a strange chord with me that Hartley would tell the viscount that Aunt Julianna is not receiving visitors. In my entire life, I cannot recall a single time she has refused anyone. It would be terrible if she has fallen ill."

With suitable expressions of sympathy Odelia's friends escorted her home.

"Welcome home, Lady Odelia, may I take your wrap for you?" greeted the butler upon her return.

"Thank you, Hartley. Do you know where my aunt is?"

"The last time I saw her she was headed to her room. She said she was suffering from a headache and needed a bit of a rest." The well-trained butler was unable to hide the concern he felt since the lady of the house was never unwell.

Odelia thought about his words for a moment before asking, "Do you know how long ago that was? I do not wish to disturb her, but I wonder if I should check to see if a doctor should be called."

"I believe it was about an hour ago. She did not seem so under the weather as to require a physician, but you should go see for yourself. If you have any doubts, you could consult with the housekeeper."

Odelia dashed up the stairs and down the hall, pausing only when she reached Julianna's door. Hesitating for a moment, she finally scratched lightly before she heard her aunt's familiar voice calling out.

"Please enter."

Odelia stepped inside her aunt's room and was surprised to see her seated in front of the looking glass pinning a cap over her curls.

"What are you up to, Aunty Jules? Hartley said you were not feeling quite the thing."

In a cheerful voice, Julianna waved away the butler's concerns with ease. "I have grown overly accustomed to country hours and the late nights finally caught up with me. I felt a headache coming on and decided I needed to take a nap. I am much recovered now and should be perfectly able to accompany you to the Duke of York's Grand Ball this evening."

Odelia was nearly convinced but still prompted with one more question. "I spoke with Viscount Beaufort in the park this afternoon. He said he had stopped by to invite you to ride with him again but you were not receiving. I was surprised."

Julianna coloured slightly but maintained her composure. "But Odelia, surely you would agree that a lady must never show her face when she is not looking quite at her best. The viscount knocked just as I was heading to my room. I really was not in a position to entertain, let alone to go bouncing around in his phaeton."

Odelia could not argue with the logic of her aunt's reasoning. Despite it being a little out of character for Julianna, Odelia would have no doubt made a similar decision so she allowed the matter to drop as Julianna peppered her with questions about her afternoon.

"Tell me, how was your afternoon? Did you have a good time with Abigail, Mr. Landon, and Mr. Jackes?"

As Julianna had expected, Odelia had plenty to say. "Oh, Aunty Jules, it was quite lovely. Despite the cool temperatures, the sun was shining and it was quite comfortable. The baron had brought a landau which seemed to be perfectly designed for just our purposes."

She rambled on for a while, and Julianna allowed her mind to wander back to her own problems but she was abruptly drawn to attention by Odelia's words. "We had a grand time riding around with the top down then we got out for a stroll in what remains of the gardens. That is where the viscount found us."

"Was he searching for you?" Julianna was somewhat confused by Odelia's choice of words and struggled to keep as neutral a tone as possible.

"That is what it looked like. I didn't pay it too much heed at first, but I did notice him enter the park with his beautifully matched pair and that strikingly handsome phaeton of his. He barely paused to acknowledge anyone about the park until he saw us. He came straight over and spoke with us. He seemed quite nonchalant about it, but Mr. Landon commented after he left that it seemed he simply wanted to check on you. As soon as he realized I did not think there was anything seriously wrong with you, he left. He did ask me to save him a dance this evening."

"Did he ask where we were planning to be this evening?" Julianna questioned.

"Not exactly. I told him in the course of the conversation."

"And then what happened?"

"Then he jumped back in his phaeton and left the park entirely. It was most strange I must say. Mr. Jackes at first wanted to speculate that the viscount had a *tendre* for me, but since all we discussed was you, we soon dismissed that thought. Do you suppose Lord Ackerley has a *tendre* for you?"

Julianna couldn't help chuckling over Odelia's surprise with this thought. It should have been unflattering, but rather than being offended, her amusement calmed her.

"I very much doubt that the viscount has a *tendre* for me. He is hardly likely to make the same mistake more than once."

Despite her lack of thought about her aunt in this regard Odelia was ever loyal. "What mistake? He would be prodigiously lucky to have you take any notice of him, and well I will tell him if given a chance."

"Oh no you will not, you silly widgeon. A pretty picture that would make. I can just see the scene now in my mind's eye." Julianna dissolved into gales of laughter that Odelia soon joined in.

After a moment Julianna stood, drying her cheeks from the tears her chuckles had brought.

"That did the trick. It blew away the last of the cobwebs lingering in my head. I don't know about you, but I am now prepared to get ready for our social rounds of the night. We should have a bite to eat before we dress."

Chapter Eighteen

The Duke of York's Grand Ball was in full swing. It was a tradition that he and his duchess opened their home once a year and invited all the highest members of the nobility for a lavish ball. Every year it was one of the most sought after invitations of the Season and always ended up being a veritable squeeze despite the vastness of their rooms. Odelia and Abigail were having a fantastic time. Even Julianna, despite her efforts to avoid the viscount, was enjoying herself reasonably well. There had been a few tense moments when she ran into her dear friend Catherine.

"Julianna, there you are. I was wondering if I would see you this evening. I meant to come around to visit you this afternoon but I was unavoidably detained. I was concerned when you disappeared last night. Is everything all right?"

Julianna had steeled herself just in case this would come up, so she was somewhat prepared. She started with avoidance. "Disappeared? I did not disappear. In fact Odelia, Hart, and I were among the last of the guests to depart from the Westfields' lovely ball. Hart had to explain to Dee that the countess wished to retire but could not as long as we were present. Of course, he may have been exaggerating, but I must tell you I was relieved. At that point, I was beginning to droop. Let me tell you, chaperoning a debutante is not for the faint of heart. I have begun to wonder how my grandmother managed when I made my debut."

This was exactly the wrong thing to say since it brought Catherine back to the point she wished to discuss.

"Since you got engaged so early in your Season, she was able to send you off with your fiancé and did not have to keep such a vigilant eye out for you. She trusted you were in good hands when she allowed you to go off with Lord Ackerley."

Despite Julianna's composure, she could not prevent the wave of colour that ebbed and flowed across her face at the mention of the viscount.

"I'm sorry, Julianna. Are you still uncomfortable around him? I thought the two of you were becoming friends again. But then last night you seemed almost distressed when you caught sight of him. Would you like to talk about it?"

There was nothing in this world Julianna wanted less than discussing it. "No, no, Catherine, I was not distressed. We *have* become friends of a sort. I am quite certain I will never be perfectly comfortable in the presence of the viscount given our past, but I can surely tolerate his presence. He can be charming when he puts his mind to it. And even I will admit he is a lovely dancing partner."

Catherine felt there was still something amiss with her friend but could not quite put her finger on it. Julianna was saying all the right things, so her worries should have been put to rest. Catherine had to content herself with squeezing her friend's hand and concluding the matter with the words, "You do know you can come to me to discuss any matter of concern, don't you, my friend?"

Julianna was humbled by her friend's concern and squeezed back. "I do, thank you, my dear." But she did not want to think about her worries, let alone discuss them with anyone, so she changed the subject. "Now, I have heard wonderfully complimentary things about the duke's generosity. Shall we leave the youngsters to their dancing for a few moments and search out a drink?"

Despite her misgivings with regard to her friend, Catherine allowed the change of subject, and the two elegant ladies left the room in search of refreshments.

They were enjoying a comfortable coze together catching each other up on their respective news when they were interrupted by a deep, male voice.

"Lady Chorney, Lady Julianna, it is a pleasure to see the two of you." The viscount tried to keep relief from his voice but couldn't quite restrain his enthusiasm.

Catherine regarded him quizzically while Julianna paled and struggled for composure. Steeling her nerves, Julianna forced herself to speak and act as normally as possible. She dropped a polite curtsy.

"Lord Ackerley, how kind of you to say so. I owe you an apology for this afternoon. I was unavailable to see any guests when you stopped in." Julianna made an effort to put sincerity into her voice.

"I understand and accept your apology. I trust all is well?" The viscount searched her face endeavouring to see beyond her social mask.

"Of course all is well. Thank you for asking." Julianna refused to meet his eye, making a lie of her statement.

"There was something I wished to discuss with you," Lucius persisted.

"I apologize again, in that case. Perhaps another day we can discuss it." Julianna smiled politely despite feeling a deep pang of distress.

She knew he must mean to discuss Fletcher, and Julianna longed to hear whatever he might have to say, but facing him now just was not to be borne. Fletcher was an adult as the viscount had said. He would have to look out for himself for a few more days. Perhaps in a week or two she would be able to face Lord Ackerley with a degree of calm and hear whatever he had to say without revealing her own roiling emotions. But that would not be possible for at least a few days. She needed some space to numb her pain.

The viscount was puzzled by Julianna's distant attitude. He knew without question that she adored her niece and nephew, so it was impossible that she was indifferent to whatever he might have to say about Fletcher. It was doubtful she was harebrained enough to have forgotten their conversation wherein he had promised to speak to her nephew. Luc looked at her askance for a moment while the three stood and exchanged social niceties.

Julianna soon excused herself saying she had to return to the ballroom to watch over Odelia. Lucius opened his mouth to offer to escort her there and perhaps request that they share a dance, but before he could draw a breath she had turned on her heel and strode away.

Lucius looked at Catherine and could not help the surprised chuckle that escaped him. Catherine gazed back at him with raised eyebrows.

"What did you do to her?" she demanded with some heat.

Taken aback, the viscount denied any wrongdoing. "I did not do anything to her. I swear it to you."

"Well you must have done something, because she is acting like a skittish kitten whenever you are near. It strikes me as being terribly out of character. I know she was nervous to meet you at the beginning of the Season, but I thought all that had been smoothed over at your first meeting."

"Not exactly completely smoothed over," the viscount had to admit. "But I have to agree this does strike me as being strange. She actually confided in me some concerns of hers just a couple of days ago, and we had arranged to meet for an early morning ride yesterday. She did not show up, and when I went to check on her she was not at home to visitors."

This was news to Catherine, and she was silent a moment while they both considered the possible implications.

"Did she not say anything to you about anything of import?" Luc demanded, uncaring if Lady Chorney drew any conclusions of her own by his intense interest.

Catherine was concerned about her old friend but was feeling very torn in her loyalties. She felt a kinship with Julianna since they had gone to school together and shared their first Season, but her friendship with Lord Ackerley was of a longstanding nature as well. Besides he was friends with her husband, which held some weight with her, too. But in all honesty, whether she wanted to confide in him or not, she really had nothing to add, so she told him the truth.

"I'm sorry, Luc. I don't think Lady Julianna is confiding in anyone at the moment. Certainly she has not told me anything that would explain her strange behaviour." Catherine paused for a moment watching the disappointment play across the viscount's face. "On the other hand, do you think we might be overreacting? I mean, really, has she done anything that has been truly so odd that we should be worrying so?"

Luc had to acknowledge the reasonableness of what Catherine had just said, but instinctively he knew beyond doubt that Julianna was not acting normally. Of course, it could just be that she did not wish to be in his company and was too polite to say that outright. But he did not think he was being inexcusably arrogant to consider that was not the problem.

Was it not just three days ago she had asked him to look into her nephew's behaviour? They had barely seen each other in the meantime, so he could not have done anything to give her a disgust of him. No, he was sure it was something bigger than just her taking him in dislike. Her strangeness had all started when he introduced her to his brother. Now she was suddenly acting like she had seven years ago except that her circumstances would not allow her to physically leave Town as she might wish. Instead she had left him in spirit, if not in body. *Can the two things be tied together? What can it be about my brother that causes such a rift?*

Luc would have to persist in getting her to talk to him. But the Duke of York's Grand Ball was not the place to do so.

"I appreciate the logic of what you are saying, Lady Chorney, but I do think there is something amiss with our Lady Julianna. Unfortunately one cannot force a person to confide in you, especially not in such a public venue. So, for the time being, I should make my rounds and move on."

Catherine watched with mixed emotions as the viscount made his way through the room. He was a popular man, and it was slow progress for him to get around as many wished to speak with him. While she stood there watching Lord Ackerley walking away her husband joined her.

"What is on your mind, dearest wife of mine?"

With a sigh, Catherine tore her eyes away from their friend and confided in her husband. "I find I am worried."

Used to his wife's methods of working out her thoughts by speaking them to him and knowing that sometimes it's a disjointed process, he waited patiently.

Catherine sighed again before continuing. "Luc seems to have developed feelings for Lady Julianna again. I think she is quite a lovely person and I would have said she would make him a wonderful viscountess. But after tonight, I'm not sure."

She paused again making her husband prompt her. "You aren't sure she would make a good viscountess?"

"No, no, that is not what I meant at all. I believe Julianna would make a perfectly wonderful viscountess, even a duchess if she had a mind for it. It is just that she seems to have misgivings about Lord Ackerley, and she does not seem to have any desire to confide in me on the subject."

Thinking he understood the source of his wife's anxiety, Lord Chorney made an attempt to soothe her hurt feelings. "Perhaps she is not used to confiding in anyone. Or since so much time has elapsed, perhaps she has forgotten how trustworthy you are."

It was much more complicated than that, but Catherine appreciated her husband's efforts to cheer her up, so she teased him. "What kind of a gentleman are you, using terms such as 'so much time has elapsed.' Don't you know you should never refer to the passing of time when it comes to any lady over the age of eighteen?"

Recognizing his wife's playful mood but feeling chagrined all the same, the viscount apologized. "My darling, surely you are not much over the age of eighteen, so I could be excused for my lapse in good judgment. Forgive my gauche behaviour and come and dance with me, please."

Catherine allowed him to lead her into the ballroom and onto the dance floor, but her mind was still preoccupied with thoughts of Julianna and Lucius. She finally gave voice to her thoughts.

"Robert, how long have you known Viscount Beaufort?"

"I was friends with the previous viscount, this one's father. We had various business dealings, which Lucius began to manage long before his father's death. I could not place a date on it, my dear, but I would say at least half his life."

Catherine thought about that for a while and decided her husband was most definitely in a position to form an honest opinion of the man.

"So you know him well, then." At his affirmative nod, she continued. "And you think highly of him, correct?"

"As a matter of fact, I do. He, of course, sowed his wild oats when he was quite young. I did not think so highly of his father. The last Viscount Beaufort was a brilliant businessman and was a success at nearly everything he put his mind to, but he was not always a nice person. He did not mind shady deals, and he had the morals of an alley cat. I highly doubt Lucius grew up with a comfortable or happy family life. He never speaks of it, but it surely would have left its mark upon him. But despite a bit of fast living when he first left school and went on his Grand Tour, he has seemed to be a very responsible, well-grounded young man." He could see by his wife's furrowed brow that he had not quite set her mind at rest.

"You still seem troubled. Why don't you tell me exactly what you want to know, and I will tell you, if I can."

"Have you ever known him to mistreat a woman in any way?"

Now it was his turn to furrow his brows. "That is a serious question. In this case I can, with a clear conscience, say that no, I have never known him to mistreat a woman. And from what I know of him, I do not think it is within his makeup to be capable of doing so. Let me explain. I believe he witnessed mistreatment of his mother at the hands of his father. Not that he ever injured her physically or even raised a hand to her, but he was a terribly cold husband and was unfaithful from the very beginning. This infuriated Luc to the point of illness when he was quite young. The sad thing is his father found this divertingly amusing."

Always warm-hearted, Catherine was immediately stirred to sympathy. "Poor Luc. But then what could have ever happened between him and Julianna, both seven years ago, and now?"

"That I could not tell you. But whatever it was, I can tell you that it hurt them both. I know Luc has never been the same. I cannot tell you if he truly loved her back then, they were both rather young, but I do know that he felt betrayed by her defection. I have occasionally wondered if *he* even knows what happened back then. But I can also tell you that it is really none of your concern." At her protest, he pulled her slightly closer. "I know, my darling wife, you care about them both and want to solve this for them, but you cannot. They must work this out for themselves, and whichever way they choose to take it, you can merely support them in their decisions, not contribute towards it in anyway. Marriage carries far too many consequences for you to stick your fingers into arranging someone's for them."

At her disappointed, crestfallen expression he allowed a suggestive look to come over his face. "I happen to know of a marriage you can rearrange however you'd like. What say you to taking our leave of the Duke and Duchess and head off to our own abode?"

For the moment Catherine allowed that it was none of her affair and went off in good humour with her own dearly loved husband. But at the back of her mind niggled her concerns, wishing Julianna could taste the happiness she had found in her marriage.

Chapter Nineteen

After further fruitless efforts to engage Julianna in conversation, Lucius left the York mansion in a spirit of recklessness. He knew where his brother could usually be found, so he went in search of him. After meeting up with Malcolm, the two men went looking for trouble.

The recklessness quickly faded and Luc stood on the threshold of the den of iniquity his brother so enjoyed frequenting and he nearly balked. Sensing his disapproval, Malcolm chided. "Come along, milord, you are blocking the entryway. Make way with haste, I tell you."

Rather than moving along, the viscount stepped back out of the doorway down onto the sidewalk, and the two men were quickly passed by lowborn individuals that sidled past them with sideways glances and vulgarity-riddled mumbles about the nobility.

Malcolm chuckled at the men's rudeness before turning to address his brother's wishy-washiness.

"What is going on with you this evening, little brother of mine? You show up out of the blue demanding to be shown a good time. When I take you around to all my favourite good time joints, you turn up your nose. I know you were born into the bluer blooded side of the family, but it sure isn't like you to be of two minds about anything."

Chagrined, Luc knew he was being uncommonly ridiculous and tried to come up with a reasonable explanation for his behaviour. It was impossible, so he merely shrugged at his brother.

"You are right, Mac, I am being ridiculous. Please forgive the odd behaviour. I meant it when I said I needed some diversion this evening."

"You most certainly do, little brother. You were always overly serious, even as a boy, but of late you seem to have taken it to extremes. Now I completely understand you not wanting to talk about it, but at least try to follow through on the diversion part. This place may not look like much, but I can guarantee you'll have a great time. The food and drink should rival any you could have been served at that ridiculous, fancy ball you were at earlier this evening. I know you don't like to gamble too much, but the games they'll be having here tonight should quickly clean out any cobwebs you have cluttering up your head. Now quit being a girl, and let's go have us a good time." With that bracing declaration Malcolm led the way into the dimly lit entrance.

After they had been checked out by an ugly brute of a doorkeeper, they made their way into a smoky, dim games room and were greeted by the obsequious major-domo who was rubbing his hands together as he imagined all the money he might be able to win off his well-heeled guests. Malcolm was a frequent guest, so he was recognized immediately. By their close resemblance, the host knew exactly who had entered that night.

"My dear Lord Ackerley, what an honour you are granting to our humble establishment this night. We occasionally have the pleasure of your brother's company, but he has not yet brought you to join us. What could we get to enhance your enjoyment this evening?" he asked deferentially as he waved impatiently to a passing servant.

Used to such treatment, Luc didn't think anything of the man's behaviour, but Malcolm, being of baser stock, was never treated to such sycophantic antics and could not let it pass. "What is the matter with you, Patrick? Somebody must've slipped something into your drink because you sure are being strange."

Angry and embarrassed, Patrick ignored what Malcolm had to say. Understanding washed over Luc and he tried to smooth all the ruffled feathers.

"Don't get your knickers in a bunch, Malcolm. This is part of the good time you are supposed to be showing me. Now Patrick, my brother and I would greatly enjoy a bottle of the best of whatever you want to offer us. Which games would you recommend we start with tonight?"

This worked. Malcolm's dark mood lightened, and he laughed while Patrick again rubbed his hands together with glee. They were soon seated at a table with a bottle to share and a deck of cards being split between them and two other shady looking men – gentlemen was not the best word to describe those two no matter how generous you were trying to be.

The play was running deep that night. Malcolm had been right, the cobwebs certainly could not linger in your head if you did not want to let a bunch of sharks fleece you. Luc would have been disgusted if he weren't having such a good time. He so rarely had the opportunity to do anything that was less than serious. Of course, many would think this was serious. Some in his world took their gaming extraordinarily seriously, but he was not one of them. Luckily for him, he had more than enough wealth that even if he didn't have nearly his skills he would be fine. Unfortunately for his opponents, he did have the requisite skills, and try as they might they were not going to get their fingers on much of his blunt this night.

When those two finally accepted their defeat, Luc stood to look around and see if anyone he was acquainted with was also present. With an inward groan he saw that sure enough, there was someone he knew.

"Baron Hanford! How interesting to find you here." Lucius was chagrined to see the young man in such a low establishment. He hoped the young fool was not running too deep. His hope was short lived when he heard how the bets were running at his table.

With a sinking feeling in the pit of his stomach, Luc realized he was going to have to do something. He didn't know how it had happened, but he found himself wishing only good things for Julianna, and he knew instinctively she would be terribly upset were she to find out where her beloved nephew was at this moment.

He had not yet been able to discuss with her what he had ascertained from Fletcher when she had asked him to find out what was going on with her nephew, but he knew she would not want Fletch to be left on his own in such an establishment. Luc barely knew the reckless young lord, but he was developing uncomfortably warm feelings for his aunt, so he felt an extended responsibility for the young man.

Malcolm looked at Luc questioningly as he very obviously set out to win back all the young lord's vowels. By the end of the night, the young baron was deep in debt to Viscount Beaufort.

"I never knew you to be in the habit of fleecing infants, brother!" he drawled sarcastically after the two men had escorted a very drunk young Fletcher home. Luc had insisted Fletch come to see him first thing in the morning, extracting the promise that he would not tell anyone about his deep play the night before.

With an exasperated sigh, Luc looked at his brother sheepishly. "I agree. It is disgusting. I have no concept of how the sharks do it! It was so easy to win with that boy! It was completely another thing to get his debts won off the other sharks there tonight," he said with feeling, glad for once about his unparalleled skills with the cards.

Still looking at him appraisingly, Malcolm wondered out loud, "But it still begs the question, why would you set yourself to the bother of having the Montgomery boy in your debt?"

Luc did not quite know how to answer the question, since he did not know himself what all had compelled him. "It could prove useful," was his cryptic reply.

Malcolm laughed good-naturedly at his brother's lack of sharing. "Sometimes you are very like your father, always knowing things you do not wish to share. It is a rather irritating trait, I must say."

It was Luc's turn to laugh. "I find it interesting that he's always my father when you wish to criticize."

Malcolm grinned. "My start in life was rather unfortunate. I needn't own him when I do not wish to, milord."

They had arrived at the viscount's townhouse not long before dawn was to arrive. "So, little brother, did you have fun tonight or what? It didn't turn out quite how I had expected there at the end, what with us robbing a child, but before that it was pretty good. The look on that numbskull's face when he realized you weren't going to be an easy mark was absolutely priceless. You should go out with me more often. I haven't had that much fun in an age. I always forget how much I enjoy your company." Malcolm put his booted feet up on his brother's desk as he lounged back in the wing-backed chair in Ackerley's library.

"Mayhap you should not allow so much time to elapse between times, and then it would not be such a difficult thing to remember," drawled the viscount with a bite of sarcasm in his voice.

Never one to allow another's wit to get him down, Malcolm tipped back his head and laughed heartily as the very tired looking butler brought them a tray and a decanter.

"That will be all, Henry," the viscount excused. "Get yourself to bed. I apologize for keeping you up so late. I can manage to lock up after my brother if he decides not to stay overnight."

"Thank you, milord. It was no trouble waiting for you, but if you're sure, I will get myself off." Henry bowed himself from the room.

"You apologize to your servants for what really amounts to being part of their job?" Malcolm demanded with incredulity. "You really don't take too much after the old man, do you? Maybe I shouldn't say he's your father when I don't care for something he did," he continued in a musing fashion.

Now it was Luc's turn to laugh. "Never mind, I learned my manners from my mother, not the viscount. Now tell me, big brother, are you going to stay overnight and partake of my cook's generosity in the morning? I would hate to have to evict you, but I really would like to take to my bed shortly, so you have to either take advantage of my hospitality or get yourself off to somewhere else since I have already dismissed the servants."

"Well since you put the invitation so graciously, I would love to stay overnight. While I do have a partiality for my own bed, I must admit to an avid curiosity about your meeting with the Montgomery boy in the morning. I wonder if he will even remember what took place tonight and if he will show his face here. If he does, I really must be here to see how you explain to him why he is suddenly so deeply in your debt."

Luc turned a look of surprise toward his brother and stared at him for a moment. "There are so many things wrong with what you just said that I am unsure where to begin. First of all, of course the lad will come. For all his father's faults, I am quite sure young Fletcher has been raised from the cradle to comprehend that a gentleman's gaming debts are debts of honour and must always be paid, no matter the cost. And secondly, would you not agree that it is he, the errant child, who must explain his deep debt, not the creditor?"

Malcolm regarded his brother steadily. "Neatly sidestepped, my lord. I am back to thinking you to be the spitting image of the old man. Regardless how you want to play with semantics, I still want to be here when it happens. So lead me to my room, and I'll let you get your beauty sleep. You're going to need it if you're going to deal with the child, then explain how it all happened to his doting aunt."

The viscount visibly paled at this reminder of the deeper trouble he had gotten himself into. Dealing with Fletcher would be a stroll in the park compared to the tricky situation he faced with Lady Julianna. The lady was already avoiding him. Should his unconventional solution reach her ears, she would no doubt have an unfavourable reaction.

Then again, it may cause the lady to quit avoiding him, if only to fill his ears with a piece of her mind, he thought with an unrepentant grin.

"Let us sleep on it. Everything will look much better in the morning," was the viscount's optimistic observation as they locked the front door and ascended the staircase.

Chapter Twenty

Morning arrived much too soon for Fletcher's peace of mind. His head felt like it was going to fall off; the pain was so bad. Unfortunately, no amount of headache could make him forget what had transpired the previous night.

He had gone carousing with some of his old friends that he had met while on his Grand Tour. They were great chums and knew their way around the seedier edges of London and had promised to show him the ropes. Fletcher did love all games of chance but usually confined himself to tamer fare than that which they faced last night. And now he was heavily in debt to Viscount Beaufort.

Fletcher was not completely clear on certain details, and this morning he had the sinking feeling that he may have been deliberately set up by his supposed friends. They certainly hadn't waited around to ensure he got home safely. Nor had they done anything to stop him from getting into this mess in the first place, instead egging him on at every step.

But, Fletcher had to acknowledge that he could not blame his friends. It had been he, Fletcher Montgomery, who had been placing those bets. He had just kept hoping his luck would turn and he could dig his way out of this mess in the same manner that he had gotten into it. Sadly that had only compounded the situation. At least he had a certain degree of trust in the viscount, which was not something he could say for some of the other men he had gamed with the previous night. So no doubt he should feel a degree of gratitude that it was only the viscount's name that appeared on all the vowels he had pulled from his pockets.

But he did not. His recollections were hazy at best, but as he thought about it and struggled to remember the events of the night before he felt as though Beaufort had a high level of determination to win his vowels off those other men.

Fletcher pondered, trying to think of any reason Lord Ackerley would behave this way. He had come over to Fletch's table and watched the play for a few moments before calling the host over and demanding that coffee be served. He had then ordered Fletcher to step away from the table. It was at this point, if Fletcher could remember correctly, that the viscount's half brother had invited him to play.

Malcolm had then engaged Fletcher in a game of chess. Fletcher had never even realized there were chessboards at a gaming hell. Apparently, some people would bet on anything. Mr. Mansfield was so skilled at chess that it had fully engaged all of Fletcher's concentration. At the end of their game, the viscount had approached them and said they were leaving.

The next thing Fletcher knew he was being dropped off at home after vowing to visit the viscount as soon as he awoke the next day. Here it was the next day, and Fletcher would have to face the music.

Fletcher wondered idly how he was going to explain this to Aunt Julianna and the earl. As that thought filtered through his aching head, he sat up abruptly in bed and pulled the bell with vigour. When a servant answered his summons, Fletcher demanded water to bathe and shave as he jumped from the bed and began pulling on his clothes.

If that skunk of a viscount thought he could somehow get to his aunt through him, he had another think coming. Fletcher had some very ugly thoughts toward Lord Ackerley as he readied himself to go and confront the older nobleman.

He decided to walk, not wanting any of the servants to know what he was about. As he drew near the viscount's address, his bravado began to falter. He was deeply in debt, and whatever the viscount's motives nothing could alter that fact. It was his signature on all those little slips of paper. And really, he doubted Ackerley would go to such effort just to coerce his aunt. Hadn't Julianna gone out riding with him just the other day?

Fletcher stood on the bottom step and wracked his brain for ways he could pay off his debts without involving the earl or Julianna. His options were quite limited, but he hoped fervently he could work something out with Lord Ackerley since he had absolutely no desire to have his father find out he had been to such a low establishment.

He finally stopped procrastinating, climbed the stairs, and gave a vigorous swing to the knocker. The door opened immediately, and he was ushered into the elegant but manly interior of Viscount Beaufort's townhouse. A well-trained footman showed no reaction to having a young man asking for the viscount at such an early hour, merely bidding him to wait a moment while he verified his lordship's availability.

Moments later the viscount himself descended the stairs, greeting Fletcher jovially.

"Baron Hanford. What an honour you do me arriving so promptly. I have not yet broken my fast. Join me in the dining room for a few minutes before we proceed with business."

Fletcher instinctively felt this was not quite how this type of meeting would normally go, but he was powerless to resist the viscount's lead. As they entered the dining room he was hailed by Mr. Mansfield, the viscount's brother.

"Ah, milord, it is a pleasure to see you again. You look like you could use a cup of coffee. No doubt you think you don't want to eat ever again, but I would highly recommend you have a bit of toast. I guarantee it will help."

Fletcher grinned at the other man's sympathetic tone. Clearly Mansfield had experience in feeling exactly how he did this morning. Fletcher sat meekly and allowed the footman to pour him a steaming cup of coffee and serve him a few slices of toast. Mr. Mansfield was correct in his assessment that Fletch's instinctive feeling was to avoid food at all costs, but after a couple of bites of the toast he began to feel much more the thing.

"There you go, young man. You are looking decidedly less green about the gills," Malcolm declared bracingly a few minutes after the three men had begun eating in companionable silence.

Ever polite, Fletcher replied, "Thank you. I am feeling somewhat better."

Lucius laughed. "Don't sound so surprised, Fletcher. We have much experience in this matter. Malcolm especially. I believe he has tried every known suggestion on overcoming a hangover. I don't recommend you follow his lead in experimentation, but if you do need a solution, he's your man."

Despite his confusion over the two older men's motivations, Fletcher could not help grinning at them and enjoying their company. His father was of a much different temperament besides always being so busy, so Fletcher was unused to this type of male company. He sat back with his cup of coffee and watched as the two brothers traded barbs after Malcolm took mock exception to the viscount's words.

"My lead in experimentation?" he growled. "I was not the overly entitled heir to the kingdom that you were. If I recall correctly, it was you who was always puking up your guts in the morning."

"That's just because my legitimately born, blue-blooded body did not have as tough a constitution as yours did," the viscount excused with a sly dig at his brother.

Fletcher's eyes grew round with shock at this volley, and he was surprised when Malcolm threw back his head and laughed loudly. Then he was further taken aback when both men turned and looked at him piercingly. He had not noticed before how closely they resembled each other until that moment when it felt like twin images gazing at him so seriously. Fletcher cleared his throat and laughed nervously. Not enjoying feeling like a sitting duck, he decided to take the bull by the horns.

"Well, so I came by, as you had requested, to discuss my debts. When I checked my pockets this morning, I was surprised to find how many IOU's I have owing to you. The irony is that I have no recollection of playing with you last night. I know I imbibed too much, but I do remember who I gamed with."

The viscount had the grace to look uncomfortable momentarily, but then a look of serious sternness came over his face.

"We do not discuss business at the dining table. Shall we adjourn to my library?" Without waiting for a reply, Lord Ackerley and Mr. Mansfield stood simultaneously, and the viscount led the way from the room.

Feeling like a chastened child, Fletcher stood and followed them silently. His feelings were very torn. He really enjoyed these men and their bantering sense of humour. But while he felt ashamed to be in debt, he also felt a sense of betrayal that somehow the viscount had tricked him into this position. He resolved to remain stoic until he heard what Lord Ackerley had to say.

A surprising sense of familiarity washed over Fletcher as they entered his lordship's library. It was strangely similar to the earl's library, which was a room Fletcher had always enjoyed. It settled his nerves a little as he sank comfortably into one of the wing-backed chairs placed strategically before the viscount's desk. Malcolm settled into the other one, shifting it slightly so that he could better observe both other occupants of the room. Fletcher had an uneasy feeling that this was diverting entertainment for the other man, and he felt a moment of resentment. That was quickly forgotten as the viscount began the interview.

Luc and Malcolm were each their mother's only children, and neither of them had offspring of their own, so Luc had never experienced this sensation. He figured it must be how an uncle feels when dealing with a recalcitrant niece or nephew. It was an odd mixture of pride and disgust, and he found it strangely unsettling.

"So, Hanford, I take it you have come to settle your debts. You are mostly correct. We did not play together for long. I trounced you quite soundly in our first game, so you went off to play chess with my brother. He refuses to accept bets from children, so there were no stakes to your game."

These words deeply offended Fletcher who, at nineteen, almost twenty, had quite decided he was a mature adult. He began to sputter but caught himself as he remembered his resolve for stoicism and subsided.

Impressed, the viscount continued. "After your defection from the card table, I continued to play with your former opponents. By the end of our game, the only thing of value remaining to them were your vowels which I accepted at their value, so when they lost those as well, then you became in debt to me rather than them."

Fletcher recognized that this was possible and did not doubt that the viscount was telling him the truth. He was again swept with a wave of relief that that was how the evening had transpired. It would be much better to deal with Lord Ackerley than those other men for whom he had far less respect and much more fear. The outcome remained more or less the same, however. He was still heavily in debt and was honour bound to pay up. Fletcher voiced some of his thoughts.

"I regret how the evening progressed, I must say, my lord. I do enjoy games of all sorts but have never engaged in play that ran so deep. I find that I am grateful that it is to you I am in debt rather than what I remember of the others I played with last night. But it does not change the fact that I owe you a rather large sum."

Fletch paused for a moment before taking a deep breath and continuing as bravely as possible. "Without applying to my father or my aunt, I am not in a position to pay off the full balance immediately. I just received my quarterly. I had been planning to set up my own residence in a rented space, but my relatives would probably be just as happy if I stay with them a bit longer, so I could give you all that. I could probably borrow the money on the expectation of my next allowance payment, or you could charge me interest. If it's all the same to you, I would very much rather leave the earl and my aunt out of this arrangement."

"I absolutely agree. It never even crossed my mind that Lady Julianna was an option in covering your debts." Lord Ackerley had a look of disgust on his face at the thought.

Without thinking before he spoke, Fletcher blurted out, "Oh, yes, she is about to come into most of her portion as her twenty-fifth birthday is approaching despite being unmarried. I believe some is tied up in investments, but full control will be turned over to her on her birthday. I would hate to admit to her what a mess I got myself into, but it would be better than facing my father."

Without revealing his thoughts, the viscount regarded him steadily. "Why?" he asked without a trace of emotion.

Unsure which statement he was questioning, Fletcher again launched into speech. "They would both be so disappointed in me. Aunty Jules would probably cry, but she would come up with a solution to help me, maybe she would even insist on paying you herself. She would no doubt direct her anger at you rather than me. I can't see that as a solution. I deserve this mess since it was me who did it. I cannot let a woman pay my debts. My father, on the other hand, would be harsh in his assessment of my behaviour and would most likely send me back to the country to think about my sins and the shame I have brought on him. He would figure out a way of making this be a problem for his politics."

Luc could see what Fletcher was saying and agreed with him. He would rather not take the youngster's money, but the boy needed to learn to take responsibility for his actions. Maybe this would teach him not to allow himself into such a situation again. But he still couldn't fleece him. He proposed a solution.

"I can see the circumstances you face, and I understand your reluctance to apply to either of your relatives. No doubt your grandparents would be just as bad or worse and would probably feel obligated to tell your aunt and father anyway. I would hate to think I was the cause of you getting caught up with the money lenders, and no doubt that would end up getting back to your father as well."

Ackerley paused for a moment allowing that thought to sink in before he continued. "Here is what I propose. It would not do for you to be completely without funds for the entire quarter. Your aunt is sure to notice since I have a feeling she is ever watchful when it comes to you and your sister. Let us divide your debt in half. You can pay the first half now from the funds you have on hand. The remainder to be paid when your next allowance comes through. Let us say the interest is that you must treat my brother and me to a bottle of the best claret White's has to offer when you are completely debt free."

Gratified by the viscount's reasonable and generous offer, Fletcher grinned, putting out his hand to shake on it. Luc grasped his hand in a firm grip. Before he let go, he eyed the young baron sternly.

"Since I pretty much own you for the next two quarters, I do not want to catch wind of you getting up to such tricks ever again."

Fletcher tripped over his own words in his haste to reassure the viscount. "I swear to you, I have developed a whole-hearted disgust of such places and such games. Tales of my adventures will not reach your ears, I promise you."

Releasing him but continuing to eye him seriously, Luc persisted. "But promise me, if you do get into trouble of any sort, or even just need a manly ear to listen, you will come to me. Do not bother your aunt with such worries. Together we will think of a solution."

Surprised by this demanded promise, but happy to grant it, Fletcher answered, "I sincerely plan to keep myself far from trouble, but I promise to apply to you for aid should I need it."

There was a moment of silence while the three gentlemen regarded each other solemnly, but then Fletcher grinned boyishly and offered a charming face of chagrin. "Thank you, my lord. You have been prodigiously understanding and accommodating. I wonder if you are almost as afraid of my aunt finding out as I am?"

The two brothers laughed uproarishly at this rejoinder. "The boy has a point, brother dear," mocked Malcolm, always ready to tease the viscount.

"Never mind about my concerns where it comes to the fair Lady Julianna. Let us just keep this amongst us, and none of us need concern ourselves with her finding out."

Wishing fervently to change the subject and still enjoying the young man's company, Luc proposed an excursion. "Has your head fully recovered yet?" he asked solicitously. "I have a mind to spend some time with Gentleman Jack this morning. Would you care to join us?"

Flushing to his roots at the prospect of such a treat, Fletcher agreed promptly. "My head will survive. I would love to join you, thank you, my lord."

"If we're going to be sparring we might as well drop the formalities. You must call me Luc or Ackerley or Beaumont, whichever you wish. I answer to all three, if I may call you Fletcher."

Again thrilled by this invitation, Fletcher struggled for nonchalance. "That would be fine." But he could not quite yet bring himself to use the less formal address with his lordship.

Seeing there was no more fun to be had in observing the exchange, Malcolm stood, ending the serious interview.

"Am I included in the invitation to spar? If so, I believe I shall require a change of attire. If I leave now, could you come past my place on your way to Bond Street?"

"That sounds like a plan, Mac. Should we give you a head start of thirty minutes? Fletcher and I should be able to keep ourselves occupied in the meantime. He did not have a big enough meal to have any energy, so maybe we shall get the kitchen to send him up a nuncheon while we wait for you."

With the plan thus set, Malcolm strode from the room promising to be ready when they arrived for him.

Turning back to his guest, Luc continued the conversation while he pulled the bell for a footman. "I don't know why he refuses to accept my offer of lodgings. It would be so much easier if he lived here or at least kept some of things here," he complained mildly.

"I believe men need their independence," Fletcher explained trying to sound knowledgeable. "At least, that's how I feel."

Luc felt a pang of conscience since he was in part responsible for the young man not being able to declare his own independence. He was saved from answering by the footman's arrival.

"Thank you, John. Could you please see if Cook has kept anything warm from breakfast? Lord Montgomery was unable to partake of much first thing, but he could use some fortification now."

"Very well, milord, I will see to it immediately." The servant bowed himself from the room.

"I am shockingly hungry now. Your brother was right. When I first arrived food was the furthest thing from my mind, but now I feel as though I could eat a whole side of bacon."

Luc laughed before warning, "Well, I pray you do not indulge that desire too literally. Keep in mind we shall soon be exerting ourselves. I can assure you Mr. Jackson does not appreciate it if anyone casts up their accounts on his gleaming hardwood."

~ ~ ~

After a rousing morning of boxing at Gentleman Jackson's, the two brothers escorted their new young friend home. As they approached his house, Fletcher began to wonder what the socially acceptable protocol was. Should he invite them in and offer them lunch? He was wracking his brain trying to decide when the viscount solved the dilemma for him.

"Well, Fletcher, you showed yourself quite to advantage today. We shall have to go a few rounds again soon."

Fletcher bobbed his head in shy acceptance of the compliment.

"Malcolm and I have things we need to attend to. Try to keep yourself out of trouble, and we shall see you again soon."

"Thank you, my lord, Mr. Mansfield. I look forward to a future match."

Relieved of his worry as to the social niceties, feeling without a care in the world, Fletcher bounded up the stairs and into the house.

Malcolm turned to his brother and regarded him appraisingly. "So now you are raising the child?" he demanded quizzically.

"He is no longer a child, and I am not raising him," defended the viscount with heat.

"In all the years I've known you, I have never known you to offer a loan to a gaming debt."

"You've also never known me to game with children."

"I thought you said he's not a child," Malcolm said mockingly.

Laughing with exasperation, Luc concluded the matter. "Let it drop, Malcolm. I have my reasons and I do not have to explain them to you."

Mac gazed at his brother appraisingly. "Do you even know what your reasons are?"

"No," Luc answered baldly. "Staring at me like that isn't going to help you know the answers either. Let us leave it for now. I am starving. Let me buy you lunch at White's, and you can tell me what your plans are for the coming week."

~~~

As Julianna descended the stairs, she was surprised to see Fletcher coming in the house greeting the footman with enthusiasm.

"Hello, Fletcher. It's nice to see you. Are you just returning home from last night?" Julianna hadn't seen him that morning at breakfast and now began to fret about his whereabouts.

Much relieved of all the cares he had been worrying about earlier that day, Fletcher did not allow his aunt's concern to fray his good mood.

"No, silly, I came home last night and slept in my own bed. I just had something I had to take care of this morning and am simply returning home again." Changing the subject in an effort to distract his aunt and solve his most pressing problem, he elaborated. "I am actually ravenously hungry, have you had your luncheon yet?"

Relieved by this evidence of his good health and such a normal request, Julianna finished descending the stairs as she answered. "I am not famished myself, but I have not yet eaten. Let us go together to see what the kitchen might have for us."

Arm in arm the two descended upon the kitchens. After a light repast on her part and an enthusiastic stuffing on his, Fletcher went off to pursue his own affairs while Julianna went in search of Odelia.

Chapter Twenty One

Julianna was already in the ballroom checking to ensure all the last minute details had been attended to. She scolded herself for this needless fluster since their staff was very well skilled to handle all the arrangements. But it gave her something to do to calm her fidgets. She was convinced she was more nervous than her niece.

Thinking of Odelia must have conjured her, Julianna thought with a whimsical smile as she watched her very excited niece bounce into the ballroom. Their modiste had done a remarkable job with Odelia's dress. The white spider gauze was the exact hue to best accentuate her skin tone and the silver embroidery around the hems, sleeves and bodice were delicate enough to be pleasing to the eye but caught the light of the myriad candles. The pearls at her neck, ears, and above her gloves were perfect for the debutante in her first Season and matched the ones that had been threaded through her elaborate hairstyle. Julianna was relieved her niece had opted not to add feathers to her headdress despite their popularity amongst the *ton*. She was getting mightily sick of seeing them everywhere she turned.

"Oh, Aunty Jewel, everything looks perfectly marvellous," Odelia enthused in reverent tones before squealing in her excitement. "I can barely believe this evening has finally arrived! Why ever did we wait so long to have my ball?"

"Well, my darling, you did say you wanted your debut to be a crush, did you not?"

"But of course!" Dee declared with a bounce.

"Then we needed to wait until we could be sure that everyone had gathered in Town. And, of course, we could not compete with the annual balls held at the large houses like the Roxboroughs and the Yorks."

"You always think of everything, don't you?"

"I do try, my dear, but I fear I rarely succeed. But this has been a communal effort, and I am certain it shall be a success. Now that you have gotten a bit of Town bronze I am sure you will be all the more confident at your own ball anyway, wouldn't you agree? If we had planned your ball for the first week we were in Town, you might not have had nearly as much fun since you would not know as many people either."

"That is quite true, Aunty." Odelia acknowledged her aunt's reasoning before changing the subject. "What are the chances of the earl and baron being here to receive our guests before they start arriving?"

Julianna could not resist grinning at her niece's way of expressing herself. "I am quite certain your father and brother will be joining us momentarily, have no fear. And no doubt the first to arrive will be family members, so it would not really matter all that much anyway." The sound of footsteps sounded nearby. "Ah, here they are now."

As Hart and Fletch stepped into the room, Julianna admired the efforts they had gone to in their toilette. "My lords, you have outdone yourselves this evening. You look extraordinarily handsome tonight."

Fletch coloured slightly at his aunt's comments, while Hart offered her a wry bow. "You don't look too shabby yourself, little sister," the earl complimented. "I do believe we shall all shine brightly tonight." Turning toward his daughter, Hart continued, "You, my darling, look ravishing. I shall have to remain near you tonight to fend off the suitors who will be vying for your attentions."

"Really, Papa? Are you planning to remain in the ballroom for the entire ball?" Odelia could not prevent her incredulity from showing.

The earl blushed. "Well, er, perhaps not the entire ball, my dear. I may have spoken in haste, but I will definitely be about the entire night."

Julianna stepped into the conversation with a laugh. "It is just as well, Hart, you probably would find it distressing to see the suitors clamouring for our darling Dee's hand anyway. Now get ready everyone, I just heard the door, our night is about to begin."

Thus began the whirl of people as the musicians struck up some background music, while the guests began to assemble. Everyone was milling about until finally the earl escorted his daughter to the dance floor for the opening number.

Julianna remained by the entrance to welcome any latecomers after Odelia left on her father's arm in order to have their dance together. The proud aunt was mightily distracted as she strained to catch a glimpse of the dancing couple. She did not notice the viscount until he cleared his throat.

Nearly jumping out of her skin, Julianna managed to hold back the squeal that threatened to disrupt the assembled guests. "Oh, my lord, you startled me. I apologize profusely that I was not attending my duties."

"Pay it no mind, my dear. I thought it was charming that you were so intent on watching your niece and brother in their dance."

Julianna blushed to her roots. She found it baffling that he could have gotten so near to her and she had not noticed, since of late she could sense his presence even across a room. Of course, she was not about to tell him that and she was momentarily at a loss for words. She had not spoken to him in days and had been fervently hoping he would not show up this evening.

Lucius looked searchingly into Julianna's face. "I have been hoping to have a few words with you, my lady. Do you think you will be able to spare me a few moments this evening? It is on a matter of some import."

He was surprised to see her eyes dart around frantically as though she were looking for an escape. Luc could see that she made an effort to bring her gaze back to his face before giving him an evasive answer.

"I must apologize once more, my lord. I do not foresee having a single spare moment this evening with all the myriad little details that I must oversee to ensure this ball is a success for Odelia."

"Could I at least partner you for one of the dances?" he asked in some desperation.

"Thank you, my lord, but I do not think that would be appropriate for me as the hostess. I must be diligent about seeing to the comfort of our guests, you see."

Luc just about gave up in disgust, thinking to turn on his heel and exit the house without having even stepped into the ballroom. But just before he did, he caught the worried furrow on her brow and the anxious gaze she was trying to conceal from him.

He retained her cold little hand and brought it to his lips. "I understand, my dear, this is a special occasion for your household. Do not trouble yourself about me. I shall save your dance for next time."

Luc was not sure what to make of the tears he saw shimmering in her eyes, and her tremulous smile made his heart turn over, although it was a relief that she was not frowning. Seeing her in obvious distress made him wish he could pull her from the room and make her confide all her worries to him. Restraining himself with a concerted effort, he smiled warmly at her and forced himself to relinquish her hand he was still holding.

"Take care, *ma petite*," he admonished in a low tone as he finally turned away.

Julianna held onto her composure by a thread, desperately hoping no one could tell that all she wanted to do was run from the room in tears. *Why does that man have to have this effect on me? Why can I not be immune to him? Why won't my heart listen to my reason?* she demanded of herself in desperation.

Plastering on a smile, she made it through the rest of the night through sheer force of will. Julianna mingled with the milling crowds, kept an eye on the supplies, oversaw the footmen and maids who were circulating to clean up wherever necessary, and checking on the preparations for the late supper. Throughout it all she was ever aware of the viscount's presence. Blessedly he was not overt in his attentions, but she was aware of his eyes upon her throughout the night. He did not approach her again until he came to take his leave of her.

"You did a remarkable job of maintaining your sanity tonight, my dear. Until I watched you doing it, I had no idea so much work went into hosting a ball. I must say I should be much more grateful when I accept invitations in the future."

Julianna blanched and then blushed hotly at his acknowledgement of having been watching her all evening, but she could not help smiling over his praise and his final statement. "It is kind of you to say so, my lord. Are you saying you had a nice time or just pleased that I did not end up in Bedlam?"

Lucius chuckled lightly over her choice of words. "Of course I am delighted that you are not a candidate for Bedlam, but I also had a lovely time. It would appear your niece is a success. You must be congratulating yourself."

Julianna allowed her eyes to rove about the room and finally settle upon Odelia, who was at the centre of a small crowd animatedly holding court. Smiling gently she turned back to the viscount. "I do believe the dear girl would be a success with or without this evening's ball, but thank you, my lord, for giving me a little credit for it."

"No doubt you deserve a great deal of the credit, but I do not wish to put you to the blush," he teased as he saw her colour rising. Wishing she would not insist upon such formality with him he quietly asked, "Would it be possible for me to call upon you one day soon, my dear?"

He had to suppress his sigh as she once more paled before him and stammered out an answer. "Oh, my lord, I must apologize. I do believe we are going to be terribly busy over the next couple of days and then we are leaving town for a house party at Yorkleigh. Perhaps upon our return?"

Luc had to be satisfied with that. At least it was not a complete denial of any chance. But that was little consolation, he acknowledged as he took his leave and wondered absently if it would be possible to get his name on the guest list for the Earl of Yorkleigh's house party.

Julianna was relieved that the wretched man had finally taken his leave. Her nerves were much steadier as she oversaw the winding down of the ball and getting Odelia settled after all her excitement of the day.

"Aunty Jewel, that was the best night ever," Odelia declared dreamily as Julianna walked her to her room after the last of their guests had departed. "Thank you so much for doing all the planning. I probably owe you an apology for not being of more help this evening."

"Not at all, darling Dee. You were the guest of honour. You had to be feted, so you could not be running around making sure the punchbowls were replenished. And I didn't mind at all. It kept me busy, because I will admit to you I was actually rather nervous about the whole thing."

"You were?" Odelia was shocked. "I would never have thought so."

"Well, thank you, my dear. I am glad it was well hidden. While I have some experience being hostess for your father's political dinners, when he invited people to Somerton, that is a far cry from having a ball. I have wondered why we bother having a ballroom in this house since he never hosts any, but it certainly served its purpose this evening. And I must say I am happy with the results."

"Me, too," Odelia grinned. "I wonder if I will be able to sleep tonight," she mused as they reached her door.

"Maizy should be waiting for you with a cup of warm milk laced with a touch of your father's brandy. That should do the trick to settling you down enough to fall asleep."

"You always think of everything, don't you?

Julianna grinned at her niece. "I do try. Now get yourself off to sleep. The sun will be up shortly."

"Goodnight."

Julianna made her way to her own bed, certain that she, too, would require assistance to settle down to sleep.

~~~

"Aunty Jules," asked Odelia hesitantly as she sat with Lady Julianna in their morning room. She was supposed to be working at her needlework, but the hated job had been tossed aside with characteristic impatience.

"Yes, my dear," replied Julianna distractedly, deep in thought over which invitations should be accepted.

"I was thinking about something you have often said over the years since you came to live with us."

"What is it?" asked Julianna, still not fully paying attention.

"You have often said that you did not enjoy Town and that you did not miss it. How could you not miss being in London?" asked the young lady, enthusiastically warming to her subject.

This finally caught Julianna's attention and she realized she would need to tread lightly over what could end up being a tricky subject. Julianna smiled gently at her dearly loved niece.

"I had you and Fletcher to keep me company, Dee. When my grandmother brought me to London for my first Season I was barely out of mourning for my parents. Hart, your father, was busy with his estates, and you two were quite young, so he couldn't come to Town to keep me company since your mama was in a delicate condition. I was quite lonely for the country and for you all, I must admit, although I did make some very nice friends. Then, as you know, things did not end well for me, and I left Town in a cloud of disgrace, so I really never had any desire to return."

After a momentary pause, Odelia asked in a small voice, "Do you wish you didn't have to come to chaperone me?"

Julianna left completely what she was doing and crossed the room quickly to join the young woman on the settee. She gave her a warm hug as she settled next to her. "Don't be a goose, Dee. I would not miss this for the world!" she declared with feeling.

"But why have you put a cap on your head? And sometimes you sit with all the old ladies and mamas. You aren't *that* old. You could be sharing my Season instead of chaperoning it."

"If I was sharing your Season we would both need a chaperone, silly," laughed Julianna. "No, I am perfectly happy sitting with the older ladies. Don't you know they are the ones with the best gossip?"

Again Julianna laughed before continuing more seriously. "Please do not concern yourself about me. I am having a fine time. I truly would never have considered not coming with you. This is an experience of a lifetime for you, and I am very happy to be able to share it with you as well as guide you through the various pitfalls that may arise. I have decided that the dreaded cap on my head puts me in a better position to do that."

"But don't you wish you had gotten married?" asked Odelia, still trying to understand her aunt's feelings.

"At times, to be perfectly honest, I do wonder what it would have been like if I had wed and had a home of my own, besides babies to care for. But then I would not have had these seven years with you and Fletch, and really I wouldn't want to trade those in for anything."

"I love you, Aunty Jules!"

"I love you, too. Now tell me what you plan to wear this evening to the theatre."

A few moments later, completely distracted, at least for the moment, Odelia tripped from the room happy that all was right in her world. She went off in search of her maid with the desire to begin her preparations for that evening's outings. As she left the room, her father sauntered in.

"That was neatly sidestepped, dearest sister of mine," he drawled, a knowing look lighting his eyes.

"Whatever do you mean, dear Hart?" laughed his sister in response.

"I may not be paying the kind of attention I should be to all this Season nonsense, but I cannot help but notice that wearing such an ugly cap on your head is a new development. You never did so until after that night that old busy body, Lady Hearst was giving you a hard time at the Westfields' ball. I saw your face that night and noticed you started wearing a cap whenever you went about after that."

"I have no idea what you are talking about," she began airily. "As you were obviously eavesdropping you must have heard me explain to Odelia that wearing a cap puts me in a better position as her chaperone."

"That is a bunch of poppycock, my dear. You are hiding out from something. I have yet to figure out what it is you are hiding from, but you could chaperone the girl perfectly well without that silly cap on your head. If you actually believe the tripe you just spouted to your niece then you are also lying to yourself. You owe it to yourself to figure out what you are hiding from and confront it."

He paused briefly in his lecture while his face took on an altogether different look and he continued with a much-changed tone and a twinkle in his eye. "And you owe it to everyone that has to look at you to take off that hideous head covering! I really must say it looks like you took to wearing a doily on your head. Whatever were you thinking?"

Julianna gasped in mock outrage while she threw a spare pillow at his head. He dodged easily, and the two siblings ended up laughing themselves silly.

"It really is terribly ugly, isn't it?" Julianna had to agree with Hart's assessment. "I thought it lent me the degree of seriousness needed to properly supervise the young people. And you may be right that I was hiding a wee bit. I do not want to be made a laughingstock. At my age I don't want anyone thinking I am hanging out for a husband."

"Why ever not?" Hart demanded. "And stop saying 'at my age.' You are several years younger than me and I'll have you know I don't feel anywhere near the edge of the grave. If you felt that you wanted to marry, any man would be lucky to have you," he declared loyally.

They sat together for a moment in companionable silence before Hart continued, again with a serious tone. "I really don't know what I would have done without you those first few years after Lucretia died, but I really hope you have not let your life pass you by because of me and my children. You actually should give some serious thought to looking around for a husband. What if I decide one day that I need another countess? You would not enjoy having your authority usurped by some other woman."

"Are you trying to tell me something in your oh-so-subtle-way, Hart?" Julianna asked with some surprise.

"Not exactly, but I have to tell you, being back in Town watching Odelia make her curtsy to society has given me some ideas. Let us just say I am far less opposed to the idea of remarrying than I once was. I still might stay a bachelor for years to come, but especially now that the children are grown, you really need to think about yourself for once, Jules. Dee is going to leave home one of these days, and I suspect you shall be bored to tears when that day comes."

Julianna gazed at her brother while she mulled over what he had said. It was sufficiently out of character for him to speak like this that she recognized she ought to give it serious consideration. With a sigh, she got up from the settee. "I promise to think about it, Hart, and I appreciate your concern for me and my welfare. But now I must prepare for our evening at the theatre."

Julianna fled to her room. It was true she did need to prepare for the evening's entertainments, but her most pressing concern was to get her scattered wits back in order. Between Odelia's comments, her brother's words, and her constant efforts to avoid Viscount Beaufort, she was feeling decidedly muddled.

She was so glad they had accepted the invitation to the Earl and Countess of Yorkleigh's house party the following week. She could really use a break from the constant whirl of activity so she could have a few moments to think. Her only regret was that she had not managed to ascertain who else had been invited. But she comforted herself with the thought that the chances of Luc also being invited were very remote. She just had to get through the next couple of days and then she would be out of town for a week. It would be a welcome reprieve.

The one good thing that had come out of her discussions with Odelia and Hart was she could remove the hideous cap from her head. They were correct in their assessments. She was hiding out, which was disgustingly faint-hearted of her. And as it turned out it wasn't really fooling anyone so there was no sense in continuing with the ruse. Putting a cap over her curls wasn't going to keep anyone from speculating about her if they so wished. She might as well endeavour to enjoy what she could of the Season.

At least with Odelia's determination to remain single in order to enjoy another Season, Julianna did not have to make up her mind about her own future plans. In light of Hart's declaration that he may pursue matrimonial plans of his own, it would need to be considered soon though. He was correct in his assessment that she would not enjoy handing over the reins of household control to another woman. But running her brother's home could really only be a temporary position, and she would have to think about where she would go when the time came.

But those were concerns for another day. In the meantime, she had a night at the theatre to prepare for.

As usual, Odelia was brimming with excitement about their evening's activities. The Montgomery men were not joining them that evening, so the ladies had the evening coach to themselves. They were joining a small group of friends to enjoy Kean's newest offering to the stage. There was a new actress reported to be joining the cast that night, and all of London was abuzz about the unknown's reputed skills and beauty. Just that afternoon Julianna had been disgusted to hear that the betting books were already filling up with wagers as to which highly born gentleman would be the first to set her up as his mistress.

"How exciting, Aunty Jules. I so love the theatre. Shakespeare can be so diverting. And the crowds of people are almost as entertaining."

"That is true enough. But when we arrive, be sure to stick close to me. I am actually surprised your father agreed that we could go with no official male escort this evening. With the crowds that are sure to be there, I fear we may get separated if we are not diligent about remaining close."

"I will try, Aunty, but you know I get easily distracted when I have to look around at everything."

Julianna knew she was speaking the truth and allowed a burst of laughter to bubble forth. "Well, do make an effort, but I will keep your lack of ability in that regard in mind and try my best to keep my eye on you."

"This is such a treat! Were you not surprised when Lady Ashwood granted us the use of her box?" Odelia was still beside herself about her grandmother's generous gift.

"Yes, I must admit I was quite surprised. It was very nice of them to think of us this way. It is unfortunate they could not be there to play host to us, but it was generous of them to say we might invite whomever we would like to join us."

"Thank you for allowing me to invite my friend Abigail. I know you are not overly fond of her, but I think she is great fun."

"I am glad you have a friend to share your season, Dee. My feelings about Abigail are more to do with my concerns about how Fletcher feels about her than about any fault she might have."

"You do not think Fletcher is actually serious about her, do you?" Odelia demanded with a degree of impatience. "Don't be a noddy. He is only nineteen."

"Exactly my point. He is only nineteen, but in his mind he is a man, and I know at his age feelings can take on a life of their own. And if he did decide his feelings were serious, she would not be a good match for him. He is much too young. And so is she, for someone like him. She needs a mature gentleman to guide here, not another child to play house with."

"Well, I really don't think you have any need for alarm in that quarter, Aunty Jules. Abigail thinks of Fletcher as a brother. She has a *tendre* for Mr. Jackes but she wants to hold out for an earl. Her mother thinks she could catch a duke, but there aren't really that many around."

Julianna couldn't help but laugh at the prosaic way Odelia was determining the odds. Perhaps the younger woman was right, and she had nothing to worry about. She pushed the worries from her mind as the carriage came to a stop in front of the theatre.

Stepping down from the coach after Odelia, Julianna took her arm. "If we hold on to each other we can both look around like school children fresh from the country and still not lose one another."

Grinning at her aunt, Odelia had no objection. "Excellent thinking!" She suited her words to action and linked arms with her aunt as she gazed about in wonder at the beautifully dressed nobility and the shiny, fancy foyer bathed in the glow of what seemed like a million candles. A smartly dressed footman quickly stepped toward them to offer an escort or to fetch them refreshments.

They were soon shown to the Ashwoods' box and were settled with a small glass of ratafia each. Both ladies enjoyed continuing to gaze about as they waited for their friends to join them.

Lady Chorney soon stepped through the curtain. "What a delightful location your box has. I have been in few boxes with such an equally good view of the stage as well as an excellent view of the other spectators."

The other occupants of the box smiled their agreement since it was an unspoken understanding that the majority of the *ton* went to the theatre to observe and be observed rather than to actually be edified by the theatrical arts. It was much like the park and really just about every other event during the Season.

Julianna paused for a moment as she pondered the absurdity of it all. Of course, there were connections to be made, both political and matrimonial, but the majority of the Season's activities were all one big gossip session – whether one was causing it or spreading it, or even just participating by listening to it. She shook her head in derision before she sheepishly allowed herself to return to that activity.

Looking across the theatre Julianna was surprised to see a young gentleman who looked very much like Fletcher stepping into a box just ahead of Viscount Beaufort. She rubbed her eyes and looked again. Sure enough, it *was* Fletcher.

"When did Fletcher become friends with Luc?" Catherine voiced Julianna's thoughts perfectly.

"That is an excellent question. I did not know they even knew each other." Odelia was gazing across the theatre with a perplexed expression upon her face.

Julianna felt a wave of heat rise to her face as she struggled to be nonchalant. She knew the viscount had barely even met her nephew before she told him about her concerns.

She felt wretched on so many levels. He was obviously still trying to follow her wishes, and she was avoiding him like the plague. Now seeing how kind he was being to her beloved nephew, she was even more certain that she could not face him. She pulled her chair a little further back into the shadows, hoping the viscount would not look across the theatre and see them. With Catherine here in her box and how she had been avoiding him for days, he was sure to come over to see them.

"Why are they at the theatre with Lady Geneva and her sisters?" Odelia asked with suspicion.

Lady Chorney looked at Odelia with a laugh. "Well, Odelia, I know he is your big brother so you do not think of him as a regular man, but Lady Geneva does have several beautiful and sweet sisters, so it is quite a common sight to see gentlemen stopping by wherever they are."

Odelia wrinkled her nose at this statement. "Aunty Jules thinks Fletch has a *tendre* for my friend, Lady Abigail Fielding. So maybe it is Lord Ackerley who wishes to visit with those ladies."

"It is possible. Lately it seems Luc is always around wherever there are ladies. But you do realize your brother could have a *tendre* for different ladies at the same time, don't you? He is still quite young and will no doubt enjoy the company of many different women over the next several years before he settles down and has anything serious. I have a feeling you shall find it highly diverting entertainment."

Odelia stared at the older lady with surprise. "Do you have brothers, Lady Chorney?"

"I do."

"Did you find them entertaining when they were young men?"

"As a matter of fact, I did. I still do sometimes, I must say, even though most of them are old married men by this point."

"Do you find my father entertaining, Aunt Jules?"

Julianna was shocked to feel a laugh burbling up her throat despite how nervous she was feeling. "It is not quite the same thing for me and your father as it is for Lady Chorney and her brothers. I am several years younger than Hart so I was still in school when he was cutting a swath through the *ton*. By the time I got out of school, he was a father and had settled into his political career, so I cannot say I ever saw him chasing after the ladies overly much."

She paused for a moment before continuing. "Although, just this afternoon he was telling me he might be considering looking for a new countess."

Odelia turned to her aunt with eyes round with shock, her mouth opened wide in an O of surprise. "Do you really think my father might remarry?"

Julianna instantly regretted her momentary lack of foresight. As strange as it may feel to her for her brother to consider remarriage, no doubt it would be even stranger for his daughter. "I'm sorry, Dee. I really did not think before I spoke. But yes, he did say it was a possibility. He was telling me about it in the context that I should be thinking about my own future, in case he does remarry. It did not strike me as something he was seriously considering for any day in the near future, nor do I think he had any potential brides picked out. But, yes, I do think your father might remarry someday."

"Oh my. That would be so interesting."

Odelia gazed off into the distance as she thought about what it could mean for her if she had a stepmother. Catherine and Julianna looked at each other regretfully.

"If my father gets married, maybe you and I could set up our own establishment." Odelia turned to her aunt with enthusiasm, surprising Julianna with such a positive reaction.

"That might be an excellent idea. In the meantime, I think the show may be about to begin."

Julianna turned to the stage with relief, already exhausted from the highs and lows her emotions had been taken on that day. Hopefully the actors would be sufficiently skilled as to divert her attention for a time, giving her feelings a welcome reprieve.

When the curtain fell for the intermission, Julianna was startled by the resounding and sustained applause. She had been so entranced by the play it was as though she had been outside herself. She blew a deep sigh and turned to her companions.

Several more ladies had arrived just as the curtain had risen and now there was a lively cacophony as they seemingly all spoke at once exclaiming over the charming performance, complementing one another on their lovely dress and grooming, and whispering whichever tidbits of gossip they had been privileged to hear that day.

Julianna enjoyed the happy buzz of female companionship. It was not something she was very accustomed to but thought she would love to share in it regularly. She was momentarily distracted by the thought that perhaps she *should* set up her own establishment here in Town. She could have access to many more friends if she wasn't holed up on her brother's estate for most of the year.

Absorbed in her thoughts, she was startled to hear Lord Ackerley's deep voice greeting the ladies as he entered their box.

"Lady Chorney, Lady Julianna, I was surprised to look across, expecting to see the Ashwoods, and here you are. What a charming surprise."

He was gratified to see colour rise in Julianna's cheeks, relieved to see that she was at least not indifferent to him despite the fact that it seemed she had been avoiding him for days. Luc was determined to have a private conversation with her soon. He wanted to put her mind at ease over Fletcher, if nothing else. He was a charming boy with whom Luc was enjoying spending time. But he was still a boy, and Julianna had little to fear about him getting overly serious with any particular young lady for quite some time.

Catherine was delighted to see her friend and stood up eagerly to greet him. "My lord, it is about time you came to say hello to us. I could hardly credit that you are here with Lady Geneva and her passel of sisters and did not have the time to come by and say hello to us."

"That is hardly fair, my lady. How was I to know you were in attendance this evening, since you did not invite me to join you? I heard such rave reviews of Kean's performance. I just had to come see it for myself. Since no one else invited me, I had to join the passel of ladies." The viscount teased her mockingly as he bent over her extended hand, kissing it with a flourish.

Julianna had risen with much less enthusiasm, forcing a welcoming smile to her face. She was delighted to see that he had brought Fletcher with him, so her greeting was not feigned. "What a pleasure to see you! I had no idea you were coming to the theatre this evening."

Fletcher dipped his head in bashful greeting. "When his lordship invited me to join him for the evening I did not know we would be coming to the theatre. He says it will do me some good to get an education in the arts." Fletch grinned at the viscount before continuing to speak with his aunt. "It was a pretty good show, wasn't it, Aunt Jules? I could not believe I was so riveted to the action!"

"I know! I was much the same. It was a shock when everyone started clapping." Julianna laughed, pleased to be in full agreement with her nephew.

Luc smiled at the pair, happy to witness their contentment.

Catherine saw the look on his face and was surprised by the depth of feeling displayed there. She regarded him steadily with her eyebrows raised. When he turned back to her, he was startled into speech.

"Why are you looking at me like that?" he asked with suspicion.

"Why are you looking at *them* like *that?*" she countered, holding her opened fan in such a way as to prevent anyone from eavesdropping.

The viscount cheeks heated with colour. "Would you believe me if I said, I have no idea what you are talking about?"

"No!" Catherine was emphatic in her denial.

Luc heaved a sigh of resignation. "Well, it would actually mostly be true if I were to say I have no idea, because I barely know how I feel." He paused for a moment and regarded his friend steadily. "Do not press me on the subject, Catherine, my dear. I am completely muddled in my thoughts at the moment and would not be coherent in the least."

Nodding with sympathy, Catherine merely squeezed his arm before moving over to speak with some of the other ladies in the box. Luc approached Julianna and Fletcher.

"No escorts this evening? Do you think that is wise?" he asked with censor, interrupting the relatives as they were discussing the play.

Feeling he had no right to question her choices, Julianna tried to ignore him but Fletcher stopped, immediately turning to his new mentor.

"He is correct, Aunt Julianna, does my father know you two have gone out on your own?"

Irritated, Julianna gritted her teeth but could not quite keep a bite out of her tone. "We are not on our own. We are with a large group of ladies. And yes, your father knows where we are. Thank you for your concern," she concluded with a hint of sarcasm.

Seeing Fletcher's arrested expression, Julianna was instantly contrite. "I'm sorry, Fletch. You probably are concerned for us, and I appreciate that. But we really are going to be just fine. Do not worry about us for one moment. Go off and have fun with your friends. We are certainly having fun with ours. We are planning to go straight home after the theatre, so you need not worry at all."

Recognizing his dismissal, Fletcher turned to leave, pausing on his way back to the corridor in order to greet all of Julianna's guests. Not instantly following him, Luc continued to regard Julianna in assessment.

"Are you quite sure you will be all right on your own?"

Beginning to bristle again, Julianna's answer was cool. "Quite sure, my lord."

Realizing his error, Luc apologized. "I'm sorry, Julianna. I promise I do not mean to question your ability to look after yourself. I just do not think this is the safest neighbourhood for ladies to be traveling around without escort."

"My brother apparently did not feel the same." Julianna refused to be appeased.

"Your brother does not see beyond the end of his own nose most of the time," Luc stated baldly, irritation causing him to overstep once more.

"Well, how fortunate for you that this is none of your concern. Thank you so much for stopping by. Have a lovely evening." Thus dismissing the viscount, Julianna turned her back on him and greeted the Fieldings.

"How lovely that you could join us. I'm sorry I did not notice your arrival I was so enraptured by the play."

"I can fully understand how that happened. The instant we took our seats, I was immediately engrossed. Thank you so much for inviting us. We do not have a box of our own so we have not had a chance to see many of the spectacles. This is a rare treat to be sure." In her enthusiasm Lady Hearst was more pleasant than usual, and Julianna allowed her irritation to drift away.

Realizing he had made a serious error in judgment, Luc looked at Catherine to see if she had observed the exchange. The amusement dancing in her eyes indicated clearly that she had. The viscount made a droll face at her before he collected Fletcher and they made their escape.

Julianna, ever aware of the viscount's presence, was equal parts relieved and disappointed when she sensed his departure. It infuriated her that he would censure her behaviour although she appreciated it was no doubt prompted by pure motives. She found herself wishing he had not so quickly accepted her dismissal.

Once again she was relieved when the play resumed and swept her away from her concerns. By the time the curtain fell upon the final scene she was sufficiently diverted as to be able to cheerfully discuss the play's various nuances with her guests while they waited for the crowds to disperse enough not to get swept along in the crush.

"Thank you so much for inviting us, Lady Julianna," gushed Abigail. "It was the best night of the Season."

Julianna was surprised the marriage-obsessed young girl would so enjoy an evening in the company of only woman. She answered with warmth. "You are most welcome. I am glad you and your mother were available to join us."

"My brother did not want us going out without him, which was why we were a little late. He and his wife were also coming to the theatre so we have to wait here for him to come and fetch us," Abigail guilelessly pointed out. "They should be along any moment."

Most of their guests had drifted out by now, and it was only the Fielding ladies and Odelia who remained with Julianna.

"Would you like us to escort you to your carriage?" Lady Hearst offered generously. "When my son gets here, he will no doubt insist upon it."

Gritting her teeth to not say anything cutting, Julianna thanked her for the offer. "We should be just fine on our own, my lady, but thank you for your concern."

WENDY MAY ANDREWS

At that moment, one of the Montgomery footmen arrived to be their escort to the carriage. Julianna was relieved that he had arrived before Lady Hearst's son could insist upon anything.

"Let us step out of the box. The crowds should be sufficiently lessened, and we will be able to watch for your son more easily."

Finally, the Fieldings were gone after more thanks were exchanged and promises of visits the following day were given.

As they walked briskly toward the carriage, again arm in arm, Odelia turned to her aunt. "That was so much fun!" she declared with glee. "It's nice to be independent for a night, isn't it?"

"It certainly is, although it is a challenge since nobody else seems to think it's a good idea."

Odelia huffed her disgust. "One of these days men will realize we are just as capable as they are."

"Maybe so, but half the battle will be convincing some of the ladies, too. But for now, let us keep our thoughts to ourselves. I am not quite ready to join the suffragette movement." Odelia giggled at her aunt's words before Julianna changed the subject. "Now tell me, what was your favourite part of the play?"

The two Montgomery ladies had a lively discussion debating the various merits of the different acts. They were so occupied by their conversation that they were surprised when the carriage pulled up in front of their house. They continued to be so engrossed in their opinions as they climbed the stairs that they failed to notice the viscount's carriage a little way down the street behind them. It didn't pull away until the door closed behind them.

"Thank you, my lord. I appreciate you following them. I have a feeling they would not appreciate our concern, though, so let us keep this as our secret."

Lord Ackerley smiled at Fletcher over this statement. He allowed the boy to continue thinking it had been his idea to follow his aunt and sister home. Luc hadn't been able to bear

210

the thought of those ladies out on their own with only a young footman as guardian. But from Julianna's reaction to his concern, he knew she would cut him dead for making any suggestions to the contrary.

"I wonder what my father was thinking to allow them to wander off on their own like that," Fletcher mused.

The viscount laughed. "You better not let your aunt catch you speaking like that or you will get your ears filled with a lecture about how capable they are."

Fletcher eyed him askance. "Of course they are capable. I think my aunt can do anything. It's just that they are small and would seem like a good target for thieves looking for an easy mark. I am sure Jules could handle it, but I would hate for her to have to."

Impressed with the boy's assessment, the viscount answered. "Well, if you put it like that, your aunt would probably be very happy. And maybe your father thought the same thing."

"More likely he was just happy to not be asked to go along," concluded Fletcher with a touch of disgust in his tone. "He would much rather debate the price of wheat or the state of things in Ireland than consider the merits of entertainment."

Agreeing, but not wishing to encourage the young man in criticism of his father, the viscount changed the subject. "Where should we go now? Are you ready to seek your bed or would you like to down a glass at White's before we call it a night?"

Gratified by the viscount's continued interest, Fletcher accepted shyly. "White's sounds good." He didn't want to disclose to his experienced friend that he had never set foot inside those exclusive walls. He was almost as giddy as a schoolgirl at the prospect.

Lord Ackerley had a pretty good idea that this might be the case and grinned at his unlikely position as surrogate uncle to the young man. He then gave orders to his driver and they set off at a brisk pace.

Chapter Twenty Two

The day dawned sunny and cloudless, a perfect day for traveling. Julianna experienced a surprising sense of anticipation as she climbed out of bed. For the past several days she had been in a grey fog bordering on despair. It was so unlike her usual optimism, so she was delighted to be feeling much more herself.

They were off to Yorkleigh that day to attend the earl and his countess' exclusive house party. Odelia had been overjoyed at the invitation for far different reasons than Julianna. While Julianna was looking forward to the slower pace and fresh air, Odelia was excited for one-on-one time with what she hoped would be a lively, entertaining crowd. She had heard the earl and his wife were meticulous in their choice of houseguests and she was thrilled beyond bearing to be included in the elite group.

Julianna smiled at her maid as she came in with her chocolate.

"Thank you so much, Maizy. This is just what I need to get myself motivated to finish up the last bit of packing. Do you know if Lady Odelia is up and about yet?"

"Yes, milady, she says she cannot possibly sleep with all the excitement. She was ringing her bell right early this morning."

"Oh, dear, I'm sorry about that, Maizy. Has she been running you girls ragged?"

"Oh, no, milady, it's not so bad. She's just mighty excited. I must say, so am I. This'll be my first time to go to another house than one of our own. I'm a little nervous about the other servants." The young, less experienced, girl was a bit shame-faced to admit her fear.

Ever soft hearted, Julianna hurried to reassure her. "You have absolutely nothing to be nervous about. You do a fine job of looking after Odelia and me, and you have quite lovely manners, so I shouldn't think anyone will have any reason to find fault with you. Just remember, should you have any problems at all, you are to come to me, and we can sort them out together."

"Thank you, milady. Now we had best be getting a move on if we are to arrive while it's still daylight, wouldn't you think, milady?"

"Yes, I think you are quite right. Now if you would just help me fasten up this dress and tidy my hair, we can go see how Odelia is managing."

Julianna made quick work of changing into her traveling clothes and her morning routine. Within minutes she was knocking on her niece's door.

"Enter," Odelia called out cheerfully, the sound muffled because she had her head buried in one of her many trunks.

Julianna walked in and allowed a gasp to escape from her lips. "Odelia Montgomery! Did a tornado go through here? I thought you were packed up last night before we went to bed."

"Good morning, Aunt Julianna. I just had to check on a few things. One thing led to another and this is what happened." Odelia lifted her shoulders in a brief, sheepish shrug before continuing. "It should be pretty easy to get it all back in order."

Julianna looked around at the chaos with a doubtful look, but then two more maids entered the room and began quickly straightening everything. They made tsking sounds as they moved, but within minutes order had been restored once more.

"See? No problems here." Odelia grinned at her aunt. "Are you ready to go?"

"Just about. The footmen are carrying my trunks down to the coach right now. I was just going to see if Cook had packed us a hamper, but I stopped in to see you on the way." Julianna smiled at how that had gone. "Have you eaten anything this morning? If you want any breakfast, you should be quick about it. I would like to be on the road within the hour."

"That should not be too difficult. I shall meet you downstairs in just a couple minutes." On an impulse, Odelia ran to her aunt and gave her a squeeze. "I am so excited about this trip. Thank you for accepting the invitation."

"You are welcome, scamp. Now hurry up. It's a good thing your father is not traveling with us. He would have an apoplexy if he saw how many trunks and boxes you are bringing for four days."

"One never knows what will be required," Odelia excused airily as she turned back to her chest of drawers to see if she had forgotten anything of import.

"Do not get too side tracked, Dee. I shall be waiting." Julianna left on those words, hurrying off to complete her own errands before settling in the breakfast room while Odelia's trunks were finally being loaded by the burly footmen.

Moments later Odelia came tripping down the stairs, still giddy with excitement over the trip. Julianna mentally reviewed what she had packed that would help Odelia to while away the hours and not drive her aunt to distraction with her excitement. Her niece was too excited to eat very much, quickly downing a piece of toast to tide her over until later.

After giving last minute instructions to the butler and housekeeper, Julianna and Odelia were finally on their way. Odelia was bouncing beside her on the seat and Julianna had to suppress a sigh, resigning herself to the exhaustive task of keeping her niece entertained in the confines of the coach.

"What do you know about the Earl and Countess of Yorkleigh?" Julianna asked.

"She was his maid, and he had to marry her to rescue her from a wicked plot concocted by her evil cousin," Odelia answered with relish.

"I did not ask what gossip have you heard," Julianna reproved. "I asked what you know. What facts do you have that will help you be socially correct while at their home?"

Odelia wrinkled her nose in concentration. "Do you mean like who should be seated first, and things like that?"

"Exactly! You have grown accustomed to the relaxed way we do things at home, but some people are sticklers for that sort of thing."

"Well, an earl comes after a duke and a duke comes after a royal duke who comes after a prince who comes after a king. Wives would come after their husbands, right?"

"Yes. But didn't you forget one?"

Odelia looked blank for a moment before brightening. "Oh, you mean marquess? But there are hardly any marquesses, I rarely think about them. And Papa said it's not a real title anyway, that the crown only makes someone a marquess when they don't want to appoint another duke."

Julianna laughed. "Now you are beginning to sound like Lady Ashwood."

Odelia laughed with her. "Sorry, Aunt Jewel, I didn't mean to sound like that, I was just embarrassed that I forgot. Back to my lesson, should one ever turn up, a marquess would be between a duke and an earl."

Julianna laughed again, "And where do you fit in with all this?"

"I am the daughter of an earl and great-granddaughter of a duke, so I guess after an earl or countess. But since I am younger, if someone my social equal but older than me was present, I would allow them precedence. Like you would come before me."

Julianna grinned wryly at her niece before commending her. "Very good. But I again ask, do you know anything about the earl and countess that would affect the order you just mentioned?"

Odelia again had to think for a moment. "I guess I have not been studying my Debretts, Aunt Jules." She continued gazing out the window in thought.

"Wait! I remember. Lady Yorkleigh inherited several old titles from her parents, one of which was Marchioness, so she would take precedence before her husband."

"Excellent, Odelia."

"I know you don't really want me listening to gossip, but do you think it's true that their baby was stolen?" Odelia looked at her aunt, gauging her reaction, wondering if she would cave to the delicious tidbit of information and indulge in a round of gossip.

"I suspect there must be some truth to that rumour since they have not come to Town for the Season. They wish to entertain, so they have invited a group to their home in the country."

Seeing Odelia's fascination with the subject, Julianna tried to make her see the error of her ways.

"Can you imagine how tragic it must have been for them, if it is true? How awful to have your beloved baby stolen away from you and not knowing if you would ever see him again? I am only an aunt, but I know my life would end if something were to happen to you or Fletcher, and you are far from being helpless babies."

Odelia had obviously not thought about things from this perspective. She turned widened eyes upon her aunt's face and continued to listen in silence.

"We should be thanking God that their baby was restored to them. But even though he is now safe, no doubt for the rest of their lives the earl and his wife will have trouble trusting people or allowing their children out of their sight."

"You are right, Aunt Jules. I should not indulge in gossip. I forgot to think how they must feel. I just listen to the story and thrill to the sensationalism of it. How tragic for them." Odelia was contrite.

"We must keep this in mind while we are guests in their home. You are not the only one to be so forgetful. Some of the other guests may wish to speculate, and we should not lower ourselves to such a level. And if we observe what might seem to be odd behaviour on the part of the earl or countess, we should keep in mind what they have been through."

"What kind of odd behaviour are you expecting?" Odelia, always ready for a joke, could not keep a hint of laughter from her voice.

Julianna couldn't help a smile at her niece's tone. "Well, I don't know exactly, I must admit. But I am actually surprised they would even want to invite anyone to their home after what they have reportedly been through. I think I would be suspicious of everyone I encountered for the rest of my days if I had been through such a terrible experience. I think I would be a candidate for Bedlam after such a trial."

"Thank you for the reminders, Aunt Jules. I shall do my best to be understanding of other's idiosyncrasies and not indulge in gossip of those very same things."

"That is all I ask. Now, what shall we do to keep ourselves occupied?"

"Did you bring any books? Perhaps we could take turns reading for a bit," suggested Odelia.

Thus they whiled away the hours of the journey, stopping only once to change the horses. They made decent time and finally arrived at Yorkleigh just as the sun was starting to set.

Odelia and Julianna both found themselves pressing their faces to the window to catch a glimpse of the beautiful, elegant estate. With the descending darkness, they couldn't see everything, but what they could observe filled them with awe.

Odelia whistled like a young boy. "Wow! I fear we will get lost at least once or twice over the next few days."

Julianna laughed. "You may be right. Hopefully, they have strategically placed footmen throughout the house to offer directions to wayward guests."

Their shared laughter helped them overcome the sudden onslaught of nerves as they pulled up to the front door. Just before a footman came to help them down, Odelia gripped her aunt's hand.

"It would be silly for me to be nervous, right? Socially we are equals to these fine folks, aren't we? I have no reason to be nervous."

Julianna smiled lovingly, covering her niece's cold hand with one of her own. "Exactly right, my dear. You are about to have a completely fascinating time. You have been raised to do well in such a situation. Never fear. Everyone will love you, and you will have so much fun you will never want to go back to London."

Odelia laughed. "Now you have gone too far, Aunty Jules. I will never be in a situation where I do not want to go back to London."

But her aunt's words had done their job. Odelia had a smile on her face as she stepped down from the travelling coach to be welcomed by their hostess.

Lady Yorkleigh stepped forward with her hands outstretched. "Welcome, ladies, it is a pleasure to have you at our home."

Julianna and Odelia both dipped into polite curtsies as Julianna took the countess' hands in hers. They were gratified by the warm welcome they were receiving.

"Welcome to Yorkleigh. You must be Ladies Julianna and Odelia Montgomery. It is a pleasure to meet you. I am Emilia, the Countess of Yorkleigh, among other things, but my friends call me Emily. We shall be spending several days together so we surely shall be good friends, so you might as well start calling me Emily from the beginning."

"Thank you, my lady."

"Emily, please."

"Thank you, Emily. You may call me Julianna, and this is Odelia. We often call her Dee."

Julianna was happy to see that her well-trained servants were already at work unloading the baggage. The Yorkleigh footmen were ably assisting. Julianna turned back to her hostess knowing she could safely leave the work in their capable hands.

"You ladies have impeccable timing," the countess was saying as she linked arms with Julianna and Odelia, escorting them into the house. "We will be dining in thirty minutes. We are not being formal this evening and not all of the guests have arrived, so if you would like to just go up to your rooms to refresh yourselves, you are welcome to join us as soon as you are ready."

"Are you sure we shouldn't change first?" Julianna asked, looking down at her slightly crumpled gown, a little the worse for the long day's wear.

"You look quite lovely. Never fear. You must be ravenous from your travels. Please, pay it no mind. What you have on will be perfectly acceptable," soothed Lady Yorkleigh in a kind, gracious voice.

"Oh, but I must at least run a comb through my hair," Odelia almost wailed in distress.

"Of course, Dee. Perhaps a footman could show us to our room and we will quickly tidy up and re-join with you in a few minutes?" No matter how relaxed the earl and countess might be, Julianna refused to sit down to a meal with mussed hair and a smudged face.

The countess crooked her finger and a footman hurried forward. "Please show our guests to the Rose suite." Turning back to the ladies, she explained, "We thought you would enjoy being together. There are two bedchambers with an adjoining dressing room where your maids could sleep on a trundle."

"Oh, thank you, my lady. That is very generous." Julianna was glad to be close by Odelia and had actually been expecting that they would share a room. To each have her own chamber was luxury indeed. And having their maid nearby would make everything so much easier. The countess had implied there was room for more than one servant, but they had only brought Maizy with them. She could manage to look after them both. The young maid would be delighted to have space of her own for a few days, Julianna thought.

"Not at all. James here will wait in the hallway for you while you get settled. Then he will be able to give you a bit of a tour about the house while he shows you to the dining room. I shall see you ladies shortly." The countess then left her guests in the capable hands of the footman. He gathered up their bandboxes and started for the stairs.

Julianna and Odelia followed him sedately, trying to be discreet as they gazed about at the earl's beautiful estate. From what they could see as they climbed the elegantly curving staircase, very little expense had been spared in the upkeep of the large home. It was obvious to Julianna's trained eye there must be an army of servants to keep up with the care and maintenance of such a massive house. She could not see a single speck of dust on any surface. Everything had been shined to a sparkling glow.

If they were that conscientious of the cleaning, she anticipated that the cooking would be spectacular as well. This thought brought an embarrassing growl to her stomach. Odelia struggled to suppress her giggles.

The expanse of the house made both girls feel an urge to whisper, as though they were on hallowed grounds. "Do you think we'll ever be able to figure out our way around?" Odelia whispered to her aunt.

Overhearing, the footman answered. "You need not fear getting lost, my lady. Despite the size of the place, it is fairly well organized. And there are plenty of footmen about who will be happy to direct you, should you need a little assistance."

Odelia flushed in embarrassment that he had overheard and she had to struggle against another gurgling giggle wanting to escape her lips. Julianna frowned at her momentarily before returning to gazing about in admiration of the grandeur of Yorkleigh.

The trio arrived at the end of the hall, and the footman stopped in front of their door, holding it open for them. After he put down the things he had been carrying, he stepped out of the room and took up a position down the hall, waiting for them to be ready to be escorted back.

It was obvious why their rooms had been called the Rose Suite. The walls had been papered with roses in varying shades of pink and burgundy. Thankfully it was muted so it was not overwhelming. The rooms were large and elegant, in keeping with the rest of the house. As the girls looked around, it was obvious they would be comfortable here.

"We should probably try to hurry. We can decide later who will take which room. I don't really care which one, so you can pick if you would like. Right at the moment, I wish I could crawl into that bed, though; it looks so inviting and I feel a little worn from the drive." Julianna suited her words to action and quickly took off her outerwear.

"I know what you mean, but I am far too anxious to see more of this place. Besides, I am starving. Do you know which bag has our combs? My hair looks like birds tried to make a nest."

Julianna laughed at Odelia's description but reassured her. "It does not look nearly that bad." She quickly rustled around and found what they were looking for.

The two ladies soon had their hair, faces, and clothing set to rights and hastened to re-join the footman in the hallway.

"We didn't catch your name," Julianna said with kindness to the waiting servant as they left their room.

The young man blushed at this attention. "I am John, milady."

"Well, thank you, John, for showing us the way and waiting for us. "

"It is my pleasure to show you around and ensure you have a comfortable visit while you are here at Yorkleigh. Normally Lady Yorkleigh would show guests around herself, but since so many have arrived, it is impossible for her to be everywhere at once, although she does give it her best effort most of the time." John grinned, obvious pride and affection for his mistress shining through in his voice. He continued with a serious tone. "She has given me a great honour to share her duties with me. I will do my best to live up to her trust."

Admiring the devotion the countess had inspired in her servants, the Montgomery ladies had little to add.

"This is the guest wing of the house. There are several guest rooms on this floor and more on the floor above this."

As they continued walking, John pointed out other aspects of the house. "Down that hallway is the family wing. The earl and countess have had the nursery moved down here so they are closer to the baby. It shall be particularly convenient when there are more children to care for."

He made no mention of the rumoured kidnapping. Odelia was itching to ask him but seeing Julianna's eye on her she restrained herself.

As they descended the stairs, John continued his instructions. "I am taking you now to a receiving room where the guests are gathering before the countess leads you into the dining room. You were quick enough that you will be able to join the group there. In the morning, you can either request a tray be brought to your room or you can come down and help yourself to breakfast, which shall be set out in the dining room. Guests will no doubt be gathering in various rooms throughout the morning. There are several receiving rooms here at the front of the house that will be available for guests to use. You are to make yourselves comfortable and have free use of whatever you find. Please give instructions to your maid as to your breakfast preferences."

By this time they had arrived near an open door. John stopped, and the ladies could hear the burble of conversations. Both ladies felt the flutter of nerves in their stomachs but hid it well.

"Thank you, John, for the escort and the information. We should be able to find our way around a little bit now. You were most helpful." Julianna smiled at the footman as he stood at attention.

"Enjoy your evening, ladies," he answered as he bowed respectfully then hurried away to fulfill his other duties.

Chapter Twenty Three

Each taking a deep breath, the Montgomery ladies stepped into the room, momentarily causing a lull in the conversations taking place amongst the waiting guests.

Smiling pleasantly, Julianna looked around the room to see if there were any familiar faces. "Hello," she said to the room at large.

A handsome man, several years her senior, stepped forward to greet them.

"Welcome, ladies. I apologize that I was not there to greet you at the door. I am Philip, the earl of this pile of stones. It is a pleasure to have you join our little party." He spoke so kindly and with such self-deprecating humour that both girls were quickly put at their ease.

Coming up from a deep, respectful curtsy, Julianna replied, "Thank you so much for your kind invitation. We are looking forward to being here for a few days. What we have seen so far shows you have a lovely home."

The earl quirked an eyebrow. "The footman who escorted you must have chosen his path very carefully." With an amused smile he continued, "You two must be the Earl of Somerton's sister and daughter. I knew Hartford when we were boys but have never had the pleasure of meeting either of you."

Julianna and Odelia dipped into curtsies once again at this introduction but he quickly interrupted.

"Please, ladies, we are being casual this evening. Now let me introduce you to whoever you may not know."

Julianna and Odelia again looked around the room, more carefully this time, before smiling sweetly at an older couple standing together off to their left. Seeing where they were looking, the earl stepped forward to perform the necessary introductions. Ignoring official protocol, out of deference for the couple's advanced age, he introduced them first.

"Lady Sheasby, Lord Sheasby, might I have the privilege of introducing Ladies Julianna and Odelia Montgomery? You might have known Lady Julianna's parents. Lord Montgomery was the fourth Earl of Somerton. Odelia's father is the fifth earl." Philip smiled kindly at his four guests while Lady Sheasby blinked for a moment before stepping forward and grasping Julianna's hands.

"It is a pleasure to meet you, Lady Julianna. I knew your mother fairly well for most of her life. She was good friends with our oldest daughter. I was so sorry to hear about your loss. I know it has been several years, but you no doubt continue to feel it sharply. Losing your mother so young is always a tragedy."

Julianna blinked away sudden tears. "Thank you, my lady. I do, of course, feel the loss always. They were much too young to die. It is a pleasure to meet you. Where do you and Lord Sheasby call home?"

Continuing to smile warmly, Lady Sheasby's eyes began to twinkle at the question. "You got your mother's gift for conversation, my dear. You must know that the seat of my lord's viscountcy is in Yorkshire, but it was an excellent question. While we visit the estate there a couple of times a year we much prefer a small estate closer to London called Hamptonshire. It has always appealed to us, and it is where we raised our children. So we have let our oldest son take over the Yorkshire estate since he came of age."

Turning to Odelia the older woman asked, "How are you enjoying your first Season, my dear? You must be terribly popular."

Odelia laughed with delight at this gentle flattery. "I am having a grand time in London, my lady, thank you for asking. Everyone has been exceedingly kind thus far and I am having so much fun."

Turning to her husband, Lady Sheasby grinned. "Oh to be so young again."

With a matching twinkle in his eye, Lord Sheasby answered. "Nay, my lady. If you were allowed to be so young again, you would probably choose to marry that upstart Earl of Trent and then where would our children and I be?"

Laughing, Lady Sheasby took a playful swat at her husband. "Get on with you, my lord. I would not change a thing, and well you know it. Now let us find a chair to sit upon while we wait for dinner to be announced."

"It was a pleasure to meet you. We look forward to getting to know you better during our stay," Julianna, ever gracious, took Lady Sheasby's arm and assisted her to a chair.

A couple of moments later the countess entered the room and the butler announced that dinner would be served. Since most of the guests had travelled that day, they were all quite hungry and conversation was somewhat subdued for a time. The countess had planned the menu to be fairly light for this first day since most had had very little activity. A couple of the younger gentlemen had ridden and were thus hungrier than the rest, but their generous hostess had planned sufficiently to satisfy all. Despite the multiple courses, the meal passed quite quickly and uneventfully and soon the guests adjourned to one of the salons to play a few games before retiring early.

Lord and Lady Sheasby excused themselves right after the meal ended. "Thank you, Lady Yorkleigh, for a lovely dinner. We must retire and recover our strength in order to be equal to whichever activities you have planned for the morrow."

Emily escorted her most elderly guests to their room before returning and directing the rest in some fun entertainment for the evening.

A table was set up for the enjoyment of the more serious gamers who would feel lost without their cards, while those looking for some light fun played a game of Shades. The assembled guests were amused by her antics as Odelia was chosen to start first. The earl was seated with a candle in front of him while Odelia had to trace his shadowed profile.

Blushing rosily at all the laughter, Odelia could not help herself from joining in.

"My art instructor would probably have an apoplexy if he were to see my skills being used in such a manner. I must say, my lord, I am not flattering you at this moment." She giggled as she tried to finish the drawing as quickly as possible.

"It would take a great deal of skill to flatter this face, my dear. Do not let it bother you. I am looking forward to seeing what is causing all the laughter, I must say." Lord Yorkleigh was kind to his young guest as he sat patiently, enduring the heat the close candle cast.

"It is the angle of the candle light, my lord," Odelia excused. "It is the least flattering shadow possible." Continuing to giggle, she finished tracing his shadow with a little flourish that drew a smattering of applause from the group watching.

"Well done, Odelia. I can see the resemblance," complimented Lady Yorkleigh with a laugh as she approached her husband while he surveyed his "portrait."

"I believe turnabout is fair play, Lady Odelia. I think it is my turn to draw you," the Earl declared much to the amusement of the other guests.

The look Odelia cast at her aunt was one of light beseeching, but she was a good enough sport to take the earl's place on the chair despite the unflattering shadow she had described. She was a sufficiently confident young woman to endure the laughter now being directed at her.

Julianna watched with approval as the younger girl displayed her best behaviour, glad that her niece was having fun.

After a few people had taken turns being the shadow caster or the artist, the countess proposed a rhyming game to be played. More laughter ensued as each player tried to out-do the previous one with more and more obscure rhymes. Of course, as the evening progressed the young gentlemen participating brought in some ribald words, causing the ladies to blush, and Lady Yorkleigh called a halt.

The butler and footmen had served port and sherry as well as a selection of cheese, fruit, and pastries throughout the evening so all the guests were well fed and relaxed as they all bade a good night to each other and returned to their rooms. Keeping country hours, it was a much earlier bedtime than most were used to in Town, but it had been a long day of travelling and most did not object.

The earl stayed up with some of the younger gentlemen who wished to continue with some card games and their port, while the countess saw to getting everyone else settled for the night.

Early the next morning, Julianna heard soft rustling and opened her eyes. Her drapes had already been thrown open and through them she could see that the sun looked to be doing its best to shine through and warm up the day. Smiling at the maid who was making an effort to be quiet, Julianna sat up and put her legs over the edge of the high bed.

"Good morning, Maizy. How are you on this fine day?"

Surprised, the young maid whirled to face her mistress. "Oh milady, did I wake you? I am so sorry! I was trying ever so hard to be quiet."

"Do not distress yourself. I am ready to be up. I would love to have something to eat soon, so I think it was my stomach that woke me up, not you." Julianna suited her words to action and hopped down from the bed, not bothering to take advantage of the little stairs provided to make access to the tall bed easier.

"Is this not one of the loveliest rooms you have ever seen, Maizy?" Julianna asked with a touch of awe as she gazed about, admiring the pretty room in the morning light.

"Nothing can be lovelier than Somerton, milady," the maid answered with full loyalty. "But I will admit that it is quite pretty," she continued grudgingly.

Julianna couldn't help laughing at the display of pride. "Thank you for your loyalty to our family's home, but it is perfectly fine to admire other places." Changing the subject she asked, "Do you know if Odelia is awake yet? I would love to run down to breakfast, but I wouldn't want to leave her to come down by herself on the first day."

"I'll go check, milady. In the meantime, hot water was just delivered for your washing up. Mind you be careful, it's quite hot still," the maid cautioned as she hurried through the dressing room to check on Odelia.

Maizy came back into the room a few minutes later. "Milady, Lady Dee says she's far too tired to go downstairs. She wants me to get her a tray from the kitchen a little later. You might as well go down and break your fast now since you're almost ready. You can come back later and check on her. There's no need for you to wait around here since she's likely to go back to sleep. I'll be around so Lady Odelia won't be alone."

"Thank you, Maizy. You are right. She'll be fine, and I really am rather ravenous. Who knows how long Dee will be? She has never been a morning person." Julianna smiled fondly, thinking about her niece. She then hurried to get dressed and allowed the maid to tie her hair up into a becoming style.

"You look so pretty, milady," the maid complimented, looking at her charge in the mirror.

"You are a flatterer, Maizy, but thank you. I need a confidence boost to go down by myself. Everyone was lovely and kind last night, but it is still a bit strange to be eating breakfast with people I barely know."

"You will be just fine. Don't worry," the maid soothed. At that moment Julianna's stomach rumbled causing Maizy and Julianna both to erupt in giggles. "You had better hurry, milady."

"See you later." Julianna left the room, still smiling. She hurried along the hall and down the stairs, turning toward the dining room. She was just about to step through the door when a low, rumbling voice caused her to check her forward momentum.

"It's good to see you, Philip. Thank you for allowing me to come."

What is Lord Ackerley doing here? Julianna worried, gnawing on her lip with indecision, wishing she could retreat to her room. The countess had mentioned last night that not all the guests had yet arrived, but she had not said the names of who was still expected. *What were the chances of us all being invited to the same house party?* she wondered. *It will be impossible to avoid him in such close confines amongst such a small group of people!*

While Julianna dithered in the hallway, more people were coming, forcing her to decide quickly. Setting her chin at a determined angle, Julianna forced her reluctant feet forward. Taking a deep, fortifying breath, she stepped into the room.

Seeing a few gentlemen already present and making as though to rise, Julianna quickly excused them. "Please do not rise on my account. Enjoy your breakfast. Good morning, everyone." She airily greeted the room at large while making her way to the sideboard.

Her nerves had caused her appetite to flee, but she randomly filled her plate with food anyway. While she was serving herself, other guests arrived and there was a new buzz of conversation.

Turning back to the table, Julianna avoided making eye contact with the viscount who had entered the room while she was filling her plate. She was happy to see several empty places and allowed a footman to hold a chair for her next to the Dowager Countess of Yorkleigh. Julianna had enjoyed meeting the earl's mother the previous evening.

"Good morning, my lady, did you sleep well?"

"Oh yes, my dear, thank you. I always sleep well when I come home to Yorkleigh."

"Do you miss living here?" Julianna asked politely.

"Rarely. I love my home at Rosemount. It is much more to my taste as an old lady. I would not want to have to deal with the upkeep for this place. But I do love coming to stay with my son and his lovely wife, especially now that the next generation is coming around. Grandchildren are such a delight."

Having no first hand experience, Julianna merely smiled politely.

"Where are my manners? I am sorry, my dear. I should have asked you if you slept well."

"That is perfectly alright, my lady. Thank you, I slept marvellously. The countess quite generously put my niece and me in a lovely suite of rooms right at the end of a hallway, so it was perfectly quiet. My bed was one of the most comfortable I have ever slept in, and I believe I must have fallen asleep as soon as my head touched the pillow. I feel quite restored from yesterday's travels."

"And where is your sweet little niece this morning?" the countess asked peering around the table inquisitively.

"She does not enjoy mornings nearly as much as I do," Julianna laughed. "She decided she needed to spend a bit more time in bed and asked the maid to bring her up a tray a bit later."

"Oh I do hope she won't miss out on any of the fun my daughter-in-law has planned for everyone today," the dear older lady worried.

"I am sure she will be up and about soon enough. Thank you for asking about her."

The dowager countess then turned from Julianna and looked around the table again. This time her eyes stopped on Luc. "Lord Ackerley! What a pleasure to see you again. I did not know you would be joining us for this little gathering. Did you just get in during the night or this morning?"

This time Julianna could not avoid looking at the viscount as he answered.

"I was rather late leaving Town yesterday, so I arrived after nearly everyone had retired last night. The poor old butler waited up for me, and the earl was still up so he treated me to a warming glass of his best brandy before we each headed off to bed. I sometimes wonder if Philip ever sleeps."

The earl's proud mother smiled at this statement. "I used to wonder that, too. When he was a little boy, he so hated bedtime. Now he has various reasons for foregoing sleep." The dowager countess' voice had taken on a harder edge, but she quickly shook it off. "I am glad someone was available to make you comfortable when you arrived."

"Thank you, my lady, I was definitely made to feel quite at home. The room I was shown to will suit my needs perfectly. It was most gracious of the countess to include me in her plans." For just a moment Lucius allowed his eyes to stray to Julianna but they did not linger. He did not want her to know he had begged his old friend to allow him to join the house party when he had heard that the Montgomery ladies would be spending several days out of town. It was his best chance to get Julianna to confide in him, or at least it would force her to stop avoiding him.

Bringing his attention back to Lady Claire the viscount asked politely, "Have you been in residence at Yorkleigh for long, my lady?"

"Not this time. I was here for an extended stay after the baby was born, but I went home to Rosemount several months ago. I arrived two days ago as a guest for the house party. Emily is a wonderful hostess, and I am looking forward to being here for a lovely visit." Lady Claire turned back to Julianna with a charming smile. "It will be a pleasure to get to know some new people as well as take advantage of Philip and Emily's hospitality.

I love my little home, but there is just something about this place that calls to me."

Julianna couldn't help empathizing. "If this is where you raised your family, there is no wonder you feel at home here."

"It's true, my dear, but after my beloved husband died I could not bear to make my home here permanently, although Philip and Emily made me feel perfectly welcome. Of course, now that there are to be grandchildren and sufficient time has passed, I feel much more comfortable here. But it's always nice to return to my own space. I love Emily dearly, of course, but this is her home now. No matter how well ladies get along, each woman needs her own space."

Julianna blinked in surprise since this comment touched quite close to home for her. Her conflicted emotions must have displayed themselves on her face since Lady Claire quickly interjected. "Do not mind an old lady, my dear. I truly hope I said nothing to disturb you."

"No, no, my lady. Please do not concern yourself. It is just that your remarks about two ladies sharing a home struck rather close to home for me. My brother has recently mentioned he might consider remarrying. I have been mistress of his home for the past seven years and I have been wondering what will become of me if he does remarry."

Lord Ackerley tried to look nonchalant but could not prevent his gaze from sharpening on Julianna's face. Is it possible this is why she has distanced herself from him? But it makes no sense. Usually ladies who are concerned about their living arrangements endeavour to engage a gentleman's interest, not discourage it. Lady Julianna Montgomery was a constant contradiction, but he was determined to get to the bottom of things within the next few days. In the meantime Lady Claire was speaking with sympathy.

"I can fully understand your concern, my dear. Do you get along with the lady in question?"

Julianna couldn't help laughing despite her various concerns. "That is the conundrum, my lady. There is no specific lady to be worried about. My brother merely mentioned that I should give thought to my own future as he has been thinking about the possibility of looking for a new countess. It does not appear to be an immediate cause for concern. My brother is quite a deliberate man and will no doubt take his time in deciding on the matter, so I need not trouble myself overly at this time. It is just a factor I need to keep in mind. He felt I should consider marriage for myself in order to have a home of my own, but I pointed out to him that since I will soon come into my inheritance I do not require a husband in order to acquire a home. Of course, being a rather antiquated man, that did not sit overly well with him, but it is always an option in my opinion. Did your son worry about you when you set up your own establishment?"

"Oh, did he ever! But as you said, there is naught he could do since I was of age. He stuck his nose into every crevice of my affairs for quite some time until he had Emily to keep his hands full. She keeps him on his toes and out of my business much better than I ever could." Lady Claire smiled with fondness as she thought of her beloved daughter-in-law. "Have you given any thought to what you will do?"

Again Julianna laughed. "Only in the vaguest sense. It has been like a pesky fly buzzing around at the back of my mind ever since he mentioned it. But I have been much too busy with Odelia and her Season to be able to give it any amount of real thought. Odelia has informed me that she will require at least one more Season to make up her mind about marriage, so I have a feeling I will be tied up with her affairs for some time to come. I am sure when we go home for the summer I will give more serious thought to my options."

Lady Claire, always generous and hospitable, made a kind offer. "I love having company, so if you find yourself in need of a quiet place to think, my home is always available to you."

Gratified by this unexpected kindness, Julianna felt her eyes mist with unshed tears. On an impulse, she reached over and squeezed the older lady's hand. "Thank you, my lady. I shall keep that in mind. Now I really must run up and check on Odelia. Surely the slug-a-bed should be up and about by now. I shall see you later."

Frustrated, Luc watched as she hurried from the room, once again avoiding a direct conversation with him. Turning back to Lady Claire he was surprised to see her eyeing him with appraisal.

"So the wind blows in that direction, does it, my lord? How interesting are things likely to get during this visit?"

"Whatever do you mean, my lady?" he asked, striving for an air of innocence.

"I happen to know for a fact that you were not on the guest list until yesterday and that my poor Emily had to do a great deal of juggling to even out her numbers at the last minute. I just have no idea why. Do you care to keep an old lady up to date?"

Lucius couldn't hide the hot colour flooding his cheekbones, which caused Lady Claire to clap her hands with glee. "I am so glad that I accepted the invitation to come for this party! I can see things are going to be interesting. It seems the lovely Lady Julianna is leading you on a merry chase. It is about time you found your comeuppance." With those words Lady Claire pushed herself back from the table and excused herself from the room.

They had been the last occupants of the dining room so there had been no witnesses to this last exchange, for which Luc was highly grateful. Lady Claire was still chuckling and mumbling about the upcoming fun as she exited the room.

The viscount was left behind in the empty room, baffled by how wrong it was all going. He didn't even know how he felt about Lady Julianna, and he was chagrined by the degree of amusement that was causing for Lady Claire. Shaking his head in disgust, he pushed back from the table and quickly stood, making way for the footmen to clear the table. What he needed was a good gallop, he resolved, so he went in search of the earl to see if he wished to join him.

Chapter Twenty Four

Knocking lightly on the door from the connecting room, Julianna waited for Odelia to bid her entry. "Come hither," she called airily.

Laughing at her summons, Julianna entered the room. Odelia was still in bed, propped up with an abundance of pillows, sipping her chocolate and munching on toast.

"Good morning, Aunty Jewel. Is this not the most gorgeous room you have ever seen? I could get used to living like this. I have slept half the morning away and was greeted with the perfect cup of chocolate as soon as I popped open my eyes. Nothing could be sweeter than this," she declared with satisfaction.

"Well, I am happy to see you enjoying yourself, my darling niece, but it really is time for you to get up and get going. I believe the countess is planning for activities this afternoon and wishes for us to gather in the morning room shortly."

Julianna bustled about the room as she spoke, opening the drapes and looking around. Admiring the view the last window revealed, she continued speaking. "What a beautiful landscape! I wonder how far the earl's lands extend. No doubt they are quite extensive. I do hope some of the planned activities for the visit include exploring some of the grounds, they surely do look inviting."

"Let me see!" Never one to enjoy being left out, Odelia quickly climbed out of bed and hurried over to stand beside her aunt. "You are so right. This is gorgeous country! Maybe we will be able to go riding. Do you think the earl would keep a sufficiently full stable to accommodate everyone?"

"Most likely. Now hurry up, sleepy head!" Julianna laughed as she tossed a spare pillow at her niece. Maizy came quietly into the room and began scurrying around the room laying out what Odelia would require to get ready.

Within a surprisingly short period of time, the beautiful young debutante was ready to descend below, and the two Montgomery ladies returned to the main floor. Julianna had always possessed a good sense of direction, besides she had been about more than Dee, so she lead the way and got them to the morning room without any false turns.

"Impressively lead, Aunty," Odelia teased as they were entering the room. Both ladies had charming, happy smiles on their faces causing some of the occupants to stop and stare.

"Good morning, ladies," greeted the countess, coming forward to welcome them. "Are you acquainted with everyone here? Please make yourselves comfortable with the other guests if there is anyone you do not know. We have just been debating whether or not we should play indoor or outdoor games this afternoon. The sun is shining brilliantly, so I have been recommending bundling up and heading outside to take advantage of it. What do you two have to say?"

Looking at each other for confirmation, Julianna spoke for them both. "I would say we should take advantage of the sunshine. We can play inside games this evening or if the weather should turn inclement. If everyone is sufficiently rested, it would be a great idea to head outside and enjoy it."

Odelia, probably the most rested member of the party, clapped her hands and did a little dance of anticipation. "We were just looking outside from my room and your estate looks particularly beautiful and well-tended. I would love to see it for myself, up close. Perhaps we could even stroll about the grounds if no one is particularly inclined for games."

"An excellent idea, Lady Odelia, or some could do one thing while others do another. We have equipment for tennis and croquet in a little shed just outside the kitchen door. Shall we decide on teams before we head back to our rooms for our wraps?"

There was a general murmur of consent.

Looking around the room with a look that bordered on impish, the countess stated, "I'll go around the room and you can each tell me your preferences for how to spend the afternoon, then we'll make up teams or groups of who wants to do what."

Seeing the impish look, Julianna was intrigued and wondered what the countess was up to. There were very few people present with whom she was well acquainted so it should be an interesting afternoon getting to know some of the assembled guests.

By the time everyone was going to get their outdoor clothes it had become obvious that their hostess was determined to ensure everyone left their comfort zones far behind. Older, married gentlemen had been paired up with young ladies barely out of the schoolroom while middle-aged ladies were teamed up with young men. It was clear Lady Yorkleigh wanted everyone to have a broader view of Society, which would no doubt benefit everyone. It explained the impish look well enough.

Julianna was looking forward to her stroll in the gardens with the earl. She was surprised by the countess' choice but anticipated an interesting afternoon.

"I promise to be quick, my lord," she had promised before dashing up the stairs.

"Take your time, Lady Julianna, there is no need to rush," Lord Yorkleigh had replied with elegant grace, eyeing her with curious speculation.

She wondered idly about his look, but it didn't occupy too much of her mind. Odelia was with her, and she was full of giggles over her partner for the afternoon.

"I shall be playing croquet with Lord Sheasby. Do you think he'll be able to see where he hits the balls?"

"Perhaps that will be your job, to chase after any wayward balls and to offer some suggestions as to direction. You will get some good practice at tact and diplomacy. He seemed like a kind and easygoing man. You should have lots of fun."

Odelia giggled again but then turned rather serious eyes to her aunt's face. "Are you nervous about going for a stroll with the earl? He seems so proper. I feel like I would be nervous to be alone in his company. At least playing a game gives me something to talk about with Lord Sheasby. We can discuss the rules or laugh at each other's wayward shots."

"It's true that he seems proper and serious, but his wife seems to be so approachable and kind. He cannot possibly be all that bad if he has chosen her to be his wife. Besides, I have much more practice dealing with gentlemen other than those trying to curry my favour than you do. Most of your experience speaking to men has been relatives or potential beaux, so I can understand your trepidation. I shall be fine. He actually seems somewhat approachable. If worse comes to worse, I can always ask him about his estate and his new heir."

"True enough. You have almost as much a gift for gab as I do," Odelia giggled.

"I must hurry. I promised the earl I would be quick. Don't forget your scarf and mitts." On that parting admonition Lady Julianna dashed from the room buttoning her coat as she went.

As she descended the stairs, she was momentarily distracted by the remembrance that Lord Ackerley had not been in the morning room for an afternoon assignment. *I wonder where he went off to. Oh well, I'm just glad we were not assigned to each other. Who would have thought we would both end up here together?*

"Are you ready, Lord Yorkleigh?" Julianna spoke softly behind the earl and he turned abruptly.

"You certainly were quick. I have known very few women who could be ready that fast. It says something interesting about you, Lady Julianna," he said rather provocatively, seemingly trying to goad a response from her.

Used to the teasing utterances of male relatives, Julianna barely batted an eyelash. "I am sorry to contradict you, my lord, but it does not say anything interesting about me. Quite the opposite, in fact, it says I am boring beyond belief."

This reply surprised a bark of laughter from the normally serious earl. "Somehow I have strong doubts about that statement, my lady. Shall we stroll outside? Since you are all bundled up, you will soon overheat if we do not venture outside soon."

Taking his arm, Julianna walked with Lord Yorkleigh out into the bright afternoon sun. "You have a lovely home. My niece and I were admiring your gardens from our window this morning."

"I am glad you are enjoying it. I can take no credit for it. My mother did a wonderful job of maintaining the house and grounds, and my wife is carrying on her legacy along with a few improvements here and there."

"I must thank you for your generous hospitality, as well. Odelia and I were very happy to be assigned to adjoining rooms. It has made us so much more comfortable."

"It is generous of you to thank me for that since you must know that is again the work of my wife." The earl looked at her with a sardonically lifted eyebrow.

Julianna looked at him steadily for a moment wondering if she should continue to make polite, socially acceptable conversation or call him out for his questionable replies. "Of course, my lord, but isn't everything worthy fundamentally the work of wives? It would be completely rude for me to not acknowledge your position of host in some way."

She said this with such an innocent look on her face that again the earl was surprised by a burble of laughter rising in his throat. *This girl has spunk, I'll grant her that,* he thought with some admiration, seeing a glimmer of what had so caught his friend's eye.

Struggling to hide his amusement, the earl fixed Julianna with what he hoped was a stern look. "What do you hope to accomplish on this visit, Lady Julianna? I understand you have a niece you are trying to marry off."

Taken aback by the earl's tone and question, Julianna looked at him with an elevated eyebrow. In that moment, she looked so much like her grandmother that Lord Yorkleigh hesitated to pursue his questioning.

"I cannot say that I had a particular agenda for visiting your home. In fact, my darling niece, Lady Odelia, has no intention of marrying this Season. She wishes to experience more of life before settling down to marriage. So when we received the invitation from, as it turns out, your wife," she inserted with gentle emphasis, "we were happy to have an opportunity to rest, relax, and maybe make some new friends. Perhaps we were wrong in that expectation." She ended her statements on such a wistful note that the earl was moved to regret the impulse that pushed him to test the woman.

The earl's usually polite veneer resumed its place. "No, no, my dear lady, you were not wrong. My countess and I hope you will be comfortable and happy here this week. I pray you, pay no mind to a grouchy old husband that has been feeling a bit neglected over all the preparations."

Not quite reassured by his explanation and not even fully believing him, there was nothing Julianna could do but smile graciously and continue walking.

The earl mentally kicked himself. Obviously confronting her was a bad idea and would get him nowhere. He wanted to get to know her and see if she was going to be trouble for his good friend Viscount Beaufort. Offending the woman was not going to accomplish anything.

"I understand you have been a substitute mother to your niece and nephew for the past several years." Lord Yorkleigh tried to be conciliatory.

Julianna struggled to maintain a polite smile. She had thought the earl was a kind, intelligent man, but that was the most obtuse statement she had heard. She hated it when people referred to her as a substitute for the children's mother. There is no way anyone could replace their mother.

"It has been my greatest privilege to have a small role in helping to raise my brother's darlings." There was a note of definite challenge in her voice as though she were daring the earl to question her statement.

"That is a lovely sentiment, my lady. As a new parent, I can say that it is a challenge, and I would think jumping into that position suddenly and with children the age yours must have been would be even more so than if you start off with babies." As Philip said it he realized it was true. His admiration for the younger woman grew, and he decided then and there that he liked her. There was a lot he needed to still learn about her, but thus far he liked what he saw.

Unfortunately, she was not leaning in the same direction of learning to like as he was. Still distant, Julianna smile did not reach her eyes. "No doubt children can be a challenge at any age."

"But rewarding none the less, or at least I hope so," he answered with a self-deprecating smile. "Our charming baby has just passed his first year. We get excited with each step he takes and every gurgle that might be able to pass for mama or papa. I am sure that eventually we shall be setting our goals for him a little higher."

Amusement finally showed on her face. "Eventually he will actually utter the words you are hoping for, my lord, have no fear. Of course, I missed that stage with Dee and Fletch, but the later years are exciting, too."

Compassion softened his face as Lord Yorkleigh spoke. "It must have been a challenge for you at such a young age to come home from the excitement of London and settle into domestic duties."

Still not feeling trustful or comfortable, Julianna decided to be honest but not to go into too many details. "There were many aspects of my Season that I did not enjoy. My parents had recently died, so I was sad and lonely. It was tragic that my brother's wife died so young, but helping him with his children in his hour of need really filled a large void for me at the time. Children bounce back much faster than adults sometimes, and they really helped me deal with my own worries."

Philip didn't respond, only continued looking at her with sympathy, so Julianna continued. "Of course, I would be lying if I told you there were no challenges. I knew very little about children and had few adults I could turn to for guidance, but thankfully their mother had done a marvellous job up until then, so they were wonderful children to look after."

After another brief, melancholic pause, Julianna continued in brisker tones, "The housekeeper who has been in service at Somerton for much of my life is still there, so I have relied heavily upon her wisdom. My only regret is that dear Fletcher and Odelia missed out on so many wonderful people in their lives. Their mother and my parents would have been so good for them to know."

Irritated by the catch in her voice, Julianna broke off for a moment, gazing into the trees lining the path they were walking. After clearing her throat, Julianna continued in much lighter tones.

"I regret nothing about coming home to be with my brother's family except that my own very short experience with the *ton* does not set me up very well to guide Odelia. I find myself constantly parroting things my mother or grandmother said to me. It has been interesting to be back in London. I was looking forward to these few days here at Yorkleigh as a respite from the social whirl."

The look of sympathy on Philip's face deepened at this. "And here you are being interrogated by your host. I am sorry, Lady Julianna, how ill-bred of me to bring up such painful subjects."

Julianna had to agree that it was ill bred of him, so she made no comment. The earl continued after a brief, slightly awkward, pause.

"So since I started off on such a rude foot, I might as well continue." This caused Julianna to laugh nervously and look at him with questions dancing in her eyes.

Philip asked, "You mentioned a moment ago that there were aspects of the Season you did not enjoy. I am surprised. I thought every young lady lived for the day she would step out into Society and loved every moment of the experience."

"Well, not every lady, my lord. In fact, I would say there are many who find it trialsome. If you are a wallflower for example, it would no doubt not be nearly as enjoyable as if you were popular and danced each evening through."

Lord Yorkleigh regarded Julianna appraisingly. "You cannot try to convince me that you were ever a wallflower."

She blushed charmingly at this but continued. "Well no, I am from a good family and was sponsored by the Duchess of Westerley. I never lacked for partners. But there are countless numbers of reasons to not love the Season. I was homesick and missed my mama. I had just come out of mourning for my parents when my grandmother summoned me to London. It was poor timing. And to be honest, I felt unprepared for the many people with two faces. There is so much that is fake about Society. We are all so polite to one another's face, but then so many will rip you to shreds behind your back. The duchess felt we were above such things and should take no notice of it, but as a young girl that was an impossible command to obey."

"So you left London without a proposal and went home to help your family?" the earl probed.

Laughing lightly, Julianna tried to avoid details, unsure how much the earl would remember about her from seven years ago and not wanting to risk any reflection on Odelia. "A girl must not brag about such things, my lord, but I was not without any proposals. I just chose not to pursue marriage at that time."

Still concerned for his friend, but convinced the young woman was not out to hurt him, the earl decided to just ask one more question before he let her off the hook completely. "If I recall correctly you were once engaged to Viscount Beaufort. Are you uncomfortable being here while Lord Ackerley is also a guest?"

Unable to prevent the blush that lightly stained her cheeks, Julianna allowed irritation to finally show through her voice. "I always thought gentlemen did not stoop to idle gossiping. I assumed that was the purview of old maids and idlers."

Philip chuckled at her set down. "You were misinformed, my lady. Gentlemen gossip nearly as much as the ladies do. It is just usually about different topics. I was not referring to gossip. I was just inquiring as to your comfort." He tried to smooth her ruffled feathers.

"Well, thank you for your concern, my lord. I was a bit surprised to see that the viscount was here at the same time as us, but we get along just fine. You need not fear any ugly scenes. Lord Ackerley knows how to behave as a perfect gentleman."

Philip noticed she was not calling Luc a gentleman, only that he knew how to behave as one. *Interesting,* he thought as he then made every effort to set the lady back at her ease. He was satisfied that she was an admirable young woman who would make his friend an excellent wife should he decide to pursue the connection. It was now none of his business.

"Do you enjoy riding, my lady?" he inquired politely after answering a few questions she had about the estate.

"I love to ride, my lord. It is one of the things I miss most being in London. We did not bring our mounts to Town for the Season. No doubt they are eating themselves sick back at Somerton, and we will have our work cut out for us to get them back in shape this summer."

"Please, feel free to make yourself at home in our stables while you are here. We have several horses that are not being ridden regularly since my wife is in a delicate condition."

"Thank you for your generous offer. Odelia and I were just this morning wondering if we would get a chance to explore this beautiful countryside."

"I believe my wife is planning for the group to go exploring tomorrow either on horseback or in carriages. Your wish will be granted at that time."

"I will look forward to it." Julianna had finally relaxed and was beginning to enjoy the stroll with the earl. It fleetingly crossed her mind to wonder why he had seemed so intent on riling her, but she decided to worry about it later. She was just beginning to wonder if they should be returning to the house.

"I feel as though I have occupied too much of your time, my lord. If you have pressing obligations, please do not allow me to detain you. I am perfectly capable of entertaining myself. I should actually probably go and check on Odelia. She was to play croquet as Lord Sheasby's partner. I might need to rescue him from her in case her chatter is driving him to distraction."

As she said that, they rounded a curve in the path and entered a small clearing. Lord Ackerley was seated on a bench. It was hard for Julianna to think this was a coincidence.

"It is kind of you to offer. There are, in fact, several things I should be looking after. Perhaps the viscount will be so kind as to escort you to the croquet field." Philip looked amused at the look of dismay that crossed Julianna's face, quickly replaced with a polite smile.

"I would not wish to impose upon his lordship's time. I can walk myself back to the house." Julianna wanted anything but private time with the viscount.

Luc had quickly stood when the two finally arrived. He had been waiting for several moments and had begun to wonder if he was on the wrong path. He hastily stepped into the conversation. "It would be my pleasure to walk with you, Lady Julianna."

There was little she could do other than accept as graciously as possible. Her smile a little tight, she thanked the earl for his time then accepted the viscount's offered elbow.

Chapter Twenty Five

"Did you have a pleasant stroll with the earl?" Luc asked politely, trying to start a conversation with his now silent companion.

"It was interesting," was all she had to offer on the subject, which caused Luc's eyebrows to rise in speculation.

"'Interesting,'" he repeated. "That is a curious way to describe your afternoon."

Not feeling comfortable to confide in the viscount, Julianna did not wish to go into detail. "Well, it *was* interesting," she insisted then tried to change the subject. "How has your day been thus far?"

"Thank you for asking, my dear. It was quite nice. I went for a bruising gallop on one of Philip's best horses. It helped sweep the cobwebs from my upper works," he laughed at his own use of the cant expression. "The tedious drive out here from London and the late night last night had not left me in a fit state for company this morning. But I am feeling much more the thing after my ride."

"Oh, that must have been quite lovely," she said, envy evident in her voice.

"Would you like to go for a ride? I would be happy to go with you. I am sure the earl would not begrudge you the use of one of his horses."

"You are correct. In fact, he has already offered me carte blanche in his stables. But I really should check on Odelia. I am supposed to be her chaperone, after all."

"Do you never get a chance to look after your own interests?" Luc asked with almost fierce intensity.

Taken aback by his tone, Julianna endeavoured to keep things light. "But it is in my interest to watch over her. I adore my niece and want only her happiness."

"But what of your happiness?" Luc persisted.

"That makes me happy," Julianna insisted, quickening her pace.

"Hold up, Julianna," the viscount called, grabbing her arm to prevent her from getting away. "Why are you running away from me all the time? There are so many things piling up that I wish to discuss with you."

Starting to feel a bit panicked, Julianna tried to shrug out of his grip, but he kept his hold firm on her arm. "I am not running away, my lord," she answered maintaining formality despite his use of her given name. "I just really do feel duty bound to ensure Odelia is fine."

"If she is perfectly content, then will you go for a ride?" Luc persisted, wishing to spend more time with her.

"Lord Yorkleigh mentioned that the group will be going for a ride tomorrow, so I think I will wait until then, but thank you for the invitation."

Nearly growling in his frustration at Julianna's efforts to keep him at arm's length, Luc released the grip he had forgotten he still had on her arm. "Well, then, allow me to walk with you as you go to check on her."

"Thank you, I would be happy for your escort," she was forced to answer with polite correctness.

They fell silent for several paces while Julianna wondered how much more complicated her life could get.

"So what will you do if she is comfortably ensconced in her game of croquet?" Luc asked, curiosity making him persist.

Drawing a deep breath to curtail her impatience with the man, Julianna turned to look searchingly at the viscount. Deciding that his stepping out of the social bounds meant she could as well, she countered his question with one of her own. "Why do you ask, my lord?" Despite her desire to put him off his questioning, she was unable to completely leave the social niceties behind.

Luc chuckled quietly at this vocal parry. "I am asking because I would dearly enjoy having a conversation with you. Since you seem intent on avoiding that for some strange reason, I would like to spend time with you even if you do not wish to talk. So in asking what you will be doing with your time, I am trying to ascertain if I could do it, too, whatever it may be."

Unable to resist, Julianna grinned at Luc, finding his detailed answer amusing despite her desire to avoid him. Regaining seriousness she again questioned, "But why?"

"Why do I persist despite your obvious reluctance?" he countered.

At her weak nod, he answered her as honestly as possible. "I really don't have an answer for that, my dear. I must be a glutton for punishment. I must admit to you that I have never found myself in the position of needing to work so hard for the attentions of a lady. You are driving me mad with your warmth one moment followed by cool reception the next. But I feel compelled to get to the bottom of it. I am almost certain there has been a serious misunderstanding underlying all this angst."

A hot blush splashed across Julianna's cheeks and she stumbled to find a response to this statement. At a loss, she merely shook her head in abstract denial of his words. She hoped fervently he would let the matter drop. That was a fruitless hope as it turned out.

"You did not answer my question, my lady. I hesitate to point out your lapse in protocol, but one really must keep up appearances," he tried to ease her discomfort by jesting about the matter, but he truly did wish to spend time with her and needed her to spell it out for him if she was going to absolutely refuse.

Her blush deepened in her confusion before she remembered that he had asked her what she would do if Odelia were occupied.

Giving in to what appeared to be inevitable, she turned to the viscount and smiled as graciously as possible. "If we arrive to find she is happily engaged in playing croquet with Lord Sheasby then I believe I will find a bench in the sunshine and enjoy a conversation with you, my lord."

"Oh, well, I might be otherwise engaged, my lady," he teased her before squeezing her arm in appreciation for her capitulation.

Regaining her backbone, Julianna teased back. "Well, if you have an appointment or some other engagement, no doubt I will be able to find someone to keep my company while I await the outcome of my niece's game. Your escort has been deeply appreciated since I doubted my ability to find my way back to the house along this well-marked path."

The viscount could not help laughing at her cheek. "You, my lady, have some nerve."

Retaining her blush, Julianna countered, "You seem to bring out the very worst in me, my lord."

Silently rejoicing over her apparent thawing toward him, he smiled at her in genuine amusement and decided to stop pressing the matter. There would be time enough to pursue a conversation when they got back to the house and saw how the croquet players were doing.

They walked in companionable silence for a few moments as they neared the house. They could hear a commotion, as they got closer. When they came to the end of the path and entered the clearing, they were surprised to see many of the guests milling around, cheering on the players. Odelia and her partner, the amiable Lord Sheasby, seemed to be in the lead by a small margin, but the few players near them in score seemed just as determined to catch up and defeat them. The other players had given up the game as a hopeless cause and had joined the spectators in cheering on those still in the race.

Julianna was thrilled to see her niece so involved in such a simple pursuit until she remembered she had as good as committed herself to facing up to a conversation with the viscount. Turning to him in resignation she gestured toward an empty bench. She was glad to see that some of the others had also taken seats so they would not be remarked upon. Of course, that was wishful thinking on her part. Amongst the *ton* everything was remarked upon. But she was correct in believing it would not be so immediately apparent that they had separated themselves for a private conversation.

Racking her brain for an innocuous topic to engage in, Julianna was at a bit of a loss, giving up when the viscount started into his conversation.

"I am so glad that we have finally found an opportunity to talk. Would it be overly bold of me to ask you straight out if you have been avoiding me?"

He barely paused so she didn't even have to try to come up with a suitable reply to this. Without interruption he answered his own question. "Of course you would not avoid speaking with me after asking me to look into what Fletcher has been up to."

This goaded her into speech. "I did not ask you to look into Fletcher's whereabouts. You volunteered to do that all on your own."

"Only after you expressed your concerns in that regard," he retorted.

"Well, it is true that I mentioned some concerns, but I did not ask you to put yourself out, and I must apologize if that is the case, my lord." Julianna could barely look at the viscount as she struggled to maintain her composure.

"Julianna, my dear, I thought we had become friends. It is not putting oneself out when one tries to alleviate the concerns of a friend. It is, in fact, the very definition of friendship in my opinion. It is one's job to help one's friends, would you not agree?"

Feeling lower and lower the longer he was kind to her, Julianna could only nod in assent.

Unaware of the turmoil she was experiencing, the viscount continued to speak although he was discouraged by her lack of response.

"I wanted to put your mind at ease. I don't think you have any need to concern yourself over much with regards to Fletcher and Lady Abigail. While it would seem that he has a slight inclination in her direction, he does seem to be quite clear on not wanting to set up anything but bachelor accommodations for himself anytime in the near future. In fact, I would not be surprised if you found he has switched his affections to some other young lady already. No doubt he will be lavishing attention on any number of young ladies over the next few years as he does seem to enjoy their company."

Julianna chewed her lip in thought, causing the viscount to sharpen his gaze on her lips before he pulled himself to attention. To distract himself from the sight he questioned her. "Does this cause you alarm? I thought you would be pleased by this information."

"I am pleased that you don't think he has fixed his attentions seriously on Lady Abigail. The trouble lies in him spreading his attentions around too much. If he raises expectations with various ladies, that could cause nearly as many problems as if he settled down too soon. Dear me, I thought Odelia would be the one to cause me worries, not Fletcher."

"I truly do not think you have cause to be distressed about this, my lady. Every young man goes through this when he is first on the town. Remember, Fletcher is only nineteen. He has a good number of oats to sow before he becomes serious about any pursuit in life. I certainly spread my attentions around a fair bit when I was his age." Luc thought this would demonstrate how little she needed to fear, but it had the complete opposite affect than he expected.

"That is what I am afraid of, my lord. I do not want my nephew treating any young lady in such a manner!"

Luc cocked his head and looked at her down the length of his nose, appearing very proud and unapproachable for a moment. Julianna stood her ground. While meeting his brother caused her to have some doubts about what she had seen all those years ago, he had verbally backed her into a corner and she was not backing down.

In deceptively soft tones, the viscount asked her, "Are you implying that I in some way mistreated ladies when I was a youngster?" His focus sharpened on her flushed face as understanding began to dawn on him. "You did accuse me of being a womanizer seven years ago, but I thought that was merely a way of getting out of an engagement that you had been convinced into by your grandmother. Are you trying to say that I mistreated you?" he asked in much kinder tones, although he had no glimmer of an idea what she could think he had done to her.

Julianna tore her gaze from his face and looked around rather frantically wanting help from some quarter but also desperately afraid of calling undue attention to their conversation.

"I do not wish to discuss this, my lord. Thank you for your kindness in checking on my dear Fletcher, but I realize it is highly inappropriate for me to be discussing him with anyone other than his father." She stood to put more distance between them. "Now if you will excuse me, I must attend to something."

Surprised by her sudden withdrawal, Luc was unable to stop her, and she cast a rather wan smile around the gathered guests and slipped from the garden. Hurrying to her room, Julianna struggled to contain her tears until she had the bedroom door firmly closed against her back. She then sank to the floor and indulged freely in a tempestuous bout of weeping.

Why is this so painful and difficult? she wondered. *What if I really did make a huge mistake seven years ago? Can I admit to him what I have done? I can't even imagine how angry he will be. No, I must continue to keep him at arm's length. Surely he will soon give up. It's not as though I have given him any reason to wish to pursue me,* she thought with despair as the tears continued to fall.

Allowing the indulgence for only a moment or two, Julianna forced herself back under control, stemming the flow of tears. Standing up, she shook out her skirts before striding briskly to the dresser where a pitcher of wash water awaited her needs. Soaking a cloth with the cool water, Julianna pressed it to her heated cheeks and endeavoured to erase any trace of her spilled emotions.

She scrutinized her face in the looking glass and decided that no one but the keenest observer would notice that she had been crying, and she doubted very much that even the keenest observer would be looking all that closely at her. To be on the safe side, though, it would be best if she did not dally too long in her room or her absence would be remarked upon.

Hurrying back down to the gathered guests in the garden, Julianna could see that the croquet game was still underway. Thinking she had not been noticed she slipped back amongst the milling group. So intent was she upon blending in, she jumped when the countess approached her and spoke softly.

"Is everything all right?" Emily inquired making sure no one could overhear.

"Of course, thank you, my lady. I am having a lovely time," she lied with a straight face before quickly turning to the truth. "You have such a beautiful home. The gardens and paths through the orchard are so inviting."

"I am happy to hear you are enjoying your surroundings," Emily replied, perceiving the polite lie. "I am sorry to be so inquisitive, but I noticed you hurrying to the house a few moments ago. Is there anything I can help you with?"

Emily had seen Julianna and Luc talking and had hoped the viscount was furthering his suit. Philip had told his wife about Luc's request to join the house party and she had been delighted to include him. But when Julianna had hurried away from him Emily had wanted to run after her. Not wanting to draw unwanted attention, she restrained herself but could not help sticking her nose into the other woman's affairs.

With a warm blush staining her cheeks Julianna tried to brazen it out. "No, no, my lady, all is well. I merely needed to relieve nature."

Seeing the moisture still climbing to the corners of Julianna's eyelashes, Emily was not convinced but did not wish to embarrass the girl further and allowed her to sidestep the issue. "Well, if you are sure all is well, please come and keep me company over here in this sunny spot while we wait for your niece to finish winning her game."

Despite her uncharacteristic reluctance, Julianna accompanied the countess to a bench and sat with her to watch the players. She fervently hoped the countess was not going to continue her husband's inquisition.

With a triumphant shout of glee Odelia finished the game, winning by a couple of strokes. Flinging her arms around Lord Sheasby, she gave him a tight hug before doing a little victory dance. Quickly recovering due to Julianna's censorious eye upon her, Odelia blushed prettily.

"I guess it is not very proper to be so happy about beating the others, is it?" she asked Lord Sheasby as she looked at him with a sheepish grin.

"That is quite all right, my dear. It is perfectly charming to see such enthusiasm. It is contagious, I must say. I have not enjoyed anything quite this much in about a decade," he declared as he was joined by his wife. His own excitement about their win caused him to lean over and give his wife a smacking kiss on the cheek. Never one for public displays, Lady Sheasby blushed and grinned crookedly at her husband.

All the spectators had applauded and crowded around the players, congratulating them all on a game well played. When the hubbub had died down a little, Lady Yorkleigh directed everyone into the morning room for a snack and a warm cup of tea or something stronger before everyone separated to make their preparations for that evening's supper and entertainments.

The next couple of days flew by. The ride to explore the surrounding countryside was a delight for Julianna since she missed the life she enjoyed on her brother's estate. It was the bright spot for her since most of the time she found herself to be nervously looking over her shoulder watching for Lucius, trying to avoid any more awkward conversations with him.

For his part, Lucius spent those couple of days intently observing the Earl of Somerton's baby sister. He was becoming more and more convinced that Julianna would make an excellent wife. She was lovely, composed, and kind. She was always polite to everyone she encountered from the lowliest scrub maid to their host, the Earl of Yorkleigh. It was driving him crazy, and so he told the earl.

"I ask you, why do I have to be so perverse as to fixate my attentions on this woman? There are any number of eligible, beautiful, kind young ladies available. Why does it have to be her? She can barely look at me, even though she is always excruciatingly polite if I can ever manage to pin her down to a conversation, but then she somehow always manages to slip away, and I am left standing there like a noddy wondering how it happened."

The earl nodded in sympathy. "She is quite lovely, and I fully understand your fascination. I have no comforting words of advice for you, my friend. When I fell in love with my countess I believed her to be the least eligible option to be my wife, but in the end that did not deter me in the least. When the heart sets its mind on something, it is very difficult to dissuade it. If it is any comfort, the fair Julianna is doing her polite best to avoid me as well. But I was inexcusably vulgar towards her, questioning her parenting and her intentions with you. Did you perhaps wrong her in some way?"

"That's just it, Philip, I have no recollection of doing so. I would like to think she was slightly unhinged in her upper works, but there is no other sign of diminished sanity." This statement caused both gentlemen to laugh for a moment before the viscount continued morosely. "I guess I have two options. I can either give up and get over her, or I can convince her to consider me as an option for her future. Unfortunately, she is likely to be around during the Season for at least the next year or so since Lady Odelia has been quite open about wanting another Season before settling down. And I need a wife. It would be much more difficult to get over her if I have to see her often. But I am not convinced I will have any more luck with convincing her than I would have with getting over her." Lucius heaved a disconsolate sigh before continuing. "It is a conundrum."

Philip tried to cheer his friend. "Well, tomorrow is the last day of our house party, and my wife has planned a small dance to include some of the surrounding gentry. You can either make a last ditch effort to secure your lady's affections, or perhaps you could meet another eligible young lady who might catch your eye." The earl laughed before presenting a third option. "Or you could meet a young lady and try to make Julianna jealous by showing her what she is missing out on."

"You are a genius. Nothing else seems to be working. Maybe I should try that!" Luc declared with glee.

Looking hesitant, Philip cautioned. "I was joking. Make sure you do not play fast and loose with any of my guests, or my wife will call us both to task."

"No, no. I will be careful. I would not want to find myself caught in the parson's mousetrap by mistake, have no fear. I will think on this. There might be a way." Luc got up and walked away in the midst of the conversation, lost in thought about possible ways to secure his lady's attentions, leaving Philip behind laughing good-naturedly at his friend's dilemma.

That afternoon, before the guests went to change for the evening's activities, the countess had arranged for any of the guests who did not wish to rest to enjoy some archery lessons or target practice for the few who were already proficient.

Facing the target that had been set up, Julianna eyed it with what almost felt like anger. Unsure why she was feeling so out of sorts, she pulled back on the bow and let the arrow fly. Her hand hesitated briefly on its way to her quiver for another arrow as she heard the viscount's deep voice ring out across the field.

"Your aim is a wee bit off," he chuckled as he headed to collect his own arrows.

Eyes narrowing, Julianna's aim settled on him. The smile faded from his handsome face as he realized she was taking aim at the center of his chest.

"I usually have exceptionally good aim, my lord. Do you care to comment further?" Even Julianna didn't recognize her own voice as it dripped with uncharacteristic venom.

Plastering a placating smile onto his suddenly paler face, Luc tried to backtrack. "I apologize sincerely, my lady, I was merely jesting at your expense. Pay me no heed."

"Gladly," she answered as she forced her aim back to the target. Letting her arrow fly, it thunked into place, dead center of the target. Most of the guests had not noticed the byplay between Julianna and Luc, but there was a smattering of applause at her accomplishment.

Her fingers suddenly feeling nerveless at the audacity of what she had just done, Julianna looked around with a rather wan smile.

"Would someone else like a turn?" she asked as she stepped away from her position. Another guest stepped forward to take her place and Julianna forced herself to hurry over to intercept the viscount.

"Lord Ackerley, please, wait a moment," she uttered in urgent, but low tones as he made to walk away. "What I just did was unspeakable."

"I would have to agree with you there, my lady. Now if you would excuse me, I have somewhere I need to be."

Refusing to meet her eyes, Luc tried to brush by her, but Julianna stood her ground. "I am terribly sorry, my lord. I cannot even explain what got into me. I have never done anything so utterly foolish in my entire life."

"Actually, I believe you have, but pay it no mind. No harm was done."

Julianna was not satisfied with his cryptic reply but had to allow him to pass if she did not want to cause a bigger scene than she already had. With a resigned sigh, she watched him walk away before returning to the small group still practicing with the bows and arrows. She waited for Odelia to be finished and then the two of them retired to their rooms to prepare for the evening.

Chapter Twenty Six

The next day most of the guests spent in quiet pursuits. The gentlemen went out riding, hunting, or fishing while the ladies wrote letters, did needlework, or pursued art projects, leaving their hostess free to finish preparing for the additional guests that evening. Julianna had enjoyed the stay at Yorkleigh despite her discomfort with Lord Ackerley's presence and was sad that it was nearly over.

All day Julianna felt as though she had exchanged roles with Lucius. She was terribly unnerved about her deplorable behaviour the previous day at the archery practice. Wishing to apologize further she had hoped to engage him in a conversation that morning but he had managed to evade her. She was left with conflicted, tumultuous feelings with regards to the handsome viscount.

Julianna spent the afternoon in quiet contemplation, writing some letters to friends and working on her embroidery. Odelia hated working with a needle so she started out with some painting, but then decided to entertain the ladies with an impromptu piano concert while some joined in with singing.

By late afternoon all the ladies, and even some of the gentlemen, were in their rooms getting ready for the evening's gathering. Despite her newly acquired sophistication, Odelia was excited about the anticipated entertainment. She loved to dance and had enjoyed making new friends at Yorkleigh.

"Even Lord Sheasby has asked me to save him a dance," Odelia told her aunt with a delighted grin. "I think I have my dance card filled already and we haven't even set foot in the ballroom."

"Did you really get the gentlemen to sign a dance card?" Julianna asked with mild curiosity.

"No silly, it was a metaphor."

Julianna laughed with delight. "I am so happy you are having a good time here. I believe it is a positive commentary on your character that you can be so adaptable to your surroundings."

Dee rolled her eyes at her aunt over this comment. "You did not raise any spoiled brats, dearest aunty. Even my brother is pretty easy to please. And surprisingly he makes friends wherever he goes, too. He is even friends with your viscount."

Julianna's face burned hot, red all the way to the roots of her hair. "Lord Ackerley is *not* my viscount. What makes you so sure they are friends?"

"Do you mean besides the fact that we saw them together at the theatre? His lordship was talking to me about Fletcher yesterday."

"He was? When?"

"After you hurried away to see if Lady Yorkleigh needed your help with anything." Odelia grinned cheekily at her aunt, revealing that Julianna's efforts were not so well hidden.

Smiling sheepishly, Julianna asked, "Was it terribly obvious?"

"No, not to other people, just to the viscount and me. But it does make me wonder why you never want to be around him. He really is terribly nice. We had a lovely conversation about his Grand Tour when he was Fletch's age and how much he is enjoying getting to know my brother. It was funny. Hearing about Fletcher from him made me want to spend more time with him myself. Fletcher that is." Odelia was quick to explain seeing the bemused look on her aunt's face.

"Well, Fletcher is a lovely boy, and the two of you should make more of an effort to get along. He's the only sibling you have. Sadly we are not a very large family, so you should make sure you take good care of the ones you have."

"I know Jules, it's just that a big brother can be terribly annoying at times," Odelia excused with such a peeved expression on her face that Julianna could not resist the tinkle of laughter that escaped her lips.

"Alright, the lecture is over. Now tell me how you are going to have your hair styled for this evening."

With that turn of conversation, the Montgomery ladies proceeded with their preparations for the evening. Before long they were ready to descend to the salon where the guests were to assemble before going into a light dinner that was to precede the dancing. The countess had arranged for two meals that evening – an early dinner and then a late supper before the guests who were not staying overnight departed. Odelia was very light on her feet, doing a little skip as they made their way to join the others.

Julianna's heart began to race as she beheld Lucius as soon as she entered the room. Always a handsome man, this evening he was very nearly gorgeous. And the look on his face as he watched her enter caused her heart to miss a beat. For one unguarded moment, their feelings were nakedly displayed for all the world to see. But then they both blinked, and the moment was broken. The viscount turned to the lady beside him and made some jest that caused a ripple of laughter. Julianna had not heard the words and could barely hear the laughter over the buzzing in her ears.

To cover her confusion she turned to Odelia, making some innocuous comment. It must have made little sense because Odelia shot her a quizzical look without replying. They were quickly distracted by the introductions Lady Yorkleigh was making between the houseguests and the local visitors. For the first time in her life, Julianna worried that she would never be able to remember the names of the people she was meeting, so distracted was she. It was with relief that a few moments later they were ushered into dinner. Julianna pasted a smile onto her face and made every effort to make it through the evening.

After a few moments at the dinner table, Julianna managed to pull herself together. Turning to her dinner partner on her right, she offered a charming smile and engaged him in conversation.

"Do you live nearby?" she asked politely.

"Yes, my lady. I live about twenty minutes ride east of Yorkleigh. My father is a baron and a horse breeder so we have quite a large property," he explained proudly.

"That must be lovely. Horses are wonderful animals. Are they race horses or work horses that you breed?" Julianna did not want to admit that she had no idea what his name was, so she was glad he had mentioned his father's barony. She wouldn't have to worry about what his title would be as a mere mister. Hopefully she could brazen it out for the length of dinner.

"Thank you for asking. We specialize in carriage horses. It's a great life, raising horses. My sisters have trouble when it comes time to sell them, but that's pretty much the only drawback."

Julianna wrinkled her nose in thought at what he had said. "I never thought about that. I guess they grow attached to them, don't they? Are your sisters here this evening?"

Her dinner companion shot her a surprised look before explaining that they had been introduced together. "You met my sister Agnes when we were introduced earlier."

"I apologize, sir. There were so many new people it was difficult to keep them all straight," Julianna blushed fiercely with embarrassment.

"I understand," the young man answered soothingly, looking at her as though she were a bit of a simpleton.

Julianna bit her lip to control her amusement over the misunderstanding despite her previous distress. For a moment she allowed her eyes to wander around the table and was surprised to find Luc's eyes upon her. Once again their eyes locked for an unending second, but this time Julianna was prepared for the spear of sensation that stabbed her to her core and sent a frisson of awareness up her spine. She managed to maintain her composure this time and, after blinking, was able to turn back to the man beside her.

"Now that you have reminded me, I believe your sister is sitting across from my niece up the table a ways. But I think you mentioned you have more than one?" she prompted him to continue the conversation.

"Yes, our youngest sister is still a bit young to go out in company. Agnes is pining for a Season in London such as your niece is enjoying. Our oldest brother is already married, and his wife offered to bring her around a little bit, but she has not yet made good on the offer. Our mother does not feel up to the task herself, so I'm glad that Agnes is having the opportunity to make some new friends this evening."

Charmed by his kind concern for his siblings, Julianna continued the simple conversation throughout most of the meal unaware of the consternation she was causing Lucius.

Despite those two moments of shared connection, Luc still felt as though Julianna was giving him the cut direct and decided to ramp up his efforts. He had been angered by her actions the previous afternoon, but he still couldn't quite give up on her. Despite the juvenile element attached to trying to make her jealous, he decided he had no other choice. He looked around the table for possible candidates. He wanted someone old enough to have flirting experience and not take things too seriously, but young enough to be believable. His eyes settled on the most likely partner for this little crime.

As soon as they stood up to signal the end of the dinner, Luc made a beeline for the lady in question. His conscience gave him a slight twinge, but he ignored it reasoning that it was for the greater good.

"Mrs. Conrad, it was a pleasure to meet you. Are you very good friends with Yorkleighs?" he asked by way of a conversational opening.

"Merely acquaintances to be perfectly honest. They are very kind, but we do not usually run in the same circles socially. Besides that, I was fairly new to the neighbourhood when my husband died, then I was in mourning for quite a while, so I was not attending any social events. This is the first time for me to attend one of their entertainments, actually. Lady Yorkleigh and I have made morning calls on each other, but that is about it." Appearing slightly uncomfortable over the direction the conversation had taken, Mrs. Conrad turned it around with a question of her own.

"What about you, my lord? How long or how well do you know the Yorkleighs?"

"I have been friends with Lord Yorkleigh since we were on our Grand Tour as boys. He is a marvellous travel companion and a great friend." He paused for a moment before continuing with a crooked grin. "Well, he was a fantastic friend before he settled down on his estate and doesn't seem to ever want to leave now that he has his countess."

"Be careful, my lord, you sound almost jealous," she teased quizzically.

He grinned sheepishly at her. "Maybe just ever so slightly."

"I would just bet that you have a perfectly lovely estate of your own somewhere, and there is no doubt a long line of debutantes queuing up for an opportunity to be your viscountess."

Luc was embarrassed to realize that a blush was creeping up his cheeks at her words. Feeling bashful, he hesitated, wondering what to say. Mrs. Conrad burst into raucous laughter at his discomfort, causing all heads in the room to swivel in their direction. Luc's discomfort grew until he noticed Julianna's eyes intently upon them. His embarrassment quickly changed into determination to continue despite his instinctive reluctance.

Affixing a smile of charm to his face as the band struck up the first song, Lucius bent over her hand and invited, "Might I have this dance?"

Mrs. Conrad bobbed a slight curtsy as she accepted his invitation. Despite her appearance of being someone from the fringes of Society, she was a delightful dance partner – graceful and light on her feet. Her laughter had drawn the attention of the other guests and it remained on them as they energetically made their way through the figures and changes of the cotillion. As the song drew to a close, Mrs. Conrad dropped another curtsy, thanking the viscount for the dance.

Turning away from her, Luc felt Julianna's eyes on him once more. As the band struck up the next number, he bowed to her, inviting her to partner with him for this dance.

Feeling suddenly shy, Julianna hesitated but could not refuse. Despite all her resistance to his efforts to advance their relationship over the past several days, she felt herself melt inside as he drew her into his arms for the quadrille. Keeping the requisite, appropriate space between them, Julianna still felt as though the air around them suddenly was charged with an indescribable energy. As they moved through the steps of the dance, she could not feel her feet on the floor and merely hoped she was doing it correctly.

Luc led her with ease around the room. They barely spoke, but for those moments it felt as though words were unnecessary and all was finally right with his world. Logic told him that the feeling would end as soon as the song did, but he decided to ignore logic for the moment and enjoy the experience.

As the band brought the dance to an end, Julianna smiled warmly at the viscount. She could not deny how she had enjoyed the dance so she merely said a soft, "Thank you."

Reluctant to allow her from his arms, Luc retained her hand for another moment. "Would you like something to drink? I could get you a glass of ratafia or some punch."

Not quite meeting his eye, Julianna pulled her hand back from his grasp but bobbed her head in acceptance. "Thank you, my lord, I would like a glass of something. I could accompany you."

Surprised that she was finally not running away, Luc grinned down at her then turned and walked toward the table that had been set up with refreshments. After he had procured drinks for them both, they stood in silence watching the dancers, sipping slowly.

"Your niece appears to be having a good time," Luc commented with an air of understatement.

Julianna grinned in response. "My niece always has a good time. It is one of her best qualities."

Luc returned her grin as he replied. "And her enthusiasm. That is also one of my favourite of her qualities."

Julianna laughed quietly. "She is a delight. In weak moments I occasionally wish I could trade places with her even temporarily." She said this last bit with a wistful note to her voice.

Turning to her, the viscount said earnestly, "Why would you ever wish to trade places with her? You are a delight yourself and cannot be traded in for anything."

Julianna's smile turned slightly wan at this, and Luc knew he had somehow made a tactical error. Cursing himself silently he watched the animation drain from her face, being replaced by her usual politeness toward him. He felt no surprise as she excused herself when the song came to an end.

"Thank you, my lord, for the lovely visit. I should go confer with Odelia during this brief pause in the music."

Luc allowed her to hurry away feeling equal parts delight and dread. It was clear to him that she had unresolved feelings for him, both positive and negative. His determination to get to the bottom of it hardened. Realizing this was not the right place or time to force a confrontation with her, he allowed her to avoid him for the rest of the evening.

After tossing and turning for the night, Luc rose at first light and left Yorkleigh as unobtrusively as he had arrived, with only the earl and the butler being aware of his activity.

"Take care, my friend," bade the earl as he saw Luc out.

"Thanks for letting me crash your party," answered the viscount with a crooked grin.

"Not that it did you much good," answered Philip with a crestfallen look.

"That is where you are wrong, my friend. It did a world of good. I shall keep you posted on my progress."

"Really?" Philip questioned. "From where I was standing last night it did not look like you had advanced very far in your pursuit of the lady."

"Perhaps not, but appearances can be very deceiving, you must remember."

"All right, keep me posted," was the sceptical reply from the earl as Luc swung up onto his skittish horse's back. "Ride carefully."

Philip stood and watched his friend ride away as Emily came up beside him. "I really like him, Philip. And Julianna seems like a delightful lady. But there is something dark between them, and I cannot say if they can bridge the gap, whatever it may be."

The earl looked lovingly down, dropping a quick kiss onto his wife's upturned face. "Well, thank you for including him in our party. Wherever it goes from here is Ackerley's responsibility. Now let us see about getting our house back to ourselves."

With a grin at each other, they returned to the house and helped the rest of their guests depart without incident.

Chapter Twenty Seven

L ord Ackerley made excellent time riding back to London. He felt badly about how hard he had pushed his mount, but he had needed the brisk ride to help clear his mind and focus his thoughts. He was no further ahead in deciding how he was going to force Julianna into telling him why she kept shutting him out, but he was hardened in his resolve to do so.

He was well caked with dust and dirt from his dash across the country when he was welcomed home by an uncomfortable looking footman.

"Welcome home, my lord," greeted the footman politely, looking around frantically for the butler. "I trust you had a nice time while in the country."

Luc eyed the young man curiously. "It was passable, John, thank you for asking. Might I ask why you look so skittish?"

Blushing hotly the young footman began a stuttering explanation. "That is to say, my lord, it should be the butler speaking to you on the matter, surely not me. I ain't had no trainin' sir." In his distress, the lad's background began to show in his accent.

He was saved from further explanation by the arrival on the scene of the viscount's trusted butler. That usually unflappable gentleman was looking rather harried as well. This caught Luc's attention firmly.

"What is going on around here Henry?" he demanded to know.

Relieved at his master's arrival, the butler was only too happy to unburden himself. "It's the young lordship you befriended, my lord. He arrived before the sun this morning demanding to see you. We tried to explain to him that you were out of town, but he decided to wait. He's been pacin' around the parlour for hours, my lord. I'm afraid he's wearing himself to exhaustion and a hole in the carpet, which the housekeeper will never forgive me for."

Trying to decipher what exactly his trusted butler was trying to tell him, Luc gazed at him with his brow knit in confusion. "Who did you say is pacing a hole in my parlour?"

"The young lord, my lord. You know, the Earl of Somerton's son. Young Lord Fletcher." Clearly the butler expected his master to have figured this out on his own from the explanation given.

"Do you know why Fletcher is so anxious to speak with me?" Luc was tired from his travels and a little frustrated with Montgomerys in general at the moment. He was hoping it was to be a simple matter.

Henry did not have a chance to answer the viscount. Obviously, Fletcher had heard the commotion of the viscount's arrival, which caused him to dash from the parlour to present himself to Lucius immediately.

"My lord, you have finally returned!" he declared with all the dramatic flair a youth can muster.

"In the flesh, Fletcher. I understand you have been waiting to see me. I must apologize for keeping you for so long. I was unaware we had an appointment."

Blushing at the reminder of how *maladroit* his behaviour was, Fletcher hastened to launch into an explanation. "I desperately needed to speak with you on a matter of the utmost importance.

I believed you would be home soon, so I asked to wait. Please, my lord, you must help me."

"Gently, Fletcher, gently. Come along to my library and you can tell me all about it. Have my people made you comfortable? Do you need anything to eat or drink? A little something to settle your nerves that appear to be on the verge of being overwrought?"

The viscount was feeling amused at Fletcher's dramatics and hoped that chiding him a little would cause him to realize that whatever his problem might be, it wasn't nearly worth all the melodrama.

Distractedly Fletcher acknowledged the hospitality shown to him. "Yes, yes, your servants were more than kind to me. I had a sandwich a while ago. Thank you, yes, a whiskey would be just the thing right now."

After pouring the young man a couple of fingers of the spirit and getting some for himself, Luc seated himself behind his large desk while Fletcher continued to pace.

"Please, Fletch, take a seat. Sip your drink. When you are ready, tell me what the problem is."

Fletcher obeyed readily, gulping down his drink with an air of desperation but then taking a deep fortifying breath as his nerves appeared to steady a bit. After another deep breath, he launched into his explanation.

"I challenged a man to a duel and I am not too certain what I am supposed to do now."

Shocked and dismayed over his young guest's words, Luc nearly choked in the act of swallowing his own drink.

"You challenged a man to a duel?" he demanded with incredulity. "What caused this? How could you have done such a thing?"

Fletcher visibly paled at the viscount's outburst, which caused Ackerley to apologize. "I'm sorry, Fletch, excuse my outburst. Please start at the beginning and tell me exactly what happened."

Gulping down what was left in his glass, Fletcher stood and began to pace again.

"You see, everyone was out of town. Julianna and Odelia went off to some house party in the country. Kenneth Landon had to go see his father, who hasn't been doing too well lately. You were not around. And my father is always so busy. Anyway, I went out on the town with some of my old friends. We obviously had way too much to drink. One thing led to another as it always does in such a situation. I overheard some other gentlemen talking about Abigail in some very unflattering terms. I jumped to the conclusion that they were speaking of Lady Abigail Fielding and I took exception to their words."

At this point, he paused for thought before continuing. "Of course, even though it turned out to be someone else, they really were objectionable things to be saying about anyone of the fairer gender in my opinion. But anyways, I called him out for it. And now we are to meet tomorrow. I named you as my second. I hope that's all right. I didn't really know what else to do."

After unburdening himself to his mentor, Fletcher now looked spent as he slumped back into his chair.

Lucius was at a loss. This was far beyond any scenario he could have imagined. There was no way he could smooth over any differences with Julianna if he somehow managed to get her nephew killed! What a mess.

Fletcher watched in dismay as his friend stood and began pacing much as he had been doing in the parlour. "I apologize, my lord. I should have asked your permission before dragging you into this mess."

"No, Fletcher. You did the right thing. I am glad you had the wherewithal to name me as your second. It is your second's job to try to prevent the duel from happening in the first place. I'm pretty sure I am in a better position to do that for you than any of your younger friends."

"Really? There's a chance I could get out of this?" Fletcher asked with disbelief and burgeoning hope. "I thought there was no honourable way to avoid a duel once you called someone out."

"It all depends on the circumstances," Luc said, already calming down. He resumed his seat behind his desk before bidding Fletcher to continue his story. "Tell me again exactly what happened. I need to know who was there and what was said."

Luc listened patiently as the tale unfolded. Once Fletcher wound down to his conclusion, the viscount pulled a cord and a servant appeared immediately.

"Please have someone find my brother. Send the first footman — he'll know where to look." Turning back to Fletcher he looked at him sternly before asking, "Who have you told? Does your aunt or sister know about this?"

Paling at the very thought, Fletcher exclaimed, "No, of course not! I might be loose in my upper works but I am not that stupid!"

"No, no, of course not," soothed the viscount. "I must be honest with you about something, Fletcher, since you have confided in me. I want to marry your aunt. She is not fully on board with the idea at this time, so I am feeling quite anxious about not allowing her to find out about this situation. I like you, Fletcher. That in itself is enough to motivate me to try to get you out of this. But you can see that I also have extra motivation."

Fletcher sat back in his chair and grinned at the viscount. "You and my aunt, eh? Well, that would be great on all counts. I'd say you will be a great uncle and I would be quite happy if you could save me from this latest disaster I have created."

Grinning back at the younger man, Luc was glad to help his friend. The trick would be to make sure Julianna never found out. "Have you slept?" he thought to ask.

"Not really. I was too anxious. I barely slept a wink last night then I got up at first light to come wait for you."

"Go home, take a nap, have a bath, and eat a meal. I will do what I can to straighten this out. Whatever you do, do not tell Odelia or Julianna!"

The young baron cast the viscount a dubious look. "I doubt I will be able to sleep, but I shall try. And, of course, I won't tell them. I'm not even sure when they are expected to arrive home." After a pause of reflection, Fletcher turned a smile of boyish charm upon the viscount. "Thank you ever so much for bailing me out, yet again. I would think my troubles would put you off wanting to pursue my aunt."

"I cannot in honesty say it is my pleasure. When I am your uncle, we shall have to see about keeping you out of trouble." On that note, the two men separated in good cheer with one another.

Fletcher made his way home, and Luc set about the precarious task of extricating the young man from this dilemma. It would take some delicate negotiations, but it just might be doable.

Chapter Twenty Eight

Fletcher rounded the corner of his street only to find his family's carriage pulled up to their door and his aunt and sister climbing down. The coward in him wanted to turn tail and run away, but he had promised the viscount to get himself cleaned up and ready for whatever further instructions Luc would have for him. He strode forward and hailed his family, forcing himself to be bold and brave.

"Hello, ladies, welcome home! Did you have a good time?"

"Fletcher!" both ladies squealed in unison, throwing their arms around him in a welcoming hug, uncaring that they were on the street.

"Looks like you missed me," Fletcher grinned at them, feeling relieved at their presence and unconditional love.

Linking arms, the trio climbed the stairs and entered the house.

"We had a lovely time, Fletch. Yorkleigh is such a beautiful estate. It is too bad you didn't come. We made some fun new friends. I think you would have liked it, too." Odelia was prattling on and Fletcher felt a pang. If he had gone with them, he would not be in his current predicament.

Watching the play of emotions over her nephew's face Julianna asked softly, "Is everything all right with you, Fletcher? You seem a little quiet."

"Oh no, Aunty Jules, I am fine. It is just impossible to get a word in edgewise with this one going on," he teased his sister who swatted him playfully.

"Have the two of you eaten?" Fletch asked solicitously. "I was thinking of having some refreshments sent up."

Surprised by his thoughtfulness, Julianna accepted. "Thank you, Fletch, that would be lovely."

Odelia and Julianna regaled Fletcher with details of their time at Yorkleigh while they waited for the tray to be sent up and then quickly dispensed with the light repast. Finally, Fletcher excused himself, and Julianna went to see about their unpacking.

While Julianna was otherwise occupied, a few of Odelia's friends came to call.

"You're back! How was the house party? Tell us all about it! Was Yorkleigh terribly elegant? Was the earl devastatingly intimidating?" Abigail pelted Odelia with questions while Mr. Jackes and Mr. Landon looked on with interest.

"It was quite lovely. We had so much fun. Everyone was all that was gracious and kind, and no one was overly intimidating." Odelia went on to give them a few details before demanding answers to questions of her own. "What have you all been up to while I was away? Did I miss anything of import?"

"No. Mr. Landon had to run home to his father for a day or two and nothing was the same without you, of course. You bring a certain sparkle with you, Dee, wherever you go, and none of the parties we attended were nearly as fun because you were not there," Abigail declared in earnest.

Blushing charmingly, Odelia was a little embarrassed by the attention and quickly changed the subject. "What about gossip? Surely there must be some interesting tidbits you can share with me."

Abigail looked as innocent as always and shook her head in denial of knowing anything salacious, but the gentlemen immediately looked uncomfortable and started gazing about for an exit strategy. Seeing their discomfort, Odelia instantly began to wheedle.

"Come on, my lord, you can tell me. Please? I am desperate for news of Town. We had fun out in the country, but I felt terribly isolated from all that was going on around here." Seeing their continued hesitation, she jumped to certain conclusions and blushed rosily. "Well if it's about someone's mistress then never mind, I would not want to know anyway."

The men continued looking discomfited, not relieved by her dismissal, so she continued badgering them. "But if it's anything else, you truly must tell me."

"It's your brother!" Tom burst out, unable to contain himself.

"Tom, hush!" growled Kenneth Landon.

"My brother? What gossip could there possibly be about Fletch? He is as boring as can be," Odelia answered without hesitation while Abigail stood wringing her hands.

"A duel!" Tom said, his nervousness making details impossible.

"Thomas Jackes, I swear I'm going to have to call you out myself," declared the young lord in disgust at his friend's inability to keep a secret.

"Fletcher is going to fight a duel?" Odelia asked with incredulity. At this statement, the four young people heard a gasp from the doorway.

Julianna had just walked into the room as Odelia was asking this last question. Paling visibly she made an effort to remain calm.

"Surely you are mistaken. Our Fletcher would never be so hen-witted as to allow himself to be called out."

"He did it," the less than helpful Mr. Jackes said.

"I swear, Tom, you are not fit for company," Kenneth said with reproach before turning to Julianna. "I apologize profusely, my lady. These are not things for your ears."

Sinking rather weakly into the nearest chair, Julianna maintained a façade of calm while inwardly reviewing all her possible options.

"Tell me, Mr. Landon, is it true? Do not worry — the cat is already out of the bag, so you might as well tell us what you know."

Looking sheepish, Kenneth sketched out the few details he knew. "I am not certain what caused it, but from what I have heard Fletcher called out a young squire just up from the country. It seems like it was over something silly, but they were all in their cups. The duel is supposed to take place tomorrow morning."

"I see. Well, I know you did not wish to divulge this information, but you did the right thing telling me. Perhaps there is something I can do to prevent it."

Looking aghast at the thought, Landon declared, "No, my lady, you cannot involve yourself. This is not a matter for ladies. It should not have even come to your ears." He shot a dirty look at his friend who bowed his head in shame. He continued, "There is no honourable way out of it once he has called someone out. This just has to run its course. If you want something to do to help, you could pray."

Julianna barely managed to restrain herself from snorting at this ridiculous suggestion. *As though praying would be of any help in this instance,* she thought with derision. Maintaining her veneer of calm, Julianna stood and hugged her niece.

"Have no fear, Odelia, no doubt this is a terrible misunderstanding. Try to put it from your mind for the time being. Why don't you four go out for a drive or go to Gunther's for a treat."

Julianna thought she was making a ridiculous suggestion, as though her niece would be able to follow through on her words. But to her surprise, Odelia acquiesced readily. Giving her aunt a quick kiss on the cheek she turned to her friends.

"What a great idea. I have been cooped up in the carriage for much of the day so I don't really want to go for a drive, but Gunther's would be lovely."

Abigail and Tom were quick to fall in with the plan. Only Mr. Landon looked momentarily sceptical at the idea. At Julianna's encouraging gestures he too fell in with the idea, and the four young people quickly left the room.

Relieved to be alone, Julianna again sank into a chair and allowed despair to roll over her for a moment. Stiffening her resolve, though, she stood and pulled the cord to summon a servant.

"Do you know if Lord Fletcher is still in the house?" she asked when the footman appeared.

"No milady, he just left a few moments ago. He said he had some errands to run."

"Thank you. Please have Maizy meet me at the front door. I, too, have some errands to run."

Within minutes, Julianna and her maid were striding purposefully down the street.

"Where are we off to, milady?" Maizy asked surprised by the brisk pace her mistress was setting.

"We are on our way somewhere that I am quite sure you are going to object to, but you must not tell anyone. Please just follow me and do not say a thing."

Surprised by this unusual command from her beloved mistress, the maid subsided for a few minutes. She was quiet until Julianna stopped in front of Viscount Beaufort's townhouse.

"No, milady, you cannot go in there!" she declared vehemently.

"Hush, Maizy, I must. And you must come with me to lend an air of respectability. Now be quick — the sooner we get inside, the less likely it is that anyone will see us."

The poor young maid was in a quandary, but she saw the logic in her lady's words so she scurried up the stairs behind her.

The dutiful butler managed to contain his surprise at seeing a well-bred young lady standing on his doorstep demanding an audience with the viscount. Unable to resist her imperious demand to be allowed to enter, he stepped back and shut the door behind her.

"I am sorry, milady, his lordship is not at home."

"Do you know where I could find him?" she asked as calmly as possible.

"His lordship did not see fit to disclose all his plans to me," Henry explained.

"Do you expect him to be home any time soon?" Julianna asked a little desperately.

"He did mention he should be back in an hour," the butler answered reluctantly.

"Then I will wait!" she declared much to the servant's dismay.

Maizy began to wring her hands in consternation and Henry was unsure of the social protocol of what to do with a lady who wished to wait for the viscount. He ushered her into the parlour, which not that long ago had contained the pacing Fletcher.

"Could I offer you some refreshments while you wait, milady?"

"Tea would be lovely, thank you."

Julianna took up the same pattern of pacing her nephew had previously occupied. Blessedly she did not have overly long to wait.

Minutes after delivering a tray of tea to the waiting guest, Henry was relieved to open the door for the viscount.

"Milord, I am so happy to see you!"

Surprised by the unprecedented degree of enthusiasm, Luc braced himself for whatever might be added to this unconventional day.

"What is it, Henry?"

"There is a lady with her maid waiting to see you in the parlour. I was unsure what to do with them since you have never had lady callers before." This last was said with a hint of reproach, which brought a smile to Lucius' face.

"I apologize if my callers have inconvenienced you, Henry. Did you happen to catch the name of this lady?"

Looking sheepish the butler had to admit, "No, milord, I did not think to ask."

"No trouble. I shall announce myself. That will be all for now, thank you, Henry." On those words, the viscount strode to the parlour and briskly opened the door.

He had been prepared for just about anything after the day he had had so far, but Julianna was the last person he expected to find in his parlour. Happiness and dread filled him in equal measure at the sight of her.

"To what do I owe the pleasure of this surprise?" he asked as nonchalantly as possible as he walked into the room, careful to close the door behind him.

Relieved to see him and feeling silly for disturbing him, Julianna strode toward him, grasping his outstretched hand.

"I have a problem I need help with and I did not know where else to turn. It is a terrible imposition, I know, to show up so unexpectedly, but the matter is of some urgency, you see."

Luc interrupted her efforts of explanation. "No apology is necessary, Julianna, you are always welcome in my home."

In her distress, Julianna did not register the implication of his words; she was too preoccupied with her concerns.

Undismayed, Luc continued, "You wished to see me about something? Should we adjourn to another room to afford us more privacy?"

Looking harassed, Julianna was startled by the question. "That would hardly be proper, my lord."

He raised a crooked eyebrow at her declaration. "Less proper than you coming to my house?"

Hot colour flooded her cheeks at the realization of how ridiculous she was being. "You are no doubt correct, and I have placed myself beyond the pale, but I will not compound it. What I have to discuss with you can be discussed with Maizy present. I trust her implicitly."

"All right, shall we be seated?" Luc was now pretty certain what Julianna was here for and he was cudgelling his brain, wondering how best to handle the situation.

Seating herself quickly, Julianna came straight to the point. "I am not completely certain as to the truth of this, but it has been relayed to me that my nephew has called someone out. I did not know who else to turn to for help. I know it is none of your concern, but could you please help me?"

Even if he had wanted to refuse, there was no way Lucius would have been able to resist the beseeching look she cast at him in that moment. Luc felt like a medieval knight called upon to slay his lady's dragons. He would do all in his power to allay her fears.

"Of course, I will help you. Now tell me clearly, what have you heard?" Unsure if he wished to reveal his prior knowledge, Luc wanted to know where she stood first.

"Odelia's friends came by to welcome her home. In the course of conversation, one of the young men revealed he had heard Fletcher is to fight a duel in the morning."

Poor Maizy had not known about any of this and she sat quietly weeping beside her mistress. Sorry to be the cause of her distress, Julianna handed her a handkerchief and rubbed her back in an effort to soothe her.

"Don't worry Maizy, his lordship is going to help us."

Gratified by the faith being placed in him by two Montgomerys today, Luc felt his chest begin to puff with pride. Reining himself in, he realized he needed to be completely honest with his beloved.

Taking her hand and looking her in the eye, Luc began rather haltingly. "Jules, I need to tell you something, and you cannot get upset. Do you promise?"

Julianna looked at him with wide, earnest eyes and nodded her agreement.

"Fletcher came to me earlier today and told me all about it."

Surprised by this information, Julianna instantly grew angry and leapt to her feet. "And you did not feel it necessary to come to me with this right away?"

"You promised not to get upset," he reminded. "Let me explain."

Subsiding a little, Julianna regained her seat and allowed him to maintain his comforting grip on her hand.

"I didn't tell you because he told me in confidence, for one thing. And for another, I believe I can sort this all out without any harm coming to anyone, so I thought it would be better to not have you worry for nothing."

"But how can you sort it out if he did, in fact, call someone out?" she asked with puzzlement. "Mr. Landon said a gentleman cannot withdraw and keep his honour."

"It is true that there are certain protocols that need to be met, and it is a tricky thing, especially when hot-headed young men are involved, but those very same protocols allow for a couple of strategies."

Julianna's worried eyes searched his to determine the sincerity behind his words. Relieved by what she saw, she felt almost limp after the tension she had been experiencing up until this moment.

"Thank you," she said simply. "What can I do to help?"

"You must return home and wait. I know it is not in your nature, but it is unfortunately all there is for you to do."

"What are you going to do?"

"It might be best if you don't know," he answered gently.

Realizing she now had two men to worry about she beseeched, "But you will be careful, won't you?"

Gratified by her concern, he answered with feeling, "I swear it."

"And will you come tell me when it is all sorted out? I shan't be able to eat or sleep until I know you are both safe."

"You must remain calm. All will be well, I promise you. But yes, I will come to you as soon as it is sorted."

After another searching look deep into his eyes, Julianna realized she would have to be satisfied with that. She was relieved to see that Maizy had been closely following the conversation. The young maid had even more faith in the viscount than Julianna did and was thus fully restored to her usual sunny nature.

Bounding down the stairs, energy restored, she grinned at her mistress. "It's quite turrible I can't tell anyone about this adventure, milady."

Smiling weakly but kindly at her devoted servant, Julianna answered, "I know, my dear, but it really must be our secret."

"Are you going to tell the earl?" Maizy wanted to know.

"If it all turns out right I will leave it up to Fletcher to decide if he wishes to share this information with his father."

"Isn't it funny that both you and the young master went to the viscount instead of the earl?"

Julianna blushed a little, not wanting to admit what she had revealed in her desperation. "Quite a coincidence," was all she would say.

Upon returning home, they had barely gotten through the door before Odelia bounced into the house.

"Aunty Jules, we had so much fun! Gunther's was the perfect destination after our long ride home. How was your afternoon?" Without even pausing to wait for her aunt's answer, she continued, "I'm so excited about going to the theatre with Lady Chorney this evening. Are you quite sure you won't come, too? I know you said before we went away that you would most likely be too fagged from the journey to go, but surely it wasn't very bad and you could join us."

The trip to the theatre had completely left Julianna's mind, but she was filled with relief that she had not committed herself. It would be the perfect excuse to stay home for the evening and wait for Lucius to come with news.

"No, my dear, while you are correct that the journey was not as bad as I had anticipated, I think it would be best for me to have a quiet night at home. I will be in a better state to carry on in your wake for the rest of the week. You will be in good hands with Lady Chorney and shall have a lovely time."

Odelia seemed to have forgotten completely about her brother's possible tragedy and prattled on about her fun with her friends and the anticipated entertainments they were to enjoy now that they had returned to Town.

Julianna stayed with her niece while she prepared for the evening, half her mind listening for a knock on the door as she listened to her niece's chatter.

As she fastened the last of her jewellery around her throat, Odelia looked shrewdly at her aunt. "You are staying home to wait for news about Fletcher, aren't you?"

Startled, Julianna showed a guilty face to her niece.

"I know you, silly. Of course, you would need to be here to ring a peal over him. I am sure you have done whatever is possible to ensure he remains safe, which is why I am not going to stay home and fret with you." Odelia grinned cheekily at her aunt after this statement.

Julianna clasped her beloved niece in a warm hug. "Have fun tonight. I probably need not remind you not to discuss this with anyone."

"No, you do not. I am not nearly as silly as Mr. Jackes. I must say, when I pressed him for gossip that was the last possibility I thought I would hear."

Julianna managed to find this amusing and laughed together with Odelia as they walked downstairs. She was relieved to be able to wave her niece off to a safe evening of entertainment while she awaited Fletcher's fate.

Endeavouring to make herself comfortable in the morning room, Julianna forced herself not to pace and sat with some needlework on her lap. Very little of it got done since she was so distracted, but it gave her hands something to do instead of wringing each other.

Thankfully her nerves were still intact an hour later when there was a commotion at the door. Unable to wait, Julianna dashed from the room to be confronted with the sight of Lord Ackerley ushering in a slightly battered, but decidedly alive, Fletcher.

Exclaiming over his many bruises, Julianna escorted the two gentlemen back into the morning room after asking that the housekeeper be called for.

Grinning at his aunt, Fletcher forgot he had meant to keep it all a secret from her. "It was so fantastic, Aunt Jules. We had a great fight. I allowed him to draw the first blood, of course, considering everything. But it was brilliant. We drew quite a crowd."

Used to her nephew's delight over such things, Julianna barely batted an eyelash over his glee, merely asking rather sceptically, "So which of you came out the winner?"

"Oh, I think we could rather say it was a draw. We were quite evenly matched. I say, I would love to match up with him again."

Unable to suppress a slight shudder, Julianna answered rather weakly, "Perhaps you should wait a bit. You won't be able to show your face at any of the *ton* gatherings for at least a week."

Grinning, Fletcher answered, "I really would not consider that to be a drawback, Aunty. Those affairs are usually terribly insipid."

Julianna could not resist her laughter at this unanswerable statement. She was relieved to hand her nephew over to the housekeeper who had arrived and was busy clucking over the young master's wounds. "I have just the thing to fix you up, young man. Come along."

The two left the room in a clatter of noise as Fletcher continued regaling the housekeeper with further details of the cause of his injuries. As the room cleared out, Julianna turned to the viscount who was watching her intently.

"I cannot thank you enough. While I cannot say I am thrilled he was in a fight, it was clearly a far better option than pistols at dawn. However did you manage it?"

"No thanks needed. It actually was even easier than I had expected. The other young man was just as young and inexperienced as Fletcher. While they both were certain it was impossible to withdraw, they were quite easy to convince that a round of fisticuffs could settle the matter just as well as a real duel with blades or pistols."

Sitting on the settee with Julianna's hand clasped warmly in his, Luc felt his optimism burgeoning.

"I had been preparing myself for various options. I even thought of approaching Lady Abigail's brother to help straighten out the matter, since Fletcher had been attempting to defend her honour. But it turned out to be rather simple and straightforward. Young men are not nearly as complicated as young ladies."

At his pointed look, Julianna's cheeks warmed and she could not quite meet his eye. She tried to remove her hand from his grasp, but he would not allow it. Still avoiding his glance, she tried again to thank him.

"It was such a relief to be able to impose on you in this way. Thank you for saving him. I do not know how I could possibly repay you."

"You could start by explaining why you have been doing your best to avoid me for weeks."

Now her eyes flew to clash with his before she looked away in distress. "I cannot. Please, I cannot explain it. Why do you even care?"

"Well, since you will be marrying me, it would make things go all the smoother if I understood where we stand with each other."

Going white where she had previously been blushing, Julianna shook her head vehemently. "I cannot marry you, my lord."

"Why ever not?" he demanded, restrained frustration beginning to show in his tone. "I think you must marry me. You compromised my reputation by coming to my home unannounced this afternoon. The only way to remove the reproach is to make an honest man out of me."

Since she had begun to weep quietly before this, his statement caused a rather watery chuckle to escape her. "Is that the only reason? I am quite certain your reputation will be able to hold up just fine under the slight strain."

"No, that is not the only reason, you silly widgeon." Pulling her more closely toward him he finally declared himself. "I find that I love you quite desperately and will not be truly happy until you agree to marry me."

"Oh Lucius, you won't when you find out what I did," Julianna declared in distress as she began to weep in earnest.

Taking her into his arms in an embrace meant to comfort, Luc prompted in soothing tones, "Tell me. Whatever it is, we can work it out together. There is nothing you can tell me that will stop me from loving you."

Unconvinced, but believing he deserved the truth, Julianna launched into her tale.

"The night I broke our engagement seven years ago at the Roxboroughs' ball, I thought I saw you passionately kissing Lady Ormiston. You had never kissed me like that, and I was devastated that you could be so unfaithful even before we were ever married. I knew it was considered acceptable in our world, but it was not acceptable to me. I refused to marry anyone that I thought would so dishonour me."

Julianna took a shuddering breath as the viscount continued to regard her steadily, his brow knit with concentration and confusion. He did not want her to stop in her explanation, so he did not interrupt nor defend himself although he was certain she was mistaken. Despite their youth at the time, he had already been quite fond of her and he, too, felt strongly about fidelity.

She continued, "You see, no one had ever told me you have a brother. I understand now that it would not have been considered appropriate to tell a debutante about illegitimate relatives, but I would think you should have told me about him yourself. Now that I have met him, I strongly suspect it was him I saw that night. It is inexcusable that I so injured us both by jumping so hastily to the wrong conclusion. We have both been robbed of seven years we cannot ever retrieve. I am unfit to be your wife as I showed so little faith in you."

Smiling gently at her as she wound down to her conclusion, Luc reminded her, "But you demonstrated great faith in me just today, and even a couple weeks ago when you confided in me your concerns about Fletcher at the time."

Brightening ever so slightly, Julianna watched him intently as he continued. "I do not feel robbed of the last seven years. We have both grown up in the meantime and will no doubt be better mates for it. You, yourself, said you would not trade the time you had with Odelia and Fletcher for anything. What would be inexcusable is to rob us of our future now that the mess has been cleared up. But if you need further convincing, I will say that you owe me, and so you must marry me – that is the price I am demanding."

With another watery chuckle, Julianna threw herself into his arms. "If you are sure that is the price you wish to set, then I suppose I must pay."

"My biggest regret now is that you are under the misapprehension that my brother is a better kisser than me. It shall now be my duty to demonstrate my abilities to your satisfaction."

With a wicked look, he proceeded to do just that.

Moments later he drew back and grinned at the dazed look on his beloved's face.

"Did I prove my point?" he asked with a wry swagger.

"What point was that, exactly?" Julianna questioned in a bemused fashion.

Luc laughed with delight before his eyes narrowed as they caught sight of her locket that had slipped out of her now slightly disarrayed clothing.

"You kept that little trinket I gave you?" he demanded, surprised delight colouring his tones.

Blushing fiercely, Julianna tried to turn away and tuck it back into its usual hiding place.

"No more secrets, Julianna," the viscount declared somewhat sternly. "Please, tell me if that is the necklace I gave you. And if it is, why do you still have it?"

With a resigned sigh, Julianna met his piercing gaze bravely. "Yes, it is the trinket you gave me. It was all I had left of you. I gave you back the ring you had given me to seal our betrothal, and this was the only other thing you had given me."

She looked at him rather helplessly while he gazed at her in wonder. With a self-deprecating shrug and a little laugh, she continued her explanation. "You see, I never stopped loving you, I just was unwilling to share you."

With a whoop of joy, Luc stood, pulling her with him. Swinging her into his arms, he spun around the room. Placing her gently back on her feet he looked her solemnly in the eye.

"I swear to you, you will never have to share me with another woman for the rest of our lives, except maybe some lovely little women."

She looked at him questioningly so he elaborated. "Hopefully we will have several daughters who will look just like you."

"Several?" Julianna laughed. "Only if you promise that *you* will be overseeing their Seasons."

Luc laughed with her. "I will love you until we die." Then, just before reclaiming her lips once more, he made one more vow. "And I promise to shower you with much finer jewels in the future."

"I don't need jewels. All I need is you," was her fervent reply before no more words were necessary.

The End

About the Author

I've been writing pretty much since I learned to read when I was five years old. Of course, those early efforts were basically only something a mother could love :-). I put writing aside after I left school and stuck with reading. I am an avid reader. I love words. I will read anything, even the cereal box, signs, posters, etc. But my true love is novels.

Almost ten years ago my husband dared me to write a book instead of always reading them. I didn't think I'd be able to do it, but to my surprise I love writing. Those early efforts eventually became my first published book – Tempting the Earl (published by Avalon Books in 2010). There were some ups and downs in my publishing efforts. My first publisher was sold and I became an "orphan" author, back to the drawing board of trying to find a publishing house. It has been a thrilling adventure as I learned to navigate the world of publishing.

I believe firmly that everyone deserves a happily ever after. I want my readers to be able to escape from the everyday for a little while and feel upbeat and refreshed when they get to the end of my books.

When not reading or writing, I can be found traipsing around my neighborhood admiring the dogs and greenery or travelling the world with my favorite companion.

Stay in touch:

Website/sign up for my newsletter:
www.wendymayandrews.com
Facebook:
www.facebook.com/groups/WMASweetRomanceReadersAndFriends
Instagram:
www.instagram.com/WendyMayAndrews
Twitter:
www.twitter.com/WendyMayAndrews

Have you read the other books in the Ladies of Mayfair series?
Check out book 1:

The Governess' Debut

The governess must charm both the spoiled child and the haughty earl.

Orphaned and destitute, gently born Felicia Scott must find a way to keep a roof over her head. No longer able to enter the Marriage Mart, but also not of the servant class, the only option is to find a position as governess.

After his spoiled, seven year old daughter has sent off three governesses in the 18 months since her mother died, the Earl of Standish doubts the young, inexperienced Miss Scott could possible manage the position. Since he's desperate and she comes so highly recommended, the earl agrees to give her a chance. Much to everyone's amazement, the beautiful, young governess succeeds where the others had failed. The entire household benefits from the calm, including the jaded earl.

How does he overcome his arrogance to see his governess' true value?

Available now on Amazon
https://amzn.to/2S8CQY4

If you like Regencies, you might also like the Mayfair Mayhem series.
Book 1 is:

The Duke Conspiracy

Anything is possible with a spying debutante, a duke, and a conspiracy.

Growing up, Rose and Alex were the best of friends until their families became embroiled in a feud. Now, the Season is throwing them into each other's company. Despite the spark of attraction they might feel for one another, they each want very different things in life, besides needing to support their own family's side in the dispute.

Miss Rosamund Smythe is finding the Season to be a dead bore after spying with her father, a baron diplomat, in Vienna. She wants more out of life than just being some nobleman's wife. When she overhears a plot to entrap Alex into a marriage of convenience, her intrigue and some last vestige of loyalty causes them to overcome the feud.

His Grace, Alexander Milton, the Duke of Wrentham, wants a quiet life with a "proper" wife after his tumultuous childhood. His parents had fought viciously, lied often, and Alex had hated it all.

Rose's meddling puts her in danger. Alex will have to leave the simple peace he craves to claim a love he never could have imagined.

Can they claim their happily ever after despite the turmoil?

Available now on Amazon
https://amzn.to/2YVKOeG

Made in the USA
Middletown, DE
30 April 2025

74967252R00179